C000137695

THE
MARRIAGE
SECRET

BOOKS BY CAREY BALDWIN

Her First Mistake

THE CASSIDY & SPENSER THRILLERS SERIES

Judgment

Fallen

Notorious

Stolen

Countdown

Prequels

First Do No Evil (Blood Secrets Book 1)

Confession (Blood Secrets Book 2)

THE
MARRIAGE
SECRET
CAREY BALDWIN

bookouture

Published by Bookouture in 2022

An imprint of Storyfire Ltd.
Carmelite House
50 Victoria Embankment
London EC4Y 0DZ

www.bookouture.com

ISBN: 978-1-80019-523-3
eBook ISBN: 978-1-80019-522-6

For You
The Reader
Whether this is the first of my books you've read or one of many,
I'm honored.

ONE

My Diary

You have what I want. You wake up in the morning and slide your feet into cashmere slippers. The robe you toss on, so carelessly, was handmade especially for you from a bolt of silk he chose while you were honeymooning in Verona—a bad omen considering what happened to Romeo and Juliet—but I digress. After regally descending your marble staircase and wandering into your kitchen with its vaulted ceilings and red-knobbed Wolf appliances, all bright light and sparkling with happiness, you find him waiting for you with your favorite coffee brewed piping hot.

Or perhaps you've changed to tea or warm milk now that a little one is on the way?

He gives you a playful, endearing swat on your perfect bottom.

You smile, your porcelain skin flushing with delight. You brush your caramel-highlighted brown hair from your sweet, girl-next-door face; pucker your pink, bow lips in a faux kiss, and then drop into a chair.

He places a cushion behind your back. "I ordered in this morning. I didn't know if you'd be craving waffles and bacon and eggs or avocado Benedict or if your stomach might be feeling delicate and you'd prefer a bit of fruit or simply a piece of dry toast but it's all here. Nibble or indulge. It's up to you. Shall I make you a vitamin-infused smoothie to go with?"

"No, darling! You shouldn't spoil me," *you say.*

No, he shouldn't.

You've done nothing to deserve any of this.

Nothing.

And yet you take your charmed life for granted.

Wake up and smell the coffee, my dear.

Just because you don't mean any harm to anyone doesn't mean they don't mean any harm to you.

I want what you have, and I'm coming for it.

TWO

What a beautiful morning!

Holly Bancroft whirled with her raised arms outstretched, and then dropped into a chair. The cushion sank beneath her weight, the leather squeaking in complaint. Ugh. She should've aimed for the couch. She was going to need a crane to lift her out of this low contraption.

"Darling? Is this everything? It's just the one small case?" A deliciously deep voice called from above, echoing off the vaulted ceiling of her living room like a baritone's at the opera.

"Yes, darling. I packed for the hospital, not Paris. I don't need much. Unless you're suggesting I ought to bring a glam kit."

Her husband, Zach, materialized at the top of the marble staircase and leaned over the balustrade. "Not at all. There's nothing that makes my pulse pound like the sight of you, my beauty, with or without window dressing."

She placed one hand over her heart. "That sounds like flattery and, on behalf of pregnant women everywhere, I thank you."

He descended the stairs with her overnight bag, the

shoulder strap flung crosswise over his broad chest, the case's tiny blue roses looking extraordinarily out of place on him, and came to stand in front of her. A hank of raven-black hair languished over one startling blue eye and, when he shoved it back, his lifted arm displayed his triceps to great effect—he was dressed in monogrammed scrubs—the custom-tailored ones, made from soft mint muslin, she'd given him for his birthday.

How lucky was she?

The father of her child happened to be not only a doting husband but also the head of the OB-GYN department at Phoenix, Arizona's Mercy General Hospital.

"If you give me a hand out of this chair I'll make you a coffee—if you think there's time," she said, though "coffee" was too lowly a term to describe the beverages that poured forth from their highfalutin espresso gizmo that cost more money than she'd made her first year out of college.

"You'll do no such thing. I set the timer on the machine last night, and I'll grab my own cup just as soon as I get your bag in the car and double-check the car seat installation."

Zach strode from the room, and she placed her palm on her stomach just in time to feel it tighten painfully and a flush of acid wash up her throat. Once the contraction passed, she stretched her legs out in front and then bent them again. She wanted to get out of this cramped position and, with effort, she could hoist herself out of the chair on her own. It would be worth it, she decided and, determined, wrangled her way into a standing position.

She heard the kitchen door close, Zach humming in the kitchen, and then, quite suddenly, he appeared in front of her, his complexion ruddy, his handsome features shockingly contorted. "Dammit, Holly!"

It wasn't so much his words as the sharpness in his tone that cut her to the quick. Once before, he'd spoken to her like that, with venom in his voice, and then, after what she'd thought was a minor argument, he'd stopped talking to her altogether. The silent treatment had continued a full day, which might not have been so awful, except the day was Christmas. Later, he'd been dreadfully sorry, and he'd made it up to her by lavishing her with affection. He'd even taken her on a surprise New Year's trip to Tahiti where he'd presented her with a beautiful strand of pearls and the promise to never treat her so coldly again.

Now, he drew a shaking hand over his face, and his expression smoothed out until it was nearly blank. She'd almost prefer the incendiary glare from a moment earlier to this current, unfeeling look.

She grabbed the back of a chair to steady herself and focused on all the wonderful things Zach had done for her. She thought of the pillows he'd propped beneath her legs when her feet had begun to swell, all the cups of chamomile tea he'd delivered with spoonfuls of honey and cream. How he'd go on and on about how no artificial sweeteners would do for his precious wife and their unborn child. He was a good husband. He loved her, and he was entitled to get stressed out once in a while.

Give him a minute. He'll get over it.

But what, exactly, had she done?

"I've told you a thousand times not to leave your shoes lying around." His voice could've flash frozen an entire side of beef, but he had, in fact, told her, many times, to put her shoes away.

Last night, she'd been exhausted, her feet aching, and she'd kicked off her loafers in the middle of the kitchen. Only now did she realize she'd forgotten to carry them to the closet.

"There will be consequences," he pronounced, kinglike.

Maybe next he'd be shouting, "Off with her head!"

Shuddering, she reminded herself of the tenderness in his tone the first time he counted out breaths in childbirth class with her and the encouraging words that followed: *Way to go, Holly. You've got this! I'm so damn proud of you.* Then, he couldn't take his eyes off her. In a room full of adoring men,

Zach had out-adored them all. He'd been positively star-struck by the life growing inside her. All the times they'd practiced for this day, he'd been pitch-perfect. Massaging her shoulders, rubbing her back, simulating timing her contractions.

Now, he stared at her with utter contempt.

She placed her hand atop her belly as if she could shield her unborn baby's eyes from a father's scorn.

"I tripped with my coffee! What if I'd burned myself?" He held up his hands. "These are our livelihood. Did you stop to think of that? No, you never do!"

He turned and marched from the room, slamming the front door behind him.

A moment later, Holly heard the car's engine revving… and a long blast from the horn.

THREE

Holly tried to think positive thoughts. She ought to relax as much as possible in between contractions, gather her strength. It was too soon to push, but she wanted to be ready. On a long inhalation, she watched the wall clock, its second hand orbiting. Time was moving forward in an orderly fashion, the earth was still spinning, and things between her and Zach would right themselves soon.

As she released her breath, her luxury hospital suite came into full focus. White-trimmed greige walls, a sitting area complete with desk and lamp. A leather pullout couch—everything designed to simulate a hotel experience. Beside her, on the nightstand, blood-red roses stood tall in a heavy, baluster-shaped crystal vase, their sweet fragrance competing with the smell of disinfectant and sweaty sheets.

The vase, with its gold-rimmed neck, looked expensive.

One of Zach's typical, thoughtful, gestures. Long after the roses rotted, the vase would remain perfect, a keepsake forever reminding them of this day.

Everything is fine.

Her belly tightened, and she placed one hand on her chest

and the other on her stomach, breathing in, counting to herself: one one hundred, two one hundred, three one hundred, four one hundred, five one hundred.

Exhale.

Zach watched her abdomen rise and fall in stony silence; he didn't count with her, didn't help her keep the rhythm, *support* her, the way they'd practiced.

How long would he keep it up?

It seemed impossible he would freeze her out at a time like this, and over such a small mistake, but he hadn't spoken a word to her since he'd stormed out of the house this morning. The entire drive to the hospital he'd given her the silent treatment. Later, when Dr. Eckard had come in to examine her, Zach had smiled and engaged in doctor speak with his colleague—talking in phrases Holly only partly understood like: *seven centimeters; variable decels; otherwise reassuring strips.* They'd joked about the Friday special in the hospital cafeteria. Then Dr. Eckard had promised he'd take the very best care of her, and Zach had replied: *You bet your sweet ass you will, David. Holly's my whole world.*

But once Dr. Eckard closed the door behind him, the temperature plummeted to meat-locker levels.

Now, Zach fixed Holly with ice-blue eyes and, still a bit foggy from the pain of her last contraction, she registered his disapproval. When she tried to slip her hand from his grip, his silence sounded a deafening warning. Sharp, like a razor blade, his thumbnail scratched the underside of her wrist; biting into her skin with enough force, she thought, to let blood.

Her eyes drifted to the tender spot, and she saw a faint red scratch—nothing more.

Of course, he hadn't broken the skin.

Nor had he scratched her on purpose—this pain medication was making her paranoid. She'd always been hypersensitive to drugs, but because she'd inherited a minor bleeding disorder—

one that otherwise caused her no problems—Dr. Eckard, her obstetrician, had said an epidural was out of the question and had given her something else to take the edge off.

She squeezed her eyes closed.

Maybe when she opened them again she'd find the husband she knew at her bedside instead of this imposter dressed in Zach's monogrammed scrubs.

The real Zach would never hurt her.

The real Zach made her feel special.

Made her believe that, in spite of her past, she'd grown into a woman who deserved happiness—a family of her own. But...

What if he's suddenly realized he's wrong? What if he's decided what I did in my youth is too terrible to forgive? That I'm not worthy of being a mother?

"Zach," she whispered, desperate for his reassurance. "Where are you?"

No response.

Well, it was an absurd question to ask of a man standing right there at the bedside.

She should get out of her head, set aside her guilt over her past sins, and focus on the only thing that mattered: safely delivering into this world the precious child she'd been carrying inside her for nine months.

Jolene.

Drawing one knee into a different position, she felt a release of pressure in her back and sighed. But the relief was soon interrupted by another contraction. One that made her fingers curl, the muscles in her thighs jump. When it was over, she opened her eyes and noticed the sheets shaking.

A series of blips sounded from the bedside monitor.

Zach silenced the alarm, then curled his lip and pressed a different button—this one on the IV pump.

What was he doing?

If only he would *talk* to her, comfort her, tell her everything was okay. She longed to rest her head on his chest, but when he leaned toward her, she suddenly imagined bolting out of bed, running as fast and as far away from him as she could, her arms forming a sling beneath her, bloated belly, her feet slapping against the wood tile floors, her gown flapping against her thighs.

Breathe, Holly.

Zach loves you.

If something were wrong, he wouldn't have shut off that alarm. But what was he doing with the IV pump?

The nurse, Gloria, poked her head in the door: "Everything okay in here, Dr. Bancroft? I was watching the central monitor, and I noticed..." When her gaze fell on Holly, she let her voice trail off.

"That was nothing. Leave Holly to me. Go check in with your other patients, and I'll call you if anything noteworthy happens."

"But—"

Zach cut her off with a *that-will-be-all* look.

"If you need me just buzz."

"Will do."

Gloria smiled at Holly, inclined her head toward the call button draped through the bedside rail, and then backed out of the room—pointing one last time at the button. "I'm here if you need me," she repeated as she closed the door behind her.

Don't go! Holly wanted to shout, but Zach's glare warned her against it.

As a wave of dizziness hit her, she yanked a tissue from a box on the bedside table and wiped perspiration from her face, then let the crumpled mess fall from her hand.

The bedside alarm sounded again and, without even glancing at the monitor, Zach silenced it.

He really shouldn't do that. He might know what he was doing but it wasn't his place—not today—not with his own wife.

The tracing on the monitor dove and dipped and yet another alarm followed.

With the next silencing touch of Zach's finger, her throat tightened. Whenever she and Zach disagreed, she usually deferred to him—it made her feel safe when he took charge, and this was his territory. He had a reputation as one of the finest obstetricians in the state. He was head of the department at this very hospital. But something felt *wrong* and, for their daughter's sake, Holly had to speak up. "I think the nurse ought to know about the alarms. Let's call her. Please, Zach?"

He shook his head—that quick movement the only real response he'd given her since they'd arrived at the hospital six hours ago. His first acknowledgment of her, his first indication that he'd even heard her voice. It was virtually impossible to ignore a woman in labor, but somehow, Zach had managed to pull it off.

He won't let anything happen to our baby.

Another contraction, this one harder than the last, doubled her over, left her gasping.

More beeps, and Zach deftly quieted them.

How many times did that make?

And what were the monitors for if not to sound a warning when something went wrong?

But if Jolene were in danger, Zach would send for Dr. Eckard right away.

Holly *knew* he would.

Zach could never, would never, be so diabolical as to take his anger at her out on their baby. To imagine for one second that her devoted husband would deliberately endanger either her or Jolene over a pair of shoes left lying about was preposterous. Her perceptions were obviously tainted, her thinking as mature as a child plucking petals from a flower:

He loves me. He loves me not.

The rapid swing of her emotions from one end of the spectrum to the other was a dead giveaway they were not to be trusted. But, even so, no matter how hard she tried to convince herself otherwise, she could not rid herself of the notion Zach was punishing her for this morning.

There will be consequences, he'd said.

"I'm sorry," she whispered. "So sorry. I promise to do better. I won't be careless again."

Zach rolled his eyes, and then cut them away.

Another alarm. Another button push, and this time true panic flooded her, making it hard to breathe. Unlike the monitor's, the alarm in her head could not be shut off.

What if *this* was the real Zach, and the kind, loving husband she'd married was the pretender?

Another contraction doubled her over.

She screamed, partly from pain, but mostly because she *had* to draw the attention of her nurse, or *anyone* who might be passing down the hall.

Maybe she was crazy to doubt her husband's intentions, but she couldn't take a chance—not with Jolene's safety.

Zach slapped his hand over her mouth, his look an unspoken command that said *don't embarrass me*. His giant palm fit over her mouth and nose, making it hard to fill her lungs. She sputtered, breathless, desperate to draw up her knees, suddenly feeling an urgent need to push, but Zach shoved her back against the bed, mashing his hand harder over her face. Dread sat heavily on her chest. Her lungs seemed to collapse.

She *must* speak up. "Don't let anything happen to the baby. Promise me." He didn't react, and she wondered if she'd only imagined saying those words. Her head felt so very heavy. "I'm... begging... you."

Beeps sounded.

Turning to silence them, he removed his palm from her mouth.

While his back was to her, she dragged her hand across the covers, inching stealthily toward the call button draped through the side-rails of the bed. Sweat dripped from her forehead, stinging her eyes, and, before she could reach the button, a searing pain crushed her.

She gasped.

Zach spun, grabbed her wrist, squeezing, bruising until the feeling in her fingertips disappeared.

The room tilted.

She was in trouble—*Jolene* was in trouble.

Holly's head lolled back, and her gaze landed on the heavy crystal vase at her bedside. Zach had imprisoned one of her hands, but the other remained free.

Must. Get. Help.

With the world fading to black, she thrashed with every ounce of her remaining strength.

Cool glass slammed against her arm.

A crash sounded, and the exploding scent of roses thrilled her.

A creaking door.

A stab of light pierced the descending veil of darkness.

Then, Nurse Gloria's voice: "What happened? Oh no, those beautiful flowers!"

Holly heard footsteps; the sounds muffled, as if coming from the bottom of a lake, but a moment later those sounds crystalized into syllables, spoken words ringing out.

"Late decels!" Gloria shouted.

"Get her on her side!" Zach ordered. "What took you so long?"

"I-I... did you call me? What... when did Dr. Eckard turn up the Pitocin?"

"She needs oxygen! Start with five liters. And, Gloria, page Dr. Eckard—STAT!"

FOUR

The nursery was perfect. Zach had seen to that, though it wasn't exactly done up in Holly's taste. Left to her own devices, she'd have opted for sunny yellow walls, the ceiling painted sky-blue with huge fluffy clouds—or maybe a mural of Winnie the Pooh. In the end, though, she hadn't put up much of a fight. Zach had told her if she truly wanted a faux sky ceiling, then a faux sky ceiling she would have. But he thought the trend outdated, and he'd looked so disappointed when she'd suggested it, she hadn't had the heart to insist. Why should mothers always get their way about nursery décor?

Fathers deserved a say, too.

She was, in truth, happy her husband took such a particular interest in everything to do with the baby, and with her. In her youth, she'd had to set off a bomb to get her parents to notice her, so the fact that Zach was extra attentive had been, and still was, a positive in her mind. Her friends used to complain about Zach's frequent phone calls interrupting their "girls' days", and sometimes joked he seemed freakishly obsessed, but Holly didn't mind. When he'd phone from the hospital to tell her "takeout" got his lunch order wrong, it didn't annoy her. His wanting to share the little things with her made her feel special and loved.

Still, she had to admit she sometimes lost patience with him constantly pointing out how other men neglected their wives. She didn't need reminding that he was a good husband. And the fact that he seemed to think she did made it seem she'd done something wrong—that she wasn't giving him the credit he deserved.

Anyway, Zach had done a stunning job with the nursery. She'd made a few suggestions along the way, but he was going for a cohesive look, and she soon realized her ideas didn't fit, so she gradually withdrew and left him in charge. One night, she'd tried to look in on how things were going and found the door to the nursery locked. When she'd complained, he'd given her the key immediately but asked her to please wait to go inside—he wanted to surprise her.

And he had.

When they'd arrived home from the hospital, just minutes ago, Zach had first taken a soundly sleeping Jolene and settled her in the crib while Holly waited in the kitchen. Next, he'd blindfolded Holly and carefully led her up the stairs and into the nursery where he'd kissed her hair, her forehead, her lips, before uncovering her eyes.

Like one of those women on the home renovation shows, she'd gasped in amazement.

The walls were white, but with just the right amount of cream to lend them warmth. Thick, undulating crown molding gave the ceiling a tiered effect. The baseboards were a slightly darker cream, perfectly blending with the earth-colored hardwood floor, all elegant style. It would've, perhaps, been a bit understated had it not been for the giant picture window—hand-painted to resemble stained glass, sending flashes of colored light dancing across the room.

Zach explained he'd asked the artist to use water-based

paints on the glass. That way, in case she still wanted her blue sky, white clouds and sunshine, the window motif could easily be redone. Perhaps they'd change it yearly, and when Jolene was old enough, she could choose her own theme.

A brilliant idea, really.

He'd furnished the room with coordinating mahogany pieces—cradle, crib, dresser, rocker, and changing table. The effect was clean and expensive-looking. Like something out of a magazine.

For their homecoming, with his typical over-the-top generosity, he'd filled the kitchen with fresh daisies and the nursery with stuffed animals. Teddy bears, unicorns, bunnies and more lurked in the corners and stood sentry on the built-in shelves.

But what brought the lump to Holly's throat and the tears to her eyes was the sight of Jolene—lovingly bundled into the mittens Zach's mother had knitted to keep her from scratching her delicate face, a matching cap to help her maintain her body temperature, and family pictures adorning the wall behind her crib.

How Zach had managed to get some of the recent ones ready in such short order was a mystery. Matching silver-framed photos hung symmetrically: Zach kneeling beside Holly, his hands splayed across her barely-there baby bump. Zach with his arms around her, pulling her nightgown taut over an enormous belly. Zach planting a kiss on Jolene's cheek. Holly's fingers entwined with baby Jolene's. And finally, a close-up shot of the soles of their darling daughter's tiny pink feet.

Zach was nothing if not kind and thoughtful.

Which was exactly what had made it so difficult to understand what happened the day she'd given birth. His cruelty, then, seemed unfathomable—and unbelievable. She wished she could outright reject her jumbled, terrifying memories as nothing more than morbid fantasy, but they felt *real*, and she was desperate to talk to Zach about them.

In her heart, she knew he was a good man.

She believed in his love for her and for their daughter.

And for those reasons, she was ready to listen to his side of things, ready to forgive and forget. But she couldn't just go on about her business like nothing had happened. They needed to clear the air.

He owed her an explanation.

He owed her an apology.

With Jolene slumbering peacefully in her crib, Holly took Zach by the hand and led him into the bedroom.

"I'm surprised." He grinned playfully. "But count me in," he said, quickly unzipping his pants and kicking off his shoes.

Her misty eyes went dry and wide. He might be the gynecologist in the family but she was the woman, and she was absolutely sure she couldn't comfortably make love just three days after a cesarean section. She backed up to the bed, extending her arms down to support the weight of her still bloated body and, ever-so-carefully, lowered herself into a sitting position onto their four-poster bed. "No! It's too soon."

"For you, yes, but that doesn't mean you can't show me how much you appreciate me." His trousers pooled around his ankles. "Of course, if you didn't miss me..."

As if there had been a sudden gravitational shift of the moon, the tide of good feelings that had been welling up inside her receded. She fanned her face with her hands, blinking incredulously at his boxers, which revealed his intense interest. She reminded herself her hormones were all over the place.

Don't overreact.

She wet her lips and took a moment to think before replying. "We spent hours together every day while I was in the hospital."

"So that's a 'no', you didn't miss me?"

"It's a 'no' to sex."

She wasn't sure if his flushed face signified ardor, anger or embarrassment.

"I'm talking about..."

"I know what you're talking about. But you must realize I'm exhausted. I just got home from the hospital, my overnight bag isn't even out of the car yet, and I need to discuss something important with you. Naturally, I want you to feel good, but frankly, this is a big ask of a woman who just gave birth."

"I didn't ask. I never would have considered it if you hadn't led me to think *you* wanted to," he said, pulling up and fastening his trousers. "I knew I should've shot it down the minute you suggested it, only I've missed your touch so much. Of *course* I don't want to if you don't."

She shook her head, trying to clear the cobwebs. "I didn't suggest anything of the sort."

He came and sat beside her on the bed and took her face in his hands. "Sweetheart, you came on to me. You whispered *let's go into the bedroom*. You took my hand and gave me a sultry look and considering how you're dressed... but if I misunderstood, that's on me. I'm sorry if I seemed interested in my wife. But you're so beautiful. What red-blooded man would refuse?"

She looked down at her zippered top. She'd omitted her bra for ease of nursing and she'd carelessly left it unzipped halfway. Her breasts were clearly outlined by the soft fabric, but that, and asking to go into the bedroom, hardly constituted an offer to pleasure him. She zipped her top with purpose. "I'm sorry we got our signals crossed. It's been a while since we made love, and I'm as anxious as you are to get back to normal." Maybe not quite as anxious. "But I wanted to speak to you, and I thought we should talk in here so as not to wake the baby."

He touched her cheek and peered into her eyes. "I'm worried about you, darling. What's on your mind? How can I help? Talk to me."

There he was. The real Zach—her loving, protective husband.

She pressed her cheek against his shoulder, felt her head rise and fall in time to his breathing. This mix-up, right now, showed how easy it was to misunderstand each other. Part of her wanted to sweep what happened at the hospital under the rug, but she'd promised him on their wedding day she'd always be honest about her feelings, about everything—and she needed to know what the hell happened in that delivery room. "When I was in labor with Jolene," she took a breath, and to give herself room before laying out her accusation, and because she wanted to own any bad behavior on her part, she said, "I knocked that vase over on purpose."

His body stiffened. "That was Baccarat crystal."

"What? I thought it looked pricey, but I had no idea." She should've known Zach would have wanted the finest—but even for him, sending a Baccarat vase to the hospital seemed outlandish. Anyone could've broken it—but it hadn't been just anyone—*she* was the culprit. Now she felt even worse about what she was about to say. "How much did it cost?"

"It doesn't matter, darling. It was yours to break, and you were out of your mind, screaming and thrashing in pain. I'm sure it was an accident."

"No." She shook her head. "You need to listen. I did it on purpose. I wanted, so desperately, for the nurse to come. I was frightened because you kept turning off the alarms, and I thought there might be something wrong with the baby."

He stroked her hair off her forehead and made shushing sounds like he was comforting a child. "You should've just said so. Those were false alarms, and I knew that, but if you wanted the nurse I would've gladly gotten her."

"I did ask."

He chuckled. "No, my darling. That's not the way I remember it, at least. But is that all that's troubling you—those alarms? As you know, we have a happy, healthy baby girl sleeping soundly in the next room. All's well that ends well. I'm sorry you were scared. I know what I'm doing, and I assumed you understood that."

She nodded, but it still didn't make complete sense to her. "If there was nothing wrong, why did you yell for oxygen when the nurse came in? Why did I need a cesarean section?"

"Because your condition changed. You almost passed out, and the baby's heart rate dropped suddenly. Dr. Eckard was the one who made the call to do a C-section, but he was absolutely right. I know you had your heart set on a normal birth, but on the bright side you don't have a tear or an episiotomy to deal with. Surgery's a bit more of a recovery, but in the long run it'll be better for our lovemaking."

She jerked her head off his chest. "Why are you talking about sex again?"

"I'm merely pointing out you're none the worse for wear in the female department."

"Do you have any idea how crass that sounds? It almost sounds like you're happy I needed a cesarean."

"I only want what's best for you. And, regardless of how it sounds, I'm not being crass or crude. It's part of life. What kind of doctor would I be if I were afraid to talk about delicate matters? In my profession, we understand the problems childbirth sometimes brings. I'm the one women turn to for help—I'm speaking professionally, not personally."

"You're right. I'm tired, and I wasn't looking at it that way."

"What if I bring you a cup of tea and tuck you in? You should try to rest while the baby's down for her nap." He rose and, facing her, placed his hands on her shoulders. "I would not and will not ever let any harm come to you or to our daughter. You do know that?"

She thought she did, only... "When you put your hand over my mouth, I was terrified. I couldn't breathe. And the nurse said someone turned up the Pitocin after I saw you fussing with the IV, and I've read Pitocin makes contractions more intense."

He frowned. "I didn't touch that pump. The Pitocin had to be increased because your labor wasn't progressing well enough. That's why *Dr. Eckard* turned it up when he was in the room. And I *never* put my hand over your mouth. You're mixing up dreams, maybe hallucinations, with reality."

A hallucination? That seemed highly unlikely to her. She remembered most of the day in vivid detail. "I realize I had pain meds on board, but is it common to hallucinate during labor?"

"Not really, but it can happen, on rare occasions, given the right mix of medication and fatigue."

"It wasn't *consequences* for the shoes? You didn't turn up the Pitocin to make my labor more painful?"

His chin jerked back. "I told you Eckard increased it for a good reason. I would die before I'd hurt you! *Consequences for the shoes?* What are you even talking about?"

"I left my shoes in the middle of the floor that morning, and you tripped over them with a coffee."

"I was irritated about that, yes, and I'm sorry to say I acted like a dick for a hot minute. It wasn't my finest moment." He looked at her with eyes that made her believe in his apology, believe in his love. "But, Holly, you are the most important thing in the world to me, and I will *never* allow anything or anyone to come between us. I think I might need to start keeping closer tabs on you—just until you're back to your old self. It's perfectly normal, but you seem to be experiencing a little post-birth confusion—a bit of baby brain as they call it."

She nodded. He was right about one thing—she was confused. It had all seemed so real—especially his hand over her mouth stopping her scream. "I'm not sure I like the sound of *keeping tabs* on me. I'm not a child."

"No. You're a woman, and a very precious one. I've put it to you the wrong way. I only want to make your life as easy as I possibly can. I'll draw up a schedule." He tapped his chin. "And a few guidelines to keep you safe. I couldn't stand for anything to happen to you."

"To me or to Jolene either?"

"Of course, my angel. That's exactly what I just said. I swear, I wish I had a recorder so I could play back this conversation to you."

She let out a sigh. She wished the exact same thing. "I know you're only trying to help, but really I don't need a schedule and rules. I can organize myself."

He shrugged a *whatever-you-want*.

"But I am sorry again about the vase. Was it really Baccarat?"

"Don't worry about it. I'm actually damn proud that when you thought something bad was about to happen to the baby you had the spunk to send it crashing." He clucked his tongue. "Good thing I didn't go all out though—that one only set me back a couple of grand."

FIVE

If anyone had told Holly that the morning after the day she came home from the hospital with her new baby girl, she'd be questioned by the police, she would've thought them crazy or cruel or both. But here she sat, in what was supposed to be a safe haven—the dream home she and Zach had built last year—with the walls of the living room closing in around her. Leaning forward on their latte-colored leather sofa, she pressed her fingertips against her forehead as if that might keep her brain from sloshing out of her skull. She couldn't figure out how to breathe normally, and she kept overinflating her lungs. They felt like balloons about to pop, and now the couch seemed to rise and roll beneath her like a magic carpet, making her sick to her stomach.

Oh man.

She wretched, and a small stream of bitter-tasting liquid dribbled out of her mouth, ran down her face, and then dripped onto her pretty pink maternity robe where it left a fluorescent yellow trail.

Sitting next to her, Zach mopped at her mouth and robe

with a damp washcloth, tossed it aside, then slid his body close to hers, tightening an arm around her shoulders.

"I swear I'll never take another pain pill." Not that she remembered taking one in the first place. It was so strange because she wasn't one to rely on painkillers; not after dental work, not after a fractured wrist when she'd fallen off a scooter, not ever. And yet, a partially empty bottle of hydrocodone sat accusingly on the coffee table in front of her in full view of her husband and a plainclothes detective.

About twenty minutes before Zach had gotten home, Detective Don Denton, a lanky man in an off-the-rack tan suit, had arrived and dismissed the uniformed patrol officer who'd been first on the scene. Denton had now been questioning Holly for over an hour. Both he and her husband were handling her with kid gloves, and she knew she must be coming off as unbalanced—but she didn't care what either of them thought of her as long as her daughter was safe.

Under the circumstances, calling the cops had seemed the only sane thing to do.

Thank heavens she'd been wrong, and it had all turned out to be a big misunderstanding between Zach and her.

Settled in a moss-green Bertoia bird chair, with his long legs bent awkwardly over the edge, Detective Denton took notes on a pocket-sized pad, slowly and carefully, like a child practicing his cursive. "I don't think my wife took narcotics after having any of our kids, and we've got three of 'em."

Holly hadn't wanted anything stronger than ibuprofen, and she'd told Dr. Eckard so. But he'd recommended filling a prescription for a small number of hydrocodone tablets and keeping them on hand just in case. He'd joked about not wanting to be disturbed after hours if she changed her mind, and she hadn't argued the point—though she hadn't planned to take them.

Then, this morning, sometime before dawn, Zach had awakened her and asked her to rate her pain. It was around a three or four out of ten—certainly not enough to make her want to take pills. So when and why she'd downed them was quite the mystery. One that made her realize Zach had been right about her memory being patchy. After this catastrophe, if he wanted to put her on a schedule and *keep tabs*, she'd go along. If she had to sacrifice a little of her pride and independence in order to keep Jolene safe, then so be it. Besides, it would only be for a short while until she got back to her usual self. This *baby brain* thing wouldn't last long, and then life would get back to normal.

Better than normal because, now, she not only had Zach, she had little Jolene.

A loving husband and a healthy child—plus an abundance of all the things money could buy. As her mother would say, she should be counting her lucky stars.

Only right now those lucky stars were hiding behind the clouds.

It was going to take a minute for her to recover from the scare she'd just had.

With a lump in her throat, she cradled empty, aching arms, rocking them, longing for her child.

She *needed* to hold Jolene.

How much longer would they make her wait?

The upheaval in her stomach threatened yet again, but she managed to quell it. The sooner she convinced Zach she was okay, the sooner she'd be able to be with Jolene, breathe in her sweet baby smell, kiss her little nose.

"Were there complications with the delivery—is that why you need these pills? I assume your doctor warned you it's easy to get dependent." Denton's lifted eyebrows were the unkempt, bushy sort and seemed out of place on a man his age. He appeared to be no older than forty, with jade-green eyes and handsome, regular features. If someone got him into a good grooming regimen, he could be quite the lady-killer.

Zach was leaning into her, supporting her, keeping her upright on the couch. "Holly had a C-section. She's no drug addict, and we don't need a lecture on pharmaceuticals. Now, if you don't mind, she should rest."

She'd been afraid Zach would be angry with her, but he'd made it clear he was on her side from the moment he'd walked in the door and found the detective grilling her. It was a relief to hear him defend her... although, that defense seemed a bit over the top—protesting too much. Denton hadn't actually implied she had a drug problem, had he? It was Zach who'd introduced the possibility by denying it.

"I'm not saying she's an addict. I'm just saying she took four pills—according to the what's left in the bottle—and I wonder why."

To be fair, so did she.

"Accidentally," Zach said, with that same overly defensive edge in his tone. "It's obvious she took a couple and then forgot and took a couple more. It could happen to anyone. She's already told you, several times I believe, that she doesn't remember taking so many."

Actually, she'd told the detective she didn't remember taking *any*. This was all so humiliating. From here on out, she should write down anything she put in her mouth—or better yet, she should throw these out. She didn't need them.

"I'd like to have her checked out by a doctor."

"I am a doctor. One double dose of pain medicine is nothing to be alarmed about. She's thrown up twice and, judging by what just came up, there's nothing left in her stomach. I can monitor her vitals closely at home—blood pressure, heart rate, oxygen saturations, and I assure you, I'll have her seen first thing in the morning by her primary care."

"Maybe a psychiatric evaluation, too. Just to be on the safe side. Make sure we don't need to worry about self-harm." Detective Denton picked up the bottle and studied the label, then looked intently at Holly. "Is it possible you took more... or something else, ma'am? Are there other prescriptions you might have around the house? You were pretty messed up when I first got here."

"I promise it wasn't intentional. I just had a baby. I feel like the luckiest woman in the world." At least that's how she *should* feel. "And no, I don't think I took anything else—I don't have any other medicines around except my vitamins." She shook her head, and a fresh wave of nausea followed, but this time she managed to swallow back the bile. Her head felt heavy, her scalp prickled, and her palms were cold and clammy. She noticed the strange way her heart thudded in her chest—the beats seemed few and far between... like her body was shutting down, like she could simply close her eyes, fall asleep and never wake up.

She squeezed Zach's hand, forcing herself to focus, fighting the fog of fear, the sense of impending doom.

This anxiety was irrational. She wasn't in any danger.

Four pills never killed anyone, and there couldn't possibly be more drugs in her system.

"Maybe you should check her purse and the medicine cabinet, just to be sure this is all she took, Dr. Bancroft, and then I have a few more questions. Regarding the ransom note—"

Zach scoffed. "There was no ransom note."

"Pardon. I mean the note your wife thought was a ransom—"

"I don't see the point of all this," Zach interrupted. "We've solved the mystery. I'm home now, and I can take it from here."

"It's good you finally made it—after we sent someone to intercept you at work." Denton's manner was polite enough, but absent the carte blanche deference others usually extended to Zach. And good point about how difficult it had been to get through to her husband in a time of crisis. Yet she'd been so relieved he wasn't displeased with *her*. Perhaps she was the one who should be angry.

"Your wife called nine-one-one and said her baby had been kidnapped. That's a serious complaint to put it mildly. I have a report to make, and I need more information for my paperwork. Being a doctor, I'm sure you understand about paperwork. Now about that note—"

"Holly misinterpreted an innocent communication—we've established that. Jolene isn't missing—you saw that for yourself when we FaceTimed my mother. I don't mean to be short with you, because, really, I appreciate your efforts today. I understand what a serious situation this *could* have been. What if our baby really had been kidnapped? Thank goodness you rushed right over to check things out. I'm truly grateful—in fact, if there's some sort of policeman's fund, I'd be happy to donate. But since it was a misunderstanding, since my wife's ill, I'd really like to wrap this up so I can get her to bed." Absently, he picked up his phone from the coffee table and set it down again.

Holly watched the home screen light up with notifications.

All those missed calls.

Her calls.

An image of Jolene's empty crib flashed before her eyes.

She straightened her back and slipped her hand out of Zach's grasp. "I'm not too ill to answer questions." Denton wanted to get to the bottom of things, and so did she. Jolene was safe, thank goodness. But going over the morning's events in her head with the police, they still didn't make perfect sense—what the hell kind of pain pills leave you with no memory of taking them? The way she felt was more akin to someone who'd been slipped a mickey. Zach was in a hurry to end the interview, but was he really protecting her, or just trying to get rid of an inconvenient guest? "*I* called *him* so I owe it to him to... It's for his report. You're always saying how important documentation is, Zach. I'm sure it won't take too much longer."

"Exactly. Just walk me through it one more time," Denton said.

Zach turned up his palms. "To what end?"

"It's okay." Holly reached out and placed her hand over Zach's again, and he curled his fingers through hers. Then she addressed Denton. "I don't know what time it was when I woke up. But when I did, I was alone in our bed, Zach's and mine, and the baby monitor was lying next to me. I sat up and noticed I didn't feel right—I was very, very woozy."

"Go on." Denton inclined his head, as if hearing her story for the first time instead of for the third.

"I picked up the baby monitor—and the video screen showed Jolene's crib was empty. I thought Zach must have her, and I called out to him. Once, twice, so many times, but I got no answer."

"I'm sorry." Zach raised her hand and kissed her palm.

"You were supposed to be home." She closed her eyes. "But you didn't answer me, and then, then I thought you might have gone for milk or something... but why would you take Jolene? Expose her to all those germs at the store? It didn't make sense. Nothing made sense."

"It's over, honey." Zach shook his head at Denton. "Must she relive it?"

Apparently she must because the scenes wouldn't stop playing in her head. "I grabbed my phone and called Zach, but he didn't pick up. So I texted him, and then I got out of bed, and I started for the nursery. The room started spinning and with every step I took I felt more off-balance—like I was walking on a teeter-totter." Just the memory was making her dizzy. "Next thing I knew I was on the floor. I think I fell, and I guess that's how I got this bump on my head." She raised her hand to touch the sore, swollen spot on the back of her skull. "I don't know how long I lay there—I'm missing some time, I think—but some-how, eventually, I found myself in the nursery. I was on my hands and knees, crawling to her crib." Glancing down, she saw her knees were scraped with a bit of dried blood, and she jerked her robe closed to cover them. "She was gone. Our baby was *gone*."

Her throat convulsed, and she waved her hand, panicking, breathless.

"Here, take a sip of this." Zach gently lifted a bottle of water from the coffee table and touched it to her lips.

She pushed it away, fearing she'd choke on it, and blew out a hard jet of air.

Keep going.

Zach tipped her face toward him, meeting her eyes. "I know how hard that was for you, darling, but just remember, Jolene is safe. She's been safe this entire time."

"I needed you, Zach. Do you have any idea what it was like to wake up alone and find our baby missing? How horrifying to imagine that someone had taken her?" He was doing his best to comfort her, now, but the truth was none of this would've happened if he'd been home. He'd promised to take the week off work, and though he'd changed his plans, he hadn't told her. "I called you, over and over, and you didn't answer. I texted you, over and over, and you didn't respond. You were gone. *Jolene* was gone. Why didn't you answer? *Why?*"

"I was in a delivery." He sighed, and his eyes grew moist. "But I shouldn't have been. I should've arranged for someone else to be on duty at the hospital, and I regret that I didn't. This is an important lesson for me. If anything had happened to you or to Jolene I would never have been able to forgive myself."

"Something did happen!"

"Yes. Yes, you got frightened."

"And I fell."

"And thank heavens you're okay. I'm so, so sorry. But I did tell you I couldn't take the week off a while ago. You've forgotten, that's all."

No. "My understanding was that you'd be home for the week. I'd definitely remember if you'd told me that changed."

She knew Zach didn't like being called out in front of a stranger, but she had to cling to the little things she knew to be true. She might be foggy regarding what had transpired *this morning*, but it wasn't as if she'd just awakened from a coma and couldn't remember their life before. "I don't have amnesia. This isn't a movie. This is real life and you promised me months ago you would take time off after the baby was born."

"You're confused."

"Maybe about today, but..." She was struggling to get her head on straight. Was he lying because he didn't want to look bad in front of the policeman? "I was crawling from room to room, searching for our daughter." She fixed him with an unyielding stare. "Because *you* took her."

There. She'd said it, and she didn't want to unsay it.

He gave her his *endless-patience* look. "Yes, darling, I took her to my mother's—just like we agreed. You were exhausted and in pain. I suggested Mom watch Jolene while I was on duty, and I planned to pick her up afterwards on my way home. That way you could sleep in and not worry."

"I don't remember that discussion at all."

"Because of the pills and, likely, you have a mild concussion —you've been vomiting, you have a headache. It all fits." He cleared his throat. "And, darling, I did leave you a note."

Denton slid forward in his chair. "About that. I'd like to..."

That note! "You're implying I did something stupid, but calling nine-one-one was the right thing to do. Any mother would've done the same if she'd found a note like that." She stared at her shaking hands, remembering the piece of paper ripped from a spiral pad and, on it, printed in block letters:

I took the baby. Will be in touch.

"No one in their right mind would interpret that as a ransom note." Zach's tone was no longer understanding.

Her temples throbbed.

Her stomach twisted.

"So you think I'm not in my right mind? You agree with Denton that I need a shrink?" She could hear the way her pitch was rising and falling erratically, but who could blame her?

"What I think is you need to go to bed and sleep off this excess medication, and when you wake up in the morning you'll laugh over this whole thing."

Laugh? About her baby being taken without her knowledge, and then finding that note? "If we agreed you'd take Jolene to your mother's why did you feel the need to leave a note at all?"

He shrugged. "I don't know. I just did."

"And why print it in those blocky letters instead of writing it out?"

"You know how bad my handwriting is."

Sure, but had he left a cursive note she would've understood immediately it was from him. She would have recognized his terrible penmanship. After all, she'd been deciphering it for years. "And you didn't sign it. No 'Love, Zach'. No nothing."

Denton cleared his throat. "I have similar questions, Dr. Bancroft, why didn't you sign the note? Maybe I'm off base but it seems to me most husbands would've left something a little more lovey-dovey. Put some hearts on it or whatnot. I do find the note odd."

"I was in a hurry and preoccupied with gathering up all of Jolene's things. This is our first baby, and I didn't want to forget anything my mother might need for her. I guess I was trying to be efficient rather than poetic, but it's no excuse." He turned to her. "I'm so sorry, sweetheart. You deserved a love letter." Then he raised his right hand and offered a rueful smile. "I solemnly swear I'll never again leave you another piece of correspondence that could be mistaken for a ransom note so long as we both shall live."

Her shoulders lowered, her anger deflating like a tire with a slow leak. He'd left that *stupid* note because he was thinking of their daughter, trying to make sure Jolene would have everything she needed. It was sweet in some ways, and she could relate. There are so many things to remember when you're packing up a baby.

"That's a reasonable enough explanation, I guess," Denton said.

"You guess?" Zach arched a brow.

"Just an expression. What time did you take the baby to your mother's house?"

"Around six a.m.," Zach said evenly, but Holly knew he was irritated. She could tell by that little muscle that always twitched in his jaw just before he lost his temper. "Before I left, I took Holly a glass of milk and two pain pills. She seemed a bit sleepy, but I had no idea she wouldn't remember our conversation—or forget she'd taken the medication and take more—but you can be sure I won't let anything like this happen again."

"I hope you won't. Earlier, you said she must've taken a couple of pills and forgotten. Now you're saying you brought them to her?" Denton asked.

"I brought them to her. Same difference."

"Uh-huh." Denton shifted in his chair. "Were the pills by her bedside or did you get them from the kitchen? The bathroom?"

"The medicine cabinet in our bathroom. Then I put the bottle back where I got it."

"Why milk? Why not water? You got the pills from your bathroom but you would need to go all the way downstairs to the kitchen to get milk."

"To coat her stomach. And I had to get the glass from the kitchen anyway."

Denton scribbled in his notebook.

This rehash of events wasn't bringing her any more clarity, and the more Denton poked at Zach the more she felt the need to defend him. He'd broken his promise and put his work before his family, but she was the one who had taken pills and couldn't remember half the morning. That bump on her head—her concussion, explained why she didn't remember their talk about Jolene going to his mother's house. If he said he'd told her then he must have. He would never have taken Jolene without discussing it with her. The note was weird, but he'd been preoccupied with getting Jolene's things together. Still, there was one more thing she needed him to explain. "If you say we talked about it, I believe you. But since I don't remember, can you please tell me *why* you decided to go in to work this week?"

"Craig Paulson was supposed to cover me, then he backed out of our agreement because he was offered a free trip to Vegas. I should've found someone else. I feel like a complete ass, and I know I let you down. But I'm here now, and I promise I won't leave your side until you're one hundred percent. Detective Denton can write it in his book and that means it's on the record. Meanwhile, Mom can watch Jolene until you're feeling better."

Denton cleared his throat. "I wrote it down, Mrs. Bancroft, so you hold him to that. But Dr. Bancroft, why not have your mother bring the baby home? I think it would help Mrs. Bancroft if she could hold the little one in her arms. I'm no psychiatrist, but it makes sense."

"Tomorrow—today Holly needs rest."

"I *need* to see Jolene." Tears welled behind her eyes.

"With all due respect, sir, your wife's been through a lot today. I recognize she needs rest, but you're going to be home so you can change the diapers and all that. It seems kinder to bring the baby back. Then Mrs. Bancroft can see for herself that she's okay. And, from what I've read, the first days after birth are very important for bonding. There's a study about baby ducks who see a human right after birth, and then follow them around because of something called—"

"Imprinting. I see you've taken a beginner's psychology class." A near smirk tugged at Zach's mouth but he seemed to catch himself before it fully developed. "Seriously, it's good to know you're informed about such matters, and I take your point. We'll get Jolene home today. Now, is there anything else you need for your paperwork?"

"I'd like to take the note." Denton removed a plastic bag from his pocket and held it out.

Zach's face crinkled into an expression Holly knew well, the one he wore whenever she'd said something ignorant, and he was trying to correct her without sounding condescending. "Surely you don't need that. Our daughter was *not* kidnapped. Where there's no crime, there can be no *evidence*."

"I suppose it's not strictly necessary. And I do have the picture of the note I took when I got here. That should be enough. I want to document this incident in case we get called over here again."

"You won't." Her face went hot.

"Good. Then, I'll file my report. I don't think I need to take it further at this time."

"Of course not. This was a simple mix-up." Zach rose.

Denton got up, too. "I wouldn't call it *simple*. It's not every day a mother reports her newborn kidnapped, but I'm glad the baby is safe and sound. Congratulations to you both."

Once Denton had gone, Zach helped her up the stairs, gripping her hand tightly.

"When will you call Frances?" she asked, feeling the fatigue through her entire body, but wanting desperately to be reunited with Jolene.

"Tomorrow."

"But you just said—"

"I have to get back to the hospital, and you're in no condition to take care of Jolene on your own."

Her knees gave way beneath her, and she crumpled onto the cold, hard, marble stairs. "You told Detective Denton you'd stay home with me. You promised."

Zach sank down beside her and let out a long sigh. "He was asking a lot of questions that were none of his business and giving pseudo-medical advice to *me*—a doctor. I told him what I thought he wanted to hear. I had to get him out of here so you could lie down. You're in no danger from four pills."

"What about my concussion?"

"You may have a mild one. We can FaceTime every couple of hours while I'm at the hospital. Not ideal, but good enough for monitoring your level of consciousness. I *wish* I had arranged coverage, but I'm on duty the rest of the week, and it's too late to change that without causing a lot of trouble for my colleagues. You don't want me to have to drag Paulson back from Vegas to take my place, do you?"

"Aren't a wife and a newborn in need of care more important than a day at the slot machines?"

He pushed back his hair, frowning. "Of course, but honestly he's a jerk, and I know he won't come back. Like I said, a mild concussion is something I can monitor with frequent check-ins, but I want you to feel safe. I can always call Eckard and have him readmit you into the hospital. That way I'll be right there with you, in the same building."

"Readmit me without Jolene?" She didn't want to go to the hospital. She wanted to be home, where she belonged, with her husband and her baby. "That feels like more punishment."

He picked up her hand. "Stop. Please, just *stop* with the nonsense. I wasn't punishing you when you were in labor, and I'm not punishing you now. If you don't want to go to the hospital you don't have to. I know you want to see Jolene, so we'll Zoom with Mom as soon as we get upstairs."

"I need to hold her in my arms."

"And you will. Tomorrow, when you're feeling yourself again." He pressed her head to his chest, stroked her hair. "Let's get you rested and back to being Holly so we can bring our little angel home. I'll text you every two hours—if anything worrisome comes up I'll put you back in the hospital."

"Tomorrow you'll bring her home?" She *was* still woozy, and she needed to be one hundred percent clear-headed if she was going to be the only one taking care of Jolene.

"I promise. And don't worry, darling. From here on out, I'm going to be keeping very close tabs on you."

SIX

When the elevator doors opened onto the fourth floor of Tanner Hall, the stink of formaldehyde hit—just in case anyone could forget the location of the anatomy lab. But, Claudia Keeler noted, the pungent funk that filled your nose and stuck in your throat hadn't dampened her lover's ardor.

Unfortunately.

Usually, she adored the fact Zach couldn't keep his hands off her, but tonight his constant poking and palming was making it hard for her to locate her student badge and swipe them into the lab. "Babe, give me a break, okay? The sooner we get in, the sooner we get out, and *then* we can get it on."

He squeezed her breast over her T-shirt. "I never thought I'd be boning a gunner."

The lock clicked, and she used her shoulder to heave open the heavy metal door, then huffing her dissatisfaction, flipped on the lights.

"What? It's not cool for me to say *boning*?"

"Like I care about that." It was crude, but she understood dirty talk was part of the thrill for him; for both of them, actually.

"Then what is it? You look ticked off."

"I don't like being called that word."

"Gunner? C'mon, some might call it a compliment."

"You know it's not. If you wanted to compliment me you'd have said, 'I can't believe I'm boning one of the smartest, most conscientious medical students in her class.' Just because I care about my grades doesn't mean I'm out to mow down anyone who gets in my way with an AK-47. *Gunner* makes me sound like a horrible person."

"I only mean we're here, in the anatomy lab, at eleven p.m. when we could be at your apartment feasting on the fruits of our passion. Studying can be overrated. Do you know what they call the person who graduates last in his medical school class?"

"What?"

"Doctor." He tweaked her nipple.

"Hilarious. And sadly true. But I have zero plans to finish out of the top ten. And, for the record, you hurt my feelings."

He pulled his hand over his face, and his expression changed, just like that, into one of total support. "I'm sorry. If those assholes in your class are calling you gunner, it's jealousy plain and simple. You're too beautiful to be this smart."

That was so Zach. He loved to tease, but when it came down to it, he really was the sweetest, most attentive man. "So you don't mind hanging out with me while I get our gal ready for tomorrow's assignment?"

"Not at all."

"Thanks." Above them, a fluorescent light crackled, then flickered off and on again. The lab was always a bit ghoulish, but tonight the milky lights bathing the rows of cadavers sent icy fingers racing down her back. Weird, because she'd been here at night before, with her lab partners, and it hadn't seemed this creepy. Maybe it was because she was anticipating the task ahead. "I promised my team I'd do the honors."

"Why?"

"Because they don't have the balls. And volunteering makes me look good."

"It makes you look like a gunner." He raised his palms. "Sorry, just kidding. I meant to say *conscientious*."

"I am conscientious, and no one else wants to do the dirty work, so it's nice of me to step up."

He kissed the back of her neck. "I think you're *very* nice, baby."

She snapped on her gloves and slipped on her goggles. Assembled her tray of tools: scissors, scalpel, forceps, hammer, chisel. Her group's cadaver—they called her Pam out of respect; it helped them remember she'd been a real person—was located at the far end of the lab, tenth row. Using a Sharpie, Claudia marked Pam's anatomical landmarks. Then, without hesitation —she'd been mentally rehearsing this all day—she sliced bone-deep with her scalpel, connecting the dots around the head, starting just above the ridges of the eyes and leaving the space between them intact. Next, she peeled the skin forward to reveal the skull.

"Impressive." Zach gave her a slow clap.

Playfully, she grabbed a bone saw and waved it at him. "So, when are you leaving Wifey?"

"Not today. She just had a kid, remember? But I do have a little surprise for you. I wasn't expecting to be unveiling it here, but this is what happens when you don't let me plan the evening. I was going to draw you a bath with rose petals..." He dropped to one knee and pulled out a small velvet box.

She gasped and her heart literally stopped. She could feel the absence of its beat.

They'd talked about this many times, but for him to propose *now*, only a few days after the birth of his child, that said it all. Tears stung her eyes. Her goggles fogged. Carefully, she set down the saw, balancing it on top of Pam's stomach. Took a step toward him, and, throat tight with emotion, reached out.

Wordlessly, he tugged the clear latex glove from her right hand and slipped a ring on her finger.

She raised her arm and smiled a small smile.

Small to match the stone.

What was this? An aquamarine? And surely less than a carat.

She'd seen the diamond sparkler his wife sported—three carats minimum. "I'm speechless. But yes! Yes, I'll marry you!"

He climbed to his feet, then pressing his body against her, Frenched her with such fervor, she stopped minding about the ring.

A big flashy one would be tacky anyway.

"Wrong hand though." She pulled back, twisting the ring, intending to transfer it to her left hand.

He tilted her face up. "You can't wear it that way yet. This has to be our secret for now. But I couldn't wait any longer to give it to you."

"I understand," she said, valiantly keeping the disappoint-ment from her voice. Naturally, this wasn't the moment to announce their love to the world, but that time would come soon enough. And tonight, he was with *her*.

While Wifey was home alone.

Really alone.

Zach had said she was too stoned to take care of a newborn, so he'd taken Jolene to his mom's. He was going to leave her there a few days so he could spend quality time with Claudia and not have to worry about the baby's welfare.

Poor little baby.

But it was for the best.

Holly was both a terrible wife, constantly berating and belittling her husband, and an unfit mother. But Claudia planned to make it up to both Zach and Jolene as soon as that terrible woman was out of the picture.

Zach ground himself against her. "I'm so happy," he whispered in her ear. "And seeing that ring on your finger is getting me hot."

She removed her goggles, then glanced at Pam. There was still work to be done. Her group was dissecting the brain tomorrow morning. "You know what would get me hot?"

"Name your pleasure, madam."

"Would you mind cutting into the calvarium and exposing the brain? Then all will be ready for tomorrow's dissection, and I'll get the pleasure of watching you at work." She pointed at the bone saw.

"Not at all." He fired it up and the room buzzed with purpose. "'Brain Day' really stuck with me back when I was a medical student. Stand by to pass me the hammer and chisel, and I'll show you how a pro breaks into a skull."

SEVEN

Pull yourself together or she'll turn around and take Jolene with her.

Holly checked the hall mirror. Dabbed tears from her red-rimmed eyes and gathered her mussed hair into a ponytail before opening her front door for her mother-in-law. It was all she could do not to tackle Frances and make off with Jolene, who was sleeping inside a baby pack strapped to Frances' chest. Instead, she pasted on a polite smile, showing the kind of restraint a delusional psycho mom—the type who'd report a child kidnapped when her dad had simply taken her to Grandma's—would've found impossible. "You're here!"

"With bells on!" Zach's mother, Frances Bancroft—balancing Jolene's diaper bag on one shoulder, the baby in front, and a gift-wrapped box in her hand—careened into the foyer. Holly couldn't help hovering, arms out, prepared to catch. Frances had occasional bouts of vertigo, and she'd recently taken a hard fall and broken her ankle—the cast had come off only two weeks ago.

Frances tossed her head and her mid-length black hair

barely moved with the gesture. "Like the new wig? It's a good match to my natural color, I think."

By natural color Frances must mean the brunette she'd been in her youth, since her real hair, now dyed a tasteful shade of red, was actually gray. Frances used wigs to change out her look more often than a celebrity. She liked to dress to accentuate her trim figure, and she minimized her age by occasionally inserting youthful slang she'd gleaned from television into conversation. Today, she looked especially smart in a hot-pink tunic, matching capris and white sandals.

"It's bombshell! Can you make it to the family room with all this?" Holly asked. "Why don't I take Jolene and come back for the rest?"

"No thanks. I'm like a Jenga tower. No telling what will happen if you pull one of my pieces. Better if I soldier on as is."

Holly gazed longingly at the top of Jolene's head, barely peeking above the baby pack. *Be cool.* Frances doesn't need to know you're anxious. "Love that outfit, but you didn't have to dress up for me."

"Oh, I didn't. I'm meeting my squad for coffee in a half hour."

Good. Holly had worried Frances would try to hang around and supervise her in an attempt to placate Zach. He was going to be mad when he learned his mother brought Jolene home against his wishes. It'd been three miserable days since he'd dropped her at his mother's. Three tearful days of pumping and dumping—after taking a slight overdose of pills. Three *guilty* days, knowing her mother-in-law was feeding the baby formula and worrying Jolene would get nipple confusion. And even though Zach had repeatedly promised to bring Jolene home, he kept asking Holly to wait yet another day—just to be safe.

She'd gone along only because she wanted to be one hundred percent for Jolene, and because she suspected her history played into Zach's concern, making him more apprehensive than he would've been otherwise.

When she'd told him her terrible secret on their wedding day, before they took their vows, she'd believed it was the right thing to do. But now, she couldn't help wishing she hadn't been quite so honest.

Maybe he'd decided she wasn't ready for motherhood after all.

Which would be heartbreaking.

It was only because of Zach's love and support she'd come to believe she deserved a family of her own. That what happened when she was sixteen shouldn't dictate her future —*their* future. And thank God for that, because her world transformed the first time Jolene wrapped her tiny palm around Holly's finger.

Now, with her daughter only an arm's length away, it was hard to be patient, but she didn't want Frances second-guessing this decision. She had to show her she was composed and fully capable of caring for a baby, not act impatient, even though she was desperately longing to feel her daughter's heart beating against her own.

"This is a planning lunch, so I don't want to be late. We've got to get our ducks in a row for our annual girls' trip."

She trailed Frances, matching her pace. "Where will you go this year? Colorado again?"

"We've decided to stay in Arizona, we're thinking Christopher Creek—it's close enough to drive, and my car's comfortable enough for the three of us and all our gear."

It was incredible how Frances had bounced back after her fall. Barely missing a beat before returning to her busy schedule: outings with her church group, book club, volunteering at the botanical garden—Holly hoped she'd be as spry at seventy-two. "Could someone else play chauffeur? What about your ankle?"

The distance from the foyer to the family room had seemed interminable, but they'd finally arrived.

"The trip's not until July," Frances scoffed. "My ankle will be fine by then, and even if it isn't, I prefer my driving to either of the other girls'."

"It's good you're planning ahead."

"Those cabins on the creek book up months in advance, and the planning is half the fun. Besides, you know me, I'm organized to a fault."

"Like mother like son."

Frances let the diaper bag slip from her shoulder, dropped the gift on the coffee table and plopped onto the couch. Then the two of them went to work, maneuvering Jolene out of the snuggly and into Holly's arms without incident.

She let out a long breath.

Three whole days apart from her daughter.

Had she been wrong to acquiesce?

She nestled Jolene against her heart. Gazed down at her face.

Pure innocence.

She was determined to be the kind of parent this tiny creature deserved, but there was so much to learn, so many mistakes she might make. She wished she could confide in Frances about the insecurities of being a new mommy, but their relationship had always been an arm's length one. "Thank you, Frances. You don't know how much this means to me."

"It's putting me on the spot with Zach. He told me expressly not to bring her home today. He's quite worried about you, dear."

"I know, and I'm very grateful to you."

"You don't need to keep thanking me. I'm not doing it for *you*." She spoke without malice, her tone neutral. "Do you remember the day of your wedding?"

Holly adjusted Jolene in her arms and sighed, not loving where this seemed to be heading.

"You remember that little talk we had?"

How could she forget the *blood-is-thicker-than-water* talk? The one in which her mother-in-law had made it clear that a daughter-in-law could be well-liked, but she would always be an outsider, never a true member of the family. "Yes."

"I said that in the event of a disagreement between you and my son it would be my duty as a mother to side with him, and that you should take no offense."

Only she had taken offense. But when she'd told Zach he'd laughed it off and declared that in case of any dispute between his mother and her it would be *his* duty as a husband to take *Holly's* part.

To this day, though, Frances' words still stung. And Holly had been more than a little surprised when she'd offered to bring the baby home after Zach left the house this morning. Even now, when it was a fait accompli, Holly could hardly believe she'd diverted her mother-in-law's loyalty away from Zach.

"When the two of you disagree, I'll always take his part. I stand by that."

"Then why did you bring Jolene home?"

"Because though I'm still Zach's mother, I'm now a *grand-mother*, too. And as Jolene's grandmamma, it has become my official duty to always be on *her* side—even if it means going against Zach. He's a grown man. He can look out for himself, but Jolene is vulnerable, totally dependent on us to do right by her."

There was something in Frances' eyes, a certain protective-ness when she looked at Jolene, and it lingered just a moment when she turned her gaze back to Holly.

"Jolene needs her mommy. I simply couldn't bear to think of you two being separated. Like I said on the phone, you needed a rest, but it's been long enough. I only hope you don't make me regret my decision."

She wanted Frances' support. She was grateful to her for bringing Jolene, but this was raising the hairs on the back of her neck. She didn't appreciate the implication she needed to prove herself worthy to her mother-in-law. "I don't know what to say."

"Can we talk about what happened? Zach tried to paint this whole incident as minor—like he's worried I'll disapprove of you —but I'm not interested in passing judgment. I just want to know *all* the facts so I can feel good about leaving Jolene in your care."

Did she doubt what Zach told her? What facts did she think he'd left out? "I'm perfectly capable."

"But you *weren't*." Frances checked her watch.

"You need to get going. Shall I open that gift now or wait for Zach?"

"It's a book on parenting—you can open it later. I've never had any reason to tell you this." Frances hugged herself. "But perhaps it will help you to know that I went through something when Zach was born. Postpartum psychosis."

Holly tried to keep her expression neutral, not reveal the shock she felt. "Psychosis?"

"Who knows if that was really the problem? But that was the diagnosis the doctor gave me. Said I was delusional because I thought my husband was going to hurt Zach."

Holly wanted to reach for Frances' hand, but decided against it. She didn't know if the gesture would be welcome.

"So they packed me off to the hospital for a few days, and, fortunately, I got better quickly on the right medication. Maybe a therapist, or medication, could help you, too."

"I-I'm so sorry for what you went through. And I appreciate your trusting me with that information. But I'm not delusional."

"You thought someone kidnapped Jolene."

"I took too many pain pills."

Frances nodded. "Zach said you took six at once."

"Four." Did Zach exaggerate to ensure his mother's cooperation, or was Frances misremembering?

"That's still too many. Why did you take more than prescribed?"

"I don't remember being in pain. I don't remember wanting the pills, or Zach telling me he was dropping Jolene off with you. I only remember waking up confused, unable to walk straight or think straight. Jolene was gone, and I found that note, so I called nine-one-one."

"You actually believed it was a ransom note?"

"I did. My fear, combined with the drugs, altered my perception. So, I guess, if you want to call that a delusion..." She shook her head. She could still see the bold black letters before her eyes. It looked nothing like any note Zach had ever left her before. "But I don't see it that way."

Jolene's hand was grasping the fabric of Holly's shirt making her milk let down. She settled Jolene beneath a blanket. The sound of her little gulps was a lullaby to her ears. She'd been so anxious about whether Jolene would have trouble latching on after days on the bottle, but fortunately her daughter seemed to be a nursing pro. Which was great because Holly wanted Zach to be able to feed the baby expressed milk. It would help him bond.

Frances smiled. "Looks like she's glad to be home with her mommy. Once he sees how happy you are, I'm sure Zachary will be pleased. He's only trying to do what's best, you know."

Holly nodded. "He's very protective of me."

"And the baby," Frances added.

"Yes..." Jolene pulled away, and Holly took a minute to get her latched on again. "Frances..." Would Frances report everything that happened today back to Zach? Did Holly dare mention her concerns to a woman who'd declared herself to be on Zach's side and to hell with whether he was right or wrong?

Still, here Frances sat, knowing it would anger Zach. Holly decided to chance it. "I hope you won't take offense, but I'm worried about Zach."

"Worried how?"

"Does his behavior seem off in any way to you? He's been a bit controlling ever since Jolene was born."

"He's used to being in charge. He gives orders all day at the hospital so it's no wonder he thinks he can come home and keep right on giving them. You just need to set him straight. But to be perfectly honest, I'm surprised to hear you complain. I thought you liked him being your big bad protector."

She did.

Or at least she *had*.

Maybe it was her, not Zach, who was changing.

She studied Frances' posture—it was open, her arms now relaxed at her side. She no longer seemed in a rush to get to her friends—just like Holly was no longer in a hurry for her to leave. She lifted Jolene to her shoulder, patting her on the back, and said, as casually as she could manage, "Zach's told a few lies. Like saying I took six pills instead of four. He told you six, right?"

Her mother-in-law folded her hands in her lap. "Yes. He did —he can be quite the fabulist. But we all lie sometimes—even your so-called surprise right now is a form of a lie, isn't it? You've been married long enough to know Zach changes the facts whenever it suits him."

Her jaw went slack at Frances' candor. Zach had always been an exaggerator, but it had never seemed like a big deal to Holly before. He was an accomplished, successful man and if he tweaked a story here and there she'd always gone along. What did it matter if he claimed to have bumped into a movie star on the plane when it was probably only a look-a-like, or added a zero when he bragged about the price of the paintings that adorned their walls? But this seemed less innocent. "Zach lied to a *policeman*, Detective Denton. He told him he was going to stay home with me, when he had no intention of doing so. And he also said I had agreed to let him take Jolene to your house, but I don't believe I did."

"I thought you couldn't remember."

She inhaled the scent of Jolene's skin, relishing the weight of her in her arms. "It's possible I could forget something we talked about, but I wouldn't have agreed to let him take her away just so I could take pain pills and sleep. I wouldn't willingly part with her. At first, I thought he wouldn't lie about it, but now I'm convinced he did."

Frances cleared her throat. "If he thought he was doing what was best for you, I can see him taking Jolene without discussing it and just leaving a note. Then, when the sky fell, he covered his mistake with a lie because he didn't want to look like a bad husband."

"You think he'd do that?"

"When he was little he never could admit when he'd done something wrong. Deny, deny, deny. I'd see him put a candy bar in his pocket at the store, and when I'd tell him to put it back he'd say *No, Mom, I don't have a candy bar in my pocket.* Then he started lying about lots of little things. I'd ask him where he'd been, and he'd say he'd been at Trey's house, but later I'd find out he'd been at Jason's—even though there was nothing to be gained or lost by the fib. I got so worried I talked to his pediatrician about it, and you know what she told me?"

Holly waited.

"She said it was normal for his age—he was seven—and that all children lie from time to time." Frances shrugged. "And that's when I stopped worrying. I knew my child wasn't the only one who told whoppers, because the doctor said so. I thought he'd outgrow it."

"But he hasn't, has he?"

"Zach really, really hates to admit it when he makes a

mistake. But there's no such thing as the perfect son or perfect husband, my dear. Zach is a good man. I think that makes up for his flair for storytelling, don't you?"

She nodded, staring down at her daughter's innocent face. No perfect parent, no perfect spouse. We have to love each other with all of our foibles and flaws. Holly had always believed that...

But there was a line, and anyone who came between her and Jolene was crossing it.

EIGHT

Holly's latte called to her from its resting place on their outrageously priced coffee table—the one with an actual teak tree root for a base and a giant slab of onyx on top. The coffee's steam had long since disappeared, and the brew would be room temperature by now, but she longed for her first hit of caffeine since Jolene's birth. Still, she couldn't bring herself to disturb the darling little lady lying prone on her lap. After a good nurse, Jolene had fallen into a milk-drunk slumber draped across Holly's knees, and she couldn't reach the World's Greatest Mom mug Zach had surprised her with yesterday without getting up.

Those are the breaks.

Later would be soon enough to indulge herself.

With a cupped hand she shaded Jolene's eyes from the light floating in through the family room's French doors. Then, staring down at her child, she let her focus soften, imagining those sunbeams ringing into a halo around the baby's wispy hair.

Too corny?

No such thing.

Dreamily, she inhaled her daughter's fresh, powdery scent and touched her pinky to Jolene's palm. The tiny hand reflexively curled around her finger and Holly's heart soared.

This.

This commonplace moment filled a void she hadn't known existed. She could sit here all day reveling in the joy of motherhood. That might be cliché, but can't the triteness of a phrase be forgiven if it reveals an absolute truth?

The irony was that Holly hadn't wanted children—not because she didn't like them—it was far more complicated than that.

Her relationship with her parents was tolerable, almost pleasant, now that they were living abroad, traveling from country to country; free-spirited and happy in a way they'd never been while they were working nine to five. She'd heard, often enough, from her parents' lips what a challenge raising a child—a *girl*—could be, and how limiting. They'd been ecstatic when, after high school, she'd earned a full scholarship to college, allowing them to quit their jobs and take up a less conventional, more "authentic", lifestyle.

Then there was her past.

Comprised of memories she stored in a hard-to-reach compartment of her brain, to be taken out and examined only when absolutely necessary. On her wedding day, in the spirit of total honesty between husband and wife, she'd shared her story with Zach.

Revealed a secret from her youth so dark it was almost too much for her to bear.

Something that made her doubt her ability to be a good parent—and her worthiness of the role.

But Zach had been unfazed. He'd told her it only made him love her more. And that he had no doubt that what happened when she was sixteen would only serve to make her a better mother to their children.

That was the Zach she knew and loved.

The man who'd lifted her up, made her believe she could be a better person.

So when he'd declared it was time to start a family, she'd let him persuade her, believing in herself mainly because he did, and knowing he'd be every bit as wonderful a father as he was a husband.

Now, the thought pricked like a pin, threatening to pop her bubble of happiness—because Zach had fallen from his pedestal this past week.

You should never have put him up on one.

There's no such thing as the perfect husband.

She certainly wasn't a perfect wife.

Fortunately, since that whole fiasco with the pain pills and the "ransom note", things had settled down. She'd flushed the pills and, apart from the fatigue anyone who gets up with a baby at night experiences, and some mild discomfort from her C-section, she felt right as rain. Plus, she had to admit that as much as she'd love to have Zach home, she didn't really *need* him. He had so many professional duties—delivering babies at the hospital, mentoring medical students, seeing patients in the clinic, administrative duties as department chair—it would be difficult to find coverage at the last minute. Given the fact Craig Paulson had backed out of his promise, Holly tended to agree Zach had little recourse but to leave her to her own devices.

She could handle it.

Besides, he checked in with her frequently, and the past few days he'd been so sweet, coming home at night with small and not so small gifts for her—yesterday was the coffee mug, the day before a gold locket with Jolene's picture inside. It seemed they were getting back to the old Zach and Holly—the couple with a marriage all her friends envied.

Her thoughts were drifting and her mouth dry. She could

really use a sip of that coffee and was debating getting up for it when soft chimes filled the room.

Jolene stirred and Holly gently lifted her to her shoulder, then checked the doorbell camera from her phone app.

How sweet!

This would be today's surprise gift from Zach.

A slight figure, her face obscured by a vase of red roses, appeared on the doorbell cam's live view.

Holly touched the speaker button. "Thanks so much! Can you just leave them on the porch?"

No response.

Sometimes the audio feed from the phone app was garbled or didn't go through at all.

Holly got up, and on her way to the front of the house, thought about the changes she planned to make to the family room. Its current décor left a lot to be desired from a baby's point of view. She'd decided to designate a "Jolene friendly" section and cushion the floors with thick mats. Put in a tall table constructed from colorful blocks that could serve as both a changing station and storage space for blankets and toys. Now that there were three of them, her definition of "family room" had changed, and it was going to take more than the playpen Frances had given them to make it work.

Her immediate dilemma, however, was how to maneuver their heavy, copper-plated front doors while holding a baby. She tried the intercom again. "Can you just leave them? Thanks so much."

"Mrs. Bancroft?" The vase moved to the side, revealing a young woman's eager face.

Apparently she didn't want to leave the arrangement on the porch.

Of course.

What was she thinking? The woman deserved a gratuity. Holly shifted Jolene into a more secure position and carefully tugged open the front door. "Sorry, my hands are full. Would you mind coming in and putting the roses on the side table?"

The delivery person slipped past her into the foyer.

"Give me one minute to get my purse." She frowned, trying to remember if she'd left it in the kitchen or the dining room. Hopefully not upstairs.

"It's me." The young woman smiled and widened her pretty blue eyes expectantly before blinking their dark, dramatic lashes.

So not a delivery person?

Holly had just put her foot in it. She gazed at her, pretending she recognized her. The nose was a bit long for her face and her chin pointy, but she had those thick, fluttery lashes —extensions for sure—long, dishwater blonde hair. Tan legs. Short skirt. Breast implants? The vivacious perfection of youth and a great body transformed her from attractive to super sexy. Holly waited a beat, still hoping this person's identity would come to her.

"Claudia, remember?"

"Oh my gosh! Of course!" Still nothing. There was something familiar about her though. And Holly hadn't seen their neighbor's daughter in almost four years, since she'd gone off to college. But wasn't her name... "You're Vera's daughter?"

She *must* be.

Disappointment flitted across that pretty face. "We met before—Zach—I mean Dr. Bancroft is my preceptor. I work with him in clinic. He introduced us once."

She remembered meeting one student Zach had mentored, but that was a while ago, and although she had a similar look, Holly was certain her name had been Beth because that was Holly's middle name.

"Sorry. I do remember, now." Vaguely. Possibly.

"Is this Jolene?" Claudia moved the flowers from side to side as if not knowing what to do with them. "She's adorable!"

A wave of warmth swept away the awkwardness Holly felt. Any fan of Jolene's was a friend of hers. "I know! Come in. You can put those right there." She nodded toward a mahogany sideboard.

Claudia set the flowers down. Up close, Holly could see they were the kind she often saw at the grocery store. Slightly browning red roses with interspersed sprigs of baby breath in a cheap, green tinted vase. But they probably set Claudia back forty dollars or more, and that was a lot for a medical student. If she didn't have Jolene in her arms she'd hug her. "I love them! That's so nice of you! Thank you!"

"You're welcome." Claudia beamed.

"I'm sorry you missed Dr. Bancroft, but I'll be sure to tell him you came by and brought these beautiful roses."

"I figured he might be working, but I just wanted to say congratulations... and I've been dying to see Jolene. I've heard so much about her."

Sweet that Zach was talking about the baby to the medical students.

"Can I hold her?"

"Let's sit down first." Holly's maternal instincts had her tightening her hold on Jolene, but logic mitigated the reaction. The "ransom note" incident was a lesson. It was fine to be protective, but there was no threat here. And this young woman was as nice as they came.

Claudia followed her to the family room and let out a soft gasp. "Your house is... it's stunning."

"Thank you." It was actually. Open floor plan. Twenty-foot vaulted ceilings. Marble and wood floors. Custom chandeliers. Floor-to-ceiling windows. The list went on.

"It looks like a hotel."

"Thanks again." Holly smiled, realizing Claudia had intended that as a compliment. "Please sit down wherever you like."

Claudia perched awkwardly at the edge of an armchair. "Can I hold her now?"

Holly got a fluttery feeling in her chest. "You don't have a cold or fever?"

"Oh no! I wouldn't have come. I would hate to expose Jolene to anything."

"I'm afraid she's just waking up from a nap."

Claudia's face fell.

It was perfectly safe to let her hold the baby. Holly bent and carefully slid Jolene into Claudia's outstretched arms. "But it's fine. Here you go."

Then she stood there, looming over her.

Jolene cooed.

Okay, that's enough.

Holly gathered her daughter back up and went and sat on the couch.

"You don't remember me, do you?" Claudia asked. "I guess you meet a lot of students."

Actually, she did recall meeting Claudia after all. That southern accent brought it back. One day, after visiting her obstetrician, she'd gone to campus to show Zach a copy of the latest ultrasound of the baby and, when she'd opened his office door, she'd found a young woman—*this* young woman—sitting cross-legged in a chair, reading a book. Zach had been behind his desk, apparently working on his progress notes. Claudia's shoes had been off, which Holly found inappropriate. Later on, she'd cautioned Zach not to get too familiar with his students because they might misinterpret the relationship. He'd reassured her there was nothing going on with *any* of his students, but agreed, for the sake of political correctness, to set a more formal tone in the future.

He hadn't mentioned he was Claudia's preceptor. That he was mentoring her.

Holly smiled at Claudia. "I remember. We met at the

hospital a few months ago. You were in my husband's office." Did that sound proprietary? What if it did? Zach was, after all, her husband.

"That's right," Claudia said, and stretched her arms out, waving her left hand in front of Holly.

"What a beautiful ring. Is that an aquamarine?" Holly asked.

"It is, and thanks. I just got engaged recently."

"How wonderful. Congratulations."

"Your ring is a lot better." Claudia reached out and grabbed Holly's hand.

Holly pulled it back. "We both have beautiful rings, I think. We're both very lucky."

"Only you're more lucky."

The way Claudia was staring at her diamond made Holly uncomfortable. The quicker they got off this subject the better. "Why don't I make tea?" she asked. Her coffee was long since cold and suddenly didn't appeal.

"I'd love some," Claudia said.

And that was when Holly realized her mistake. There was something off about the whole situation. It was too intimate. She shouldn't have invited Claudia inside in the first place. She shouldn't have offered her tea. She should've said she was tired. She wanted to be alone with her baby, but now she was stuck making small talk with a virtual stranger and there was no telling for how long. "I'll put the kettle on."

She decided to take Jolene into the kitchen with her.

That remark about Holly being *more lucky* gave her the shivers. It was straight out of one of those films where the ingénue wants to steal the star's life... or the nanny wants the baby for herself!

And why did Claudia bring her flowers?

Zach had never even mentioned her. He'd spoken of Beth a time or two, and now, Holly wondered what happened to her.

Medical students rotated in and out of his clinic, she knew that, but she was suddenly curious. How closely did Zach work with them and for how long? Did he choose them himself? Were all of them female? Pretty young women like Beth and Claudia?

Did Claudia have a crush on Zach?

Then she let out a breath. She could drive herself crazy with questions like these and it wasn't good for her mental health. If it were a friend's husband she might be worried on her behalf—but if ever there was a devoted husband, it was Zach. He wasn't the kind of man who would cheat. It simply wasn't in his DNA.

NINE

By four months of age, Jolene was starting to be awake more than she was asleep, which meant Holly had to make the most of her naptimes. They could easily afford a full-time house-keeper, but, since Jolene's birth, Holly had come to value her privacy more than ever, and because she was home, it made sense to do most of the chores herself. Cleaning, grocery shop-ping, and preparing make-ahead frozen meals so Zach could heat up his favorites on those many occasions he got home too late for a sit-down dinner. Of course there was laundry—seem-ingly never-ending with an infant in the house. It was a lot to keep up with, so she did use a local service to do deep cleaning every two weeks.

And she *tried* to stick to a routine.

After the pain pills fiasco, Zach had created a schedule for her, including what time to get up, have lunch, and do house-work. Remarkably, it didn't specify what time she should pee. If she needed to leave the house for groceries or the doctor, he insisted she call him upon departure and arrival.

His intentions were good—she truly believed that—but he seemed oblivious to the fact that newborns didn't care about schedules. In fact, her pediatrician recommended Jolene feed on demand. So Holly found herself falsely checking chore boxes and marking down fake feeding times in order to avoid an argument with her husband.

She missed the easiness of her pre-baby relationship with Zach, and those lazy Sundays sipping champagne at brunch after a double bout of morning lovemaking. Shrugging, she capped the bottle of hypoallergenic laundry detergent, set the wash cycle, and headed for his study. Did she dare venture off schedule to sneak in a little quality time with her man before Jolene woke up?

Structure was important to Zach, but sometimes he surprised her.

Like that day Frances had brought Jolene home "early" after *the incident*.

She'd been expecting him to hit the roof, but he hadn't put up a fuss at all. He'd said Holly should decide when she was well enough to care for Jolene on her own, and he seemed to be applying that philosophy to their bedroom activities, too. It'd been four months now, and he hadn't approached her for sex. She suspected he wanted her to take the initiative after their misunderstanding that day she came home from the hospital. And she appreciated the courtesy. She'd needed time to feel healthy and in control of her body again.

Now, in spite of a rocky start, she was feeling great, and each day she grew more confident in her new role as Mommy. Zach was getting back to his old supportive self, and apart from this mind-blowing schedule he'd foisted on her, things were good between them.

She found herself missing their lovemaking—the pleasure, certainly, but more than that, the closeness.

The shared secrets.

Letting go.

Trusting—which was why she had decided against

mentioning that student, Claudia, except to say how lovely it was of her to bring flowers.

Zach had done nothing to make her question his fidelity and interrogating him about the women he encountered at work would be doing exactly that. She wanted to return to what they'd had before, and that meant her showing a little faith in him, and him returning the favor.

Pausing at the threshold of his office, she drank in his profile and noticed her heart beating faster. It wasn't just because he was handsome, though he surely was, with his thick, black hair, and dark lashes setting off alpine-blue eyes. It was more the intimacy of knowing the exact curve of his cheek, the precise angle of his nose, the way he pursed his lips in concentration as he studied the screen in front of him.

What was he looking at?

Facebook?

"Whatcha working on?" she said teasingly, as she approached.

His shoulders jumped, and he slammed down the screen like he'd been caught on a porn site. Zach normally eschewed social media, claiming it was a time suck for weak-minded people, but she'd caught him browsing on occasion.

"I was vetting a new hire. We don't want to get blindsided like the folks in cardiology."

She crinkled her eyes. "Remind me what happened there?"

"They brought in a new department chair. Immaculate resume. Stanford educated. Fifteen years' experience—perfect interview. Offered him a big signing bonus and a golden parachute. Then six months later, when they had to let him go, they got stuck with a big payout."

"Why did they fire him?"

"There were multiple complaints he was stalking nurses online, liking white nationalist posts, etc. You know how I feel about spending time on social media, but these days it's almost malpractice to hire someone without checking their accounts."

She squeezed his shoulders, and he swiveled his chair to face her.

"What can I do for you?" he asked. "You look like you've had quite a morning, and I mean that in the best possible way."

"Oh yeah?"

"Yeah. I love it when you get dirty. Makes me want to draw you a warm bubble bath and climb in with you, fool around—just around the edges."

"Do you have time?"

He opened his arms, and she slipped onto his lap. Closed her eyes, relaxed into him. His fingers massaged her scalp. His breath was warm and ticklish as he whispered dirty words in her ear.

"I miss you," she said.

"Me too, you." He ran a finger along her cheek and tilted her face up. "I wish I could but I'm afraid I have to finish up and..."

They both knew Frances' ringtone—she was on that weekend getaway up in Christopher Creek, the one she'd been planning for months with the ladies.

"Dammit." He blew out a breath and made a show of putting the phone on speaker. "Hi, Mom." Then he mouthed: *If I have to suffer*... "You're on speaker with Holly. How's the trip? You ladies staying out of trouble—not hiring any strippers, I hope?"

There was a faint whimpering sound, like crying.

"Mom?"

More whimpering, this time louder, interrupted by punchy breaths. "I-I... just a second."

Holly stiffened and climbed off Zach's lap. "Frances, we're here. Just take your time and tell us what's going on."

"Mom? Are you okay? Is anyone hurt? You're scaring me." Zach held the phone between them.

"N-no. Not hurt. Nobody's hurt. But I'm not okay. Can you come pick me up, *please*?"

"Right now? In Christopher Creek? That's two hours from here... but I'll rush right up if you're in danger. Stop crying. Count to ten and take a breath. Then tell me what's going on," Zach said.

"I can't. Not over the phone. Not with *them* listening."

He rolled his eyes. "You had an argument? The way you were crying I assumed this was an actual emergency. This isn't high school, Mom. If you hurt someone's feelings just apologize. If they hurt yours, let it go. And anyway, you have your own car, if you're mad and want to come home early."

"I-I have nothing to 'pologize for, and I'll be damned if I'll stay. You're my son. I have no one else to call. You need to come get me."

"Have you been drinking? It's not even noon." He clapped one hand atop his head.

"Are you coming to get me or not?"

"I would if I thought it was the right thing for you, but this seems like something between you and your friends. You should try to work it out."

More whimpering.

Holly shook her head, put her arms around herself. "What if something's really wrong?"

Zach hit the mute button. "I'm not going to drive all that way because she's been drinking and got emotional. I told her not to go, but she wouldn't listen. She's too old to be traipsing around with her girlfriends. If she'd done as I asked, she could be here with us enjoying her granddaughter right now."

Holly unmuted the phone. "Frances, it's me. I'm worried. Are you sure you're not hurt? Is anyone? Will you *please* tell us what's going on?"

"It's not like that. But it's bad just the same. Dina and Alfre think... they think... I'm sorry. It's so awful, the things they're accusing me of. I need to get out of here, but then they won't have a car, and I won't be blamed for stranding them on top of everything else. And... yes... I might have had some wine so I can't drive myself no matter what. I'm begging for your help. You have no idea what it's like. I simply cannot be around these women any longer."

Those women were Frances' best friends. Had been for decades. They'd been through so much together. "Are you sure you can't talk this through?"

"Impossible. Please, please, *please* help me."

"We'll come get you," Holly said. "Try to relax, and we'll be there in about two hours. You can leave your car so the others can have a way home. We just need to make sure whoever drives it doesn't drink before getting behind the wheel."

Zach was shaking his head *no* and a vein in his forehead had doubled in size. She could tell he'd dug in his heels, but Frances wasn't one to dramatize. At least not in Holly's experience. Something *big* must have happened.

"Thank you." Frances sounded distant, like she was either whispering or had moved too far from the phone.

"We're *not* coming," Zach said. "Just sit down and work things out with your friends. You're seventy-two years old, and I'm not going to pick you up from your slumber party."

"*Please. Please.*" Frances began full-on sobbing.

"Text the address to my phone," Holly said. "I'm on my way."

Zach disconnected the call and got to his feet, loomed over her, his face flushed with anger. "I forbid you to do this. She needs to experience the natural consequences of her behavior."

Was he serious? "She's not a child, and you're not her parent."

"This is for her own good. I specifically told her not to go.

So now, if things have gone south, she can deal with the fallout. That's how people learn."

"You can't forbid me to go. And I refuse to leave your elderly mother in a potentially volatile situation far from home. We don't even know what's going on. What if the *fallout* you want her to experience is dangerous?"

"She's with Alfre and Dina. Whatever this is, I'm sure it will blow over. Trust me, this is a good lesson for her."

Holly put her hands on his shoulders and met his gaze. "I won't leave her twisting in the wind. If you insist on teaching her something, fine with me. Feel free to practice your lecture in the car. In fact, I hope you will. But with or without you, I'm going to get Frances."

TEN

Holly climbed out of her Tesla and breathed in the woods' cool pine-scented air, glad to be able to step outdoors without the oppressive heat of summer in Scottsdale.

If only she were here under different circumstances.

The heaven-blue sky, the crunch of pine cones beneath her shoes, the soft whisper-songs of fat blue jays—it would be so lovely to relax and unwind here. The ladies had rented this cabin on Christopher Creek until Wednesday. Maybe they'd worked things out while Holly was riding to the rescue. Maybe she and Jolene could spend the night stargazing and nursing and then head home tomorrow morning—which would give Zach a chance to cool down.

When she'd loaded the baby into the car, he'd made his disapproval clear, staunchly refusing to either ride along or babysit. *Ugh.* She understood it was just a word, but it made her cringe to hear Zach describe caring for his own daughter as *babysitting.*

Now, as she went around to unbuckle Jolene, who slept soundly in her car seat, she heard shrill voices coming from inside the cabin. She stepped back, debating. It didn't seem like a good idea to take a baby into the midst of an ongoing argument. The cabin was on a remote private property. Her car was parked in clear view of the front door—and at this altitude the outdoor temperature was safe, just about seventy. If a car came up the road she'd have plenty of warning. It would pose no danger to Jolene to let her finish her nap in the back seat.

"Bitch!"

Okay. Jolene was definitely staying in the car.

Holly eased the door closed and then climbed the porch. Rapped at the frame of the screened-in cabin.

Dina, dressed in denim shorts and shirt, her gray hair in a mini ponytail, her green eyes snapping, flung open the screen door. "I'm outta here!" She shoved past Holly without so much as a *hello* or *how's the baby?*

Next, came Alfre in similar garb, identical mood. "We're not coming back until she's gone."

Holly turned to watch the ladies race down the path, past the car and Jolene, not bothering to glance over their shoulders.

"What on earth?" she asked and entered the cabin, which was really too cute with its colorful throw rugs, antler chandeliers and little statues of black bears all over the place.

"I told you so," Frances said. "I'm so done with those two."

At least she wasn't crying, but her lips were pale and tear trails of dirt and mascara stained her cheeks. Holly wanted to give her a hug, but they didn't have that kind of relationship. She pulled some tissue from her purse and held it out.

Frances took it and blew her nose. "Where's Zachary?"

"He had work to do. He's very sorry he couldn't make it. Listen, Jolene's napping in the car so we need to keep an eye and ear out. I'm going to leave the front door open."

"You drove all the way up here? Just you and the baby?"

"It's fine." Not only had Zach refused to ride along, he'd told her if she defied his wishes he'd have to "crack down" on her, whatever the hell that was supposed to mean.

"But Zachary should've been the one to... Oh, Holly. I never meant to cause you any problems, but thank goodness you're here. You can see how it is. This situation is unbearable."

Empty wine glasses cluttered the kitchen counters and the tables, but Frances' words were crisper than they'd been on the phone. Hopefully her buzz was wearing off, and a lot of this mess could've been left over from the previous evening's festivities.

"Is that your stuff?" An overnight case and small backpack were positioned next to the front door. Frances nodded and folded her arms.

Holly had just driven two hours. She needed at least a small break before heading down to Phoenix again. The living area and kitchen were all one room, and Holly poured herself a glass of water from a pitcher in the fridge. She peeked out the front door at the car, and then went to sit and stretch her legs at the dining table, where an open laptop faced away from her. "Okay, we're alone, and I need a minute before getting behind the wheel again. Do you feel comfortable telling me what happened?"

"I'll never feel comfortable. But go ahead. Look for yourself."

"What are you talking about?"

"Check the laptop." Frances covered her eyes, as if she couldn't bear to watch Holly's reaction.

Suddenly nervous, Holly pivoted the laptop and tapped a key. The screen lit up and she covered her mouth with her hand. "Oh my word!"

"You're looking at *Harry's* Facebook account. Supposedly, *I* sent all those lewd private messages to him."

"Dina's Harry?" Oh boy. This was a lot worse than she'd imagined. She was now skimming a whole string of triple X-rated messages between Harry and some evil prankster masquerading as Frances.

Faked—obviously—but still, incredibly disturbing.

"Uh-huh. Harry wants to do things to me I didn't even know existed."

"You've been hacked. I know this must be upsetting but Dina and Alfre surely know you'd never send messages like these, and especially not to Dina's husband. None of you work for Google, but you're savvy enough to realize social media accounts get hacked all the time. If anything, I'd think your friends would be sympathizing with you that something like this was being put out there."

"They think the messages are real."

"But that's ridiculous!"

"Ridiculous to you and me. But apparently not to Dina and Alfre. They're calling me a home-wrecker."

"I just can't believe they'd take that stance."

"Harry *responded* to the messages. He believes I offered to-to...!"

"Maybe his account was hacked, too. I'll stay until Dina and Alfre get back, and then we can all sit down. I'll explain how these things happen. They know you well enough to recognize that you'd never do anything like this."

"You don't understand! Harry admitted it—begged Dina for forgiveness. He said that in the beginning he thought it was a joke, but then, as time went on he just got sucked into a fantasy, because he's weak, but he never meant to actually *act* on anything. Dina flipped out, and Alfre's almost worse. They are accusing Harry and me of having an affair. Dina said she's going to leave him so we can fly our 'freak flag'. Do I seem like the type who wants to fly her *freak flag*?"

"Look, this kind of thing happens all the time."

"It doesn't. I don't know a single other person this has happened to. And those messages are circulating among my church group *and* my Red Hat Club. I can't show my face anywhere. I won't even be able to go to worship services!"

"You know what? Let's talk about this more in the car. Grab your stuff and we'll get going. I'm sure after a little bit of time, Dina and Alfre, the church group, *everyone* will realize this wasn't your fault. You didn't send any raunchy messages and you're certainly not responsible for *Harry's* bad behavior—that's between Dina and him."

"You make it sound like it's all about them forgiving me! Like that will make everything okay. But I did nothing wrong. And now I'm supposed to ignore their accusations. I've been friends with both of those women more than thirty years and neither one of them gave me the courtesy of listening to my side."

"They will. Just give it some time. It's the shock value—they're not thinking clearly."

"*Who* would do this to me? Poison everyone I know against me? I just don't understand what I've done to deserve this. I can't think of anyone who hates me this much."

This time, Holly didn't hold back. She jumped up and gave Frances a good long hug. The woman needed support. She needed to know someone was on her side. "Like I said, we can straighten this out. We just need to help them see that your account was hacked. It's a common occurrence."

"But..."

"Truly, it is. We'll change your password. Open a different account if we have to. They're going to forgive you, and with time, you're going to forgive them. Let's try not to worry about someone hating you. Everyone who knows you loves you. This a random event, not a personal attack."

It couldn't possibly be.

ELEVEN

This bustling restaurant was on Holly's list of the best things in life. Usually, Kandel's Delicatessen, with its delicious aromas, meat-filled glass showcases, and to-die-for desserts, not only made her mouth water, it made her want to book a flight to New York City.

Only today, her heart wasn't in it.

She'd barely touched her pastrami sandwich and root beer.

Jolene's state-of-the-art baby monitor, or rather its corpse, lay in the center of a big circular booth, while Holly and three of her best girlfriends discussed possible means of resuscitation.

"You've tried turning it off and on again?" asked Lindsey of the Brazilian blown-out hair, filled cheeks, and competition-fit body. When Holly first met her, Lindsey was pretty with naturally curly hair and a curvy figure. This more glamorous version debuted after her husband's affair with his personal trainer. When that came to light, Lindsey took a spa vacation and returned home with new cheeks, a new hair color—red—and what she coyly referred to as a laser-tightened "feminine mystique".

Out of her peripheral vision, Holly caught Tamara rolling

her big green eyes. Holly reached under the table and gave Tamara's arm a warning squeeze, lest she unleash her famous sarcastic wit, and then said, "First thing I tried. But it won't turn on at all—and I also changed the batteries."

"Did you shake it?" Lindsey seemed determined to pursue an unhelpful line of questioning.

"Believe me. I did everything but give it mouth-to-mouth. It's dead, kaput, gone for good." Her shaky voice belied the joke. This crashed techno-gadget signaled trouble. It wasn't because Zach would be angry when he found out what had happened. It was because he would be "concerned", and, worse, that concern would be understandable.

Audra crossed her slender arms and pursed full lips, painted in a subtle glossy peach shade that matched her Dior blouse. "Okay. But, honey, you need to relax. I don't see why you can't just ask Zach to pick up a new one on his way home."

"She was on a wait-list for months before Jolene was born. Remember? It's got built-in lullabies and temperature controls and all kinds of stuff."

Tamara was right, but that wasn't the main problem. "These are always on back order and it will be months before we can get a new one, but that's not why I don't want to tell him."

"Then what is?" Audra asked, twirling a lock of blonde hair around a manicured finger—also painted peach—and looking confused.

"I don't want him to know that I found it in the freezer next to my breast milk."

"Big deal. I left my glasses in the refrigerator once. Didn't find them until the next morning when I went to get myself a glass of juice." Audra removed her designer frames and turned them over in her hands as if inspecting for damage. "You've got baby brain. He'll understand."

"Five months of baby brain?" What if there really was something wrong with her? "That monitor is my connection to

Jolene, and I lost it. If I could do something so dumb with something so important..."

"It's just a gadget. It's not like you put *Jolene* in the freezer." Lindsey picked up the monitor and pressed the power button.

They all held their breaths, and then... nothing.

Her friends were only trying to reassure her, but they didn't understand. It had all started with the ransom note incident. Afterwards, things improved for a while, but then, after the day she'd picked Frances up at Christopher Creek, everything started going downhill again. Holly kept forgetting things, misplacing things, and Zach began treating her like a child in need of constant supervision. He expected her to text him, *with pictures*, every hour throughout the day, send him her route if she went anywhere, and again, snap photos of the location.

For the past month, she'd mostly stayed home to avoid the drama, and being housebound, self-imposed or not, was getting to her. So when Frances offered to watch Jolene today, Holly jumped at the chance to lunch with friends and get some objective advice. But now, the pitying looks on their faces only made her feel worse.

Tamara's arm slid around her, and suddenly, without warning the dam burst. Silent tears began rolling down Holly's cheeks to a chorus of sighing, comforting clucks of the tongue and *oh honeys.*

She wasn't used to being the object of her friends' pity.

It was humiliating.

And the baby monitor was only a small part of it.

What would they think if they knew about the ransom note incident?

Or that right now, at this very minute, her garage was crammed with shipping boxes?

She hated the idea of looking even more foolish in front of these women, but she needed to confide in someone. "I ordered twenty Italian strollers," she blurted.

"Why did you do that? Never mind. Baby brain." Lindsey waved her hand like she thought it was nothing, but the look on her face told a different tale.

"I guess. But I don't know how much longer I can keep covering my mistakes with a catchphrase. At some point I need to take responsibility for my actions."

"*Baby brain* isn't a catchphrase, it's a real thing. At least I think it is. And we've all done strange things when we're under stress. Believe me, I know what I'm talking about." Tamara's voice held no hint of neediness. She wasn't trying to minimize the issue or turn the attention to her own problems—which were far worse than Holly's. The way Tamara had carried herself, with such grace, after Tom died, even though her heart had been breaking, made Holly admire her. She realized she should've told Tamara that, but she'd been preoccupied with her pregnancy, and Tamara was so strong she didn't seem to need anyone's approval.

She wished she were more like Tamara. "Zach suggested I see a shrink. When all this started he wasn't in favor, but now, he thinks I might need medication."

"Maybe he has a point. If you need help getting through the postpartum period, that's nothing to be ashamed of," Lindsey said.

"When does postpartum officially end?" Holly sighed.

"Zach's an obstetrician. He'd know the answer if you'd ask him," Audra said softly. "He's not a monster, Holly. I don't understand why you're acting like you can't talk to him."

"Don't do that, Audra. She never said he was a monster." Tamara turned to Holly. "What happened with the strollers? And when? And why didn't you tell us before?"

Holly took a long breath, trying to channel some of Tamara's moxie. "Zach decided our stroller wasn't what he wanted. He'd heard about some that come with special wheels and built-in fleece and, you know him, he loves his designer labels. So we researched them together and picked out a brand a lot of the celebrities use. I was supposed to order two—he wanted one for his mother to keep at her place. But it seems I hit an extra zero and wound up ordering a quantity of twenty."

Audra got busy stirring her coffee, avoiding eye contact. "I'm sorry but I have to ask—what did that set him back?"

"Including the tax..." Holly stuck up her chin. "Over thirty-thousand dollars."

The table went completely silent. A woman in a nearby booth gasped, making Holly's face go hot.

She should lower her voice.

"Oh, wow." Tamara's lips curled at the edges. "Thirty grand on strollers. Hats off to you, my friend."

Holly's trembling lips began to itch, and then a tickle started in her throat.

Lindsey covered a blatant smile, and a moment later Tamara let loose her laugh. Audra followed suit, and then, finally, Holly did too.

When you really thought about it, it was funny, like something out of an "I Love Lucy" episode.

Lucy might have been crazy, but in a good way. Nobody considered her a danger to Little Ricky.

And Zach blowing his top and cancelling her credit cards? That was just what Ricky Ricardo would have done.

The world wasn't coming to an end.

All she'd needed was a little perspective.

Thank heavens for friends.

"What did Zach say? And can you return them?" Lindsey asked.

She might as well spill all the dirt. But something in her wanted to protect Zach from being judged too harshly, so she started with the good part. "We're going to return ten of them for a refund and pay for the other ten. The company was very understanding, especially when Zach said he'd donate the extra ones we didn't need to a women's shelter."

"That is just like him—generous to a fault." Audra made no secret she'd always thought Zach hung the moon and, she'd said once, when she was snookered, of course, that if she weren't one of Holly's closest friends, she'd go after him herself, now that her divorce was final.

Holly counted to three. *Ready, set, reveal.* "And then he took my name off our bank accounts and all of our credit cards. Except for one card with a low credit limit. Now, every time I make a purchase, it sends him a text requesting authorization."

"You mean like one of those starter cards for teenagers?" Tamara asked.

Holly nodded. "I expect it won't last long. Zach says I just need to demonstrate responsibility and then…"

"You'll get your privileges back? I don't like it. He's acting like your father." Tamara frowned and shook her head.

"I don't know, Tam. We're all on Holly's side. You know we are but—" Audra broke off without finishing.

"Thirty thousand dollars is a lot of money," Lindsey said. "I don't think he's being *that* unreasonable—as long as it's tempo-rary. But now I totally get why you don't want to tell him about the baby monitor. Is there anything I can do? I'll run out right now and pick one up for you if we can locate one."

Audra was already searching on her phone. "I just found one on Craigslist. Should I try to grab it?"

Holly shrugged. "Thanks, but I think I better face the music. I've always believed honesty is the bedrock of marriage. I was having a moment, but you guys, as usual have saved my sanity. I don't know what I'd do without you."

"You've always been there for us, so it's only fair," Tamara said.

Tamara's response, probably automatic, was a generous one that Holly didn't deserve. She'd only reached out to Tamara a handful of times since Tom died, and she regretted that. Holly should've done more. Been a better friend.

Tamara brushed her fingers across the back of Holly's hand and said, "I promise you'll get through this. I almost said you'll look back and laugh someday but we've already done that. Just focus on the good stuff. You've got a beautiful baby and three friends who love you to death."

"And a wonderful husband," Audra said. "Should we all go over to the hospital and break the news to him together?"

Lindsey coughed exaggeratedly. "Keep that crush of yours a little more under wraps or next time we won't invite you."

Holly smiled, feeling relieved that she'd told her friends and no one thought things were beyond repair, either with her brain or her marriage. "I'll tell him myself. I'm sure he'll understand."

After lunch, the women streamed out of the delicatessen and lingered near the doorway, their goodbyes interrupted multiple times with just one more bit of gossip, just one more hug, until finally, a good twenty minutes later, they went their separate ways.

When Holly reached her car, she looked up to find Tamara signaling to her, walking quickly in her direction.

Holly waited by her Tesla, wondering what Tamara, apparently, hadn't wanted to say in front of the others.

Tamara arrived, kicked up one foot and pointed to her heel. "Word to the wise: Stilettos are made for looking good, not for chasing folks down in parking lots."

Holly smiled and waited for Tamara to catch her breath.

"I'm not sure exactly how to put this, and you can tell me to butt out if you think I'm overstepping."

The sun was hot and beads of sweat were forming on the back of Holly's neck. Tamara wasn't one to apologize for having an opinion. What she was about to say was clearly making her uncomfortable, so no telling how Holly was going to feel about it. "Please, just tell me what you think. I value your honesty, and I promise I won't take offense."

"That's good, because the last thing I want is to make you feel badly. You and I have been friends a long time, and I like Zach, I really do. Tom adored him and that means *everything* to me."

"But?" While she appreciated the tact, this delay was only making her more anxious.

"All right. Here goes. I don't think Zach cancelling your credit cards and taking you off the bank accounts was justified at all. It sounds to me like you've lost access to your money, and that worries me."

"Most of it, yes. But that's only temporary."

"Doesn't matter. He's taking away your basic rights. Making you completely dependent on him. I know he provides for your needs, but this isn't good."

"So what are you suggesting I do?"

"I think you need to look out for yourself. Find a way to have some kind of emergency fund just in case."

"In case of what?"

Tamara lifted one shoulder, apparently unwilling to detail what kind of hypothetical emergency might require Holly to have cash secreted away. But the suggestion was enough to get Holly started making her own mental lists of scenarios.

And none of them were good.

TWELVE

Waving off the valet, Holly pulled into the garage at Mercy General Hospital. Courtesy of driving an electric vehicle, she could count on a primo parking spot, specially reserved for plug-ins, next to the elevator on the second level. Gone were the days of planning extra time for circling the garage and then having to cram her car into a too-small space. Also gone: the dings that sometimes mysteriously appeared on her old Nissan's door.

She didn't miss any of that.

But she did miss the sense of belonging, being part of the hospital team. The smile on a child's face when his words were finally understood. Back then, she'd been Holly March, speech-language pathologist assistant (SLPA), a person in her own right.

Now, she was Mrs. Bancroft—Dr. Bancroft's wife.

She'd loved her job as a speech therapist and would have continued working longer, but Zach had wanted her to stop as soon as she'd gotten pregnant. Since she'd planned to stay home the first few years anyway, and it had seemed so important to him, she hadn't put up a fight. But now, she wished she had, and that she'd secreted away some cash for a rainy day.

Only who would've thought she'd need a separate bank account?

One her husband didn't control.

The elevator arrived and she took it to ground level. After exiting the parking garage, she followed the sidewalk through the well-kept grassy grounds, past the prayer chapel, past the hospital's main entrance, and then went in a familiar side door. This older hospital tower housed both pediatrics on the lower levels and maternity on the high floors. When she reached the Teddy Bear Lobby, so named for the murals on its walls, a wave of nostalgia hit.

This was where she'd first met Zach, and she'd fallen hard for him from the very beginning. She'd been standing right here, in the center of the gold and red mosaic floor medallion, waiting with Jeffery, one of her young patients whose mommy was late to pick up. Big, fat tears were rolling down Jeffery's cheeks when Zach rushed past, nearly knocking poor Jeffery down in the process. But Zach had caught him just as the boy's feet went out from under, and had swung him high, zooming him around like an airplane, sound effects and all. A moment later, Jeffery's tears were forgotten and Zach was kneeling in front of him, letting him listen to the beat of his own heart with a stethoscope.

Zach had patiently listened to Jeffery's excited utterances about his new puppy, his mean big sister, and his favorite vegetable—in spite of the little guy's stutter. And after Jeffery's mother arrived and carted him off with apologies for her tardiness, Zach had treated Holly to coffee in the cafeteria. She'd asked him where he'd been rushing off to, and he'd replied, *I was in a hurry to meet you, of course!*

That memory still melted her heart.

Try to hang on to that.

Every marriage has its ups and downs.

No perfect husbands.

She rode the elevator to the fourth floor and, shoulders back, head held high, marched in the direction of Zach's office. She should've texted, but she knew he'd probably be working on his charts around this time, and she wanted to explain about the baby monitor in person. At least at the hospital, he'd be forced to take a breath before reacting. He would never behave unprofessionally at his place of business. Not even behind a closed door.

"Holly!" A vaguely familiar voice hailed her.

She stopped and waited for Craig Paulson, the rat, to catch up with her. "Hi, Craig, how are you?"

"I'm well. How about you? I haven't seen you since the baby was born and I've been meaning to send a card. How is the little one? She's not with you?"

"She's perfect, if I do say so myself, and no, she's with her grandmother."

"Pictures?"

"Of course." His interest in Jolene seemed genuine, softening Holly up a bit. But she hadn't forgotten that he'd promised to cover Zach's shifts when Jolene was born, but then backed out at the last minute. She fumbled in her purse for her phone.

Finding baby photos on it was easy work.

He stepped close, and she held up her display, swiping quickly through her favorites.

"Gosh, she's really just beautiful. It's so good to see you, Holly. Zach's a lucky man."

"Thank you for that, Craig." She hesitated to say anything, but the hard feelings she'd been harboring had vanished. After all, it wasn't Craig's responsibility to ensure Zach took time off when Jolene was born. Zach could've asked someone else to cover. "I hope you had fun in Vegas. I completely understand why you wouldn't want to turn down a free trip."

Silence.

Oh boy. She shouldn't have brought it up. He must be embarrassed about letting Zach down. She smiled broadly to convey her sincerity. "No really, I hope you had a great time."

He shook his head. "I... thank you, but I, um, I haven't been to Vegas in years."

She stared at him.

He shrugged, inclining his head.

"You didn't win a free trip to Vegas at the beginning of March?"

"Not guilty. Sounds great though. I wonder who you're thinking of?"

You. I'm thinking of you.

She tapped her phone against her leg, noticing a bitter taste in her mouth. "Did my husband ask you to cover for him the week Jolene was born—so he could have time off with the baby and me?"

Craig had a scar under his left eye, and now it began to twitch like mad. "Uh... I'm not sure. Did he tell you he did?"

"He said you promised to cover for him, but then you won a free trip to Vegas, and you had to cancel on him."

Craig pressed his fingers against his scar, concealing the twitch beneath his eye. "I won't lie to you, Holly. Zach never approached me for coverage. But you know what? You're probably just confused."

She felt her jaw clench. It was always *she* who was mistaken. *She* was confused. *She* was hallucinating. Only this time *she* freakin' wasn't.

"I bet it was someone else. Maybe he said Paul Conner and you heard Craig Paulson."

"Uh-huh." She nodded, keeping her voice calm, her expression neutral. "That must be it. Anyway, it was nice seeing you. But I've got to go track Zach down. I'm sure he'll be able to clear it up."

Craig reached out and touched her shoulder, then headed down the hall.

She waited until he was out of sight and turned around, heading back for the elevator, searching for Audra's number in her contact list.

"Hey, hon." Audra picked up on the first ring. "What's up? Lunch was fun!"

"You said you found someone offering to sell a baby monitor like mine on Craigslist?"

"Uh-huh. Did you change your mind?"

"Can you give me the seller's info? I want to buy it today."

"Let me put you on hold while I look it up."

Holly was almost to the elevator when Audra came back on the line. "Okay, I found it, but it looks like the seller is offering a package deal—the monitor plus a picture frame nanny cam. Looks like a good one. It's got all the bells and whistles and then some."

"Haven't got a nanny, Audra."

"The seller is specifying 'package deal only'."

"Guess I'll take both the monitor and the nanny cam, then. And, Audra, I hate to ask, but do you think you could lend me some cash?"

"Of course." Audra waited a beat. "But, honey, what happened to total honesty in a marriage?"

Holly boarded the elevator and jammed the button for the ground floor. "I'm beginning to think it's overrated."

* * *

And yet, Holly couldn't see a marriage based on lies going the distance. An occasional fib of convenience might be tolerated, but not something as major as promising to take time off when the baby was born when you had no intention of doing so.

Which was why, later that evening, she'd confronted Zach about Craig Paulson. They couldn't turn back the clock and spend that first precious week of Jolene's life together, but if only Zach would tell the truth, it would go a long way toward restoring the trust she'd once had in him.

"Craig's the one who's lying." Zach rose and began clearing plates from the dinner table, something he rarely did.

Holly followed him into the kitchen. "He's got no reason."

"Sure he does. He doesn't want to look like the bad guy in front of you. I'm not inventing this, Holly. I bumped into Craig in the medical staff services office while I was turning in the monthly duty roster to Donna. That's when I asked him, and he agreed. Donna heard the whole conversation. If you don't believe me, you can ask her."

"Maybe I will." But there was no point. Donna had gotten the job in staff services on Zach's recommendation. She'd cover for him in a heartbeat.

He set the plates on the countertop near the sink. "Great. Now, if I may change the subject, I'd like you to join me upstairs whenever you're ready."

Apparently that meant after she'd finished the dishes.

Whatever hope she'd been holding out that she and Zach could regain the picture-perfect relationship they'd once had was fading fast.

"I want to show you the surprise I promised you before you brought up that creep, Paulson."

She took her time loading the dishwasher, and then brought a package in from the car. She still hadn't told Zach about the frozen baby monitor, and at this point, she probably never would. Truth in a marriage is a two-way street, and if only one person plays by the rules, it puts her at a disadvantage.

Holly climbed the stairs and left the Craigslist baby monitor in the nursery where Jolene was sleeping, then joined Zach in their bedroom. She found him waiting with a wide grin on his face, as if everything between them were fine. As if he hadn't cut off her funds or treated her like a child or been caught in a terrible lie.

Then he covered her eyes, just as he'd done the day of the nursery reveal. He guided her to the big walk-in closet that was hers and hers alone. She heard a click of the light switch and he uncovered her eyes.

She gasped. Not from delight as she had when she'd first seen the finished nursery, but from dismay. What had he done?

Save for her shoes, carefully ordered in rows, and her winter coats, the closet was empty.

"Where are my clothes?" Her knees threatened to buckle beneath her and she backed against the wall.

"You were complaining that nothing fit, so I got rid of them."

"Where are my things?" she asked again, incredulous.

"Donna bundled them up, and the Salvation Army came by and picked them up while you were out to lunch with team Holly."

Donna. Could her relationship with Zach be more inappropriate?

Holly slid to the floor, her legs no longer able to support her weight. "And what am I supposed to wear?"

He crouched down beside her and picked up her hand, turned it palm up, and planted a kiss in it. "That's the big surprise. I hired a personal shopper—actually Donna found her. But I've been consulting with the shopper all week about your favorite colors, your favorite designers. I've authorized her to purchase an entirely new wardrobe, and she's got multiple sizes in everything for you to try. I'll return the ones that don't fit... and, of course, anything you don't like."

"So now you're deciding what I can and cannot wear."

"You're not listening to me. You may choose what you like and what you don't."

"From a selection of clothing you've preapproved."

He dropped her hand. "I would think you'd be thrilled."

She shut her mouth, willing herself not to scream. Sat on her hands to keep from pummeling him with her fists.

"I've spent a small fortune on this. And as I recall, you used to like my taking such a particular interest in *all things Holly*."

He definitely had one thing right.

She *used* to like it.

THIRTEEN

Frances' ringtone startled Holly awake. She grabbed her phone and the screen lit up, flashing the time: eight a.m.

What in the world?

She hadn't slept past five since Jolene had begun teething. The blackout curtain behind the shutters was down, the bedroom dark. Holly fumbled for the remote, and as the curtain scrolled up, light flooded the room. She scooted into a sitting position—simultaneously reaching for the baby monitor on the bedside table. "Frances? You okay?"

"Not really. Are you?"

"I'm fine. I overslept, though." The screen on the baby monitor showed an empty crib. Zach must have Jolene downstairs with him. Holly didn't remember him mentioning he'd be going in late today.

Maybe he regretted lying about Paulson—even though he'd never admit it—or giving away all her clothes. Perhaps he'd realized what a pompous, controlling move that had been and decided to let her sleep in. Extra sleep was a far better gift than roses, and it wouldn't be the first time he'd tried to make amends after acting like a jerk. "What's going on? Did something new happen with Dina and Alfre?"

"I wouldn't know. We're still not speaking, but it's not that. It's Zach. I think he's still mad at me."

"About what?"

"I don't know. Christopher Creek, I guess."

Holly had tried to pretend Zach was on board with her driving up to rescue his mother, but Frances may have seen through her act. Anyway, he hadn't brought it up to Holly since, so she presumed all was forgiven. "Doubtful. That was a month ago and, besides, by the time I got home, he was over it."

"Are you sure? Because he usually calls me in the mornings on his way to work, but he hasn't done that in at least a month; not since Christopher Creek. And if I text him, he either sends me a one word reply or that stupid auto-responder of his—like he did just now."

Holly groaned. "The one that says 'I'm in a meeting. I'll get back to you as soon as possible'? He's probably just got his hands full with Jolene." Holly never went this long without nursing or pumping, and she was feeling more than a little uncomfortable. Just saying Jolene's name aloud made her milk let down. "If he's mad at you, he hasn't said a word to me about it. Let me go find them, and I'll have him call you to straighten this out."

"You don't know where they are?"

"I'm still in bed. He's probably got Jolene in the kitchen." Hopefully he didn't give her a bottle already or she'd have to pump. Of course he had. It was after eight a.m. Oh, well, at least she wasn't panicking. Her head was clear, and she'd learned from her past mistakes not to jump to conclusions. Then her gaze fell on a piece of paper, taped to the lampshade on his side of the bed. "Hang on. Looks like he left me a note..."

I've taken Jolene. I thought you needed the day to reflect on the ungrateful way you behaved last night. We'll both be home tonight for dinner. Hopefully, by then, you'll have realized what a lucky woman you are.

P.S. This is not a ransom note.

Her heart plummeted. "They've gone out. He doesn't say where, but he says they'll be home for dinner. I really don't want to spend the whole day without her, though. Promise me if you hear from him you'll call me right away."

"Of course, but—"

"I've got to hang up now. I'm sorry." She clicked off the phone, and for one stupid moment dropped her face into her hands, helplessly letting the tears fall. Then she straightened her shoulders.

Not this time.

No freakin' way was she going to let him do this to her again.

He had no right. He might be Jolene's father, but he didn't get to spirit her off to heaven knew where whenever he felt like it. Not without telling Holly exactly where he was taking their daughter and who would be looking after her, because it almost certainly wouldn't be *him.*

He'd lowered the blackout curtain and snuck out of the house.

Hopefully, by then, you'll have realized what a lucky woman you are.

This wasn't amends for bad behavior.

This was punishment—again.

He'd forbidden her to go to Christopher Creek, and she'd done it anyway.

She'd gone to lunch with her girlfriends, deviated from her schedule, and left Jolene with Frances when, apparently, Zach was angry with her.

And, finally, she hadn't kissed his ring when he'd given her clothes away to charity in order to replace them with items he'd preapproved.

Now he was paying her back, *cracking down*, really sticking it to her by recreating a scenario that had devastated her in the past.

Last time, he'd had her mother keep Jolene away for days.

Well, Holly wasn't going to stand for that.

If Frances had Jolene, Holly would go over there right now and get her. She might've been lying on the phone. Maybe Zach was with her, pressuring her to say he wasn't there, all the while listening in, checking out Holly's reaction to finding his note.

She was glad, now, she'd pretended to be calm for Frances—that had been the right thing to do.

No. Actually *being* calm was the right thing.

In the bathroom, she splashed water on her face, brushed her teeth, and then, since all her other clothes were gone, she dressed in the same outfit she'd worn yesterday.

She called Zach.

No surprise—he didn't pick up, so she left him a voicemail.

Next, she checked her phone finder app and again, no surprise, he'd turned off location sharing.

But that didn't mean she couldn't find him.

Her body had gotten ahead of her brain. She'd already made her way to his study, and she found herself seated in the swivel chair in front of his laptop.

Check his calendar.

His computer was on. She hit a key and his desktop lit up. He hadn't bothered to password protect it, either because he didn't care what she found out, or because he didn't think she had the nerve to check up on him.

Maybe the old Holly wouldn't have had the gumption, but she was a mother now, and when it came to Jolene she was a fire-breathing dragon, and no one, not even her husband, better try to get between them again.

Dammit.

The calendar didn't help—it showed him with no agenda.

She opened his internet browser, navigated to the history button, and held her breath.

Please don't let it be cleared.

A window popped open, and she clicked on "show full history".

Her palms suddenly went clammy.

Every site Zach had visited in recent months appeared with a date and time stamp. This morning it was CNN and a shopping site—no help there.

She drummed her fingers on the desk, then scrolled down.

Yesterday—more shopping, two news blogs, a medical journal.

She kept scrolling, not sure what she was looking for at this point, since the further back she went, the less likely it was she'd figure out where he'd taken Jolene *today*, but once she'd started, her curiosity kept her in the game.

Facebook.

A recurring page, almost every day for months—then suddenly, nothing.

Was that because of the new hire he'd been vetting?

Her stomach fluttered uncomfortably.

She clicked the link and cringed when Frances' Facebook page loaded—and automatically logged her in.

There it was again, the sexy message chain with Dina's husband, Harry. Frances said she never wanted to go near that account again, and Zach promised Holly he'd take everything down. But his browsing history showed he'd been on this site several times a week for *months*—starting *before* Frances had called crying from the cabin at Christopher Creek.

Holly opened the chain of raunchy messages between Frances and Harry, then pulled out a pen and pad from the desk drawer and furiously copied down the dates.

She snapped a photo as well.

Next, back in Zach's browsing history, she verified what she already knew in her gut to be true—each date there was a message going out from Frances to Dina's husband, Zach had visited Frances' Facebook account—and he'd no doubt been automatically logged in as Frances, just like what had happened to her, when she clicked on the page.

As she stared at the screen in front of her, it blurred, and then started to throb in time with the pulse that was raging in her ears.

Zach wasn't just punishing Holly—he was punishing his own mother—and not for Christopher Creek. For something that happened long before...

Of course!

Frances had brought Jolene back home to Holly even though Zach had told her explicitly not to do so.

She'd dared defy his orders for the sake of Jolene, and so he'd *pretended* not to mind, then ruined his mother's reputation in her church and gone after her oldest and dearest friendships.

Holly's mouth quivered. Her hands shook, and then, a deadly calm came over her.

Now, she knew who she was dealing with.

Zach Bancroft was no longer the man she thought she'd married.

Probably, he never had been.

FOURTEEN

Jolene was cooing and kicking on the pallet they'd constructed for her on the floor made of Claudia's extra blankets. Claudia knelt on a pillow several feet away from the baby. She squeezed her eyes closed, struggling to focus on Zach, who half-reclined, naked, with his legs spread over the edge of the bed, feet bouncing while Claudia worked her mouth on him in the way that he liked.

As he moaned and swore, she couldn't help thinking how thin the walls of her student apartment were.

And it was hard to get into it with Zach's baby in the same room. Even though Claudia had taken care to place Jolene far enough away that she couldn't see what was going on—Claudia felt weird.

Someday, she was going to be Jolene's mommy, and she didn't want to break her. What was the point of sliding into the perfect family if you ruined it in the process?

Her concern didn't extend to Holly, herself, of course. Claudia couldn't afford to be magnanimous where she was concerned. It wasn't that she relished causing Holly pain; it was simply because, in a perfect family, there is room for only one wife.

Me!

Concentrate.

She tried to stop her mind from wandering. Tried not to compare the crappy rental furniture and worn brown carpeting in her student apartment to the full-on house-beautiful that was the Bancroft mansion nestled up in the foothills of north Scottsdale—one of Phoenix's most exclusive suburbs.

She hated this place, and she didn't have to live here. Her best friend, Callista, wanted Claudia and her to be roomies. Share a decent apartment close to Arizona State. Only Zach said that was too far for him to travel.

The cheap medical student apartments, located on the hospital campus, were supposed to be rented for no more than six weeks at a time to students rotating through Mercy General. But Zach had pulled strings and managed to get her a lease for the entire semester.

She ought to be more grateful.

It gave Zach easy access, and that meant they could be together more often.

But right now, this kind of sucked—*ha ha*. Her knees hurt, and the boredom was getting to her, but then his thighs tensed. Thank goodness he was almost there.

"Holly!" Zach jerked twice, and it was over.

In spite of the circumstances, Claudia had done well. With a corner of the sheet, she wiped her face and rocked back on her heels. Looked up at him, smiling. Happy she'd satisfied him.

The first time Zach had called out Holly's name during sex, Claudia had been devastated. But he'd explained that when he had his strongest orgasms he lost track of everything—including where he was and who he was with.

Holly hadn't been enough for Zach for a long time, and he'd been with a lot of other women before he met Claudia.

But unlike Claudia, those other women hadn't meant anything to him.

He'd told her that, to avoid a mistake at home, he'd trained himself to *always* cry out for Holly. It hadn't been easy, but he'd mastered the trick.

Once Holly was out of the picture, he would let go of that habit.

And that day couldn't come soon enough. Claudia was doing her best to be patient, but things weren't the same as they used to be between her and Zach.

Their rendezvous were growing almost tedious.

Before the baby, Zach used to do things to Claudia. Exotic, special things that no one else had bothered to try with her, all designed to please. He'd been the best lover she'd had, in spite of being far older than any of her previous boyfriends. She and Zach had done everything she'd ever heard of and more—sexually speaking. They'd turned this drab, dingy apartment into a veritable palace of delights, and the danger of his being both married *and* her preceptor had only added to the thrill.

But lately, he'd become progressively more demanding, unimaginative, and worse, he'd all but forgotten about *her* pleasure. And that was Holly's fault. He'd said that since Jolene's birth, Holly paid him even less attention than before. *Naturally* he needed more from Claudia.

And Claudia was prepared to give him her all.

Except that it was hard to wait things out.

She wanted Holly gone *now*.

Soon, my love, Zach said. The three of them would be a family very soon. *Be patient, my love.*

And she was trying.

But then, today, he'd shown up expecting her to *babysit*. No notice. Just knocked on her door with Jolene and a bunch of formula and diapers and stuff.

Now, he kissed the top of her head and lay back on the bed in all his post-climax glory. "That was amazing."

"For me too," she said, climbing up onto the bed beside him, reluctantly pulling her top and her bra back down to cover her breasts. He hadn't even touched them. She closed her eyes and tried to work up some maternal feeling. "I'm so glad you brought Jolene. I've missed her so much."

Was that true? She wanted it to be, but she didn't have much time to think about a baby when she was so busy with school. She cast a glance down and across the room at Jolene, a little bundle of boring baby who didn't even talk yet. Zach sprawled with his hands propped behind his head, either not noticing or not caring about Claudia's lack of interest in his offspring.

Maybe her lack of maternal instinct was for the best. At least she wouldn't make the same mistake as Holly—lavishing all her affection on a child instead of her man. As soon as they were married, Claudia would put Jolene in daycare. And when she was older they might consider boarding school. A lot of wealthy families did that kind of thing. It didn't make them bad parents.

Now that she'd pleased him, it was time to break the news. "As much as I love her, I'm afraid I can't watch her for you today. You should've given me notice."

"I really need you to do this for me." He took her hand and brought it to his lips.

Had he forgotten she had her outpatient dermatology clinic at noon on Thursdays? "I've got clinic."

"Call in sick."

When you were a med student you didn't *call in sick*, you *crawled in sick*. "You know that's not how it works."

"Make it happen."

"Why don't you ask your mother to keep her?"

He made a face. "You are the only one I trust with my daughter."

Our daughter, she thought. "I want to but..."

He reached over and slipped his hands into her shorts, began to tease her. "Thanks, hon. Holly is getting worse. She's gone totally off the deep end. Crying all day, barely gets out of bed."

"Oh, no." She opened her legs and pushed against his hand. "I hope she's going to be okay. I feel so sorry for her."

"Me too." He worked her, urgently. "That's why I have to do this the right way. You understand why it's taking time."

"Yes," She was so close. "I-I understand."

"Good." He pulled his hand away just at the most inopportune time. She lurched up, but the moment had passed. "And it's super important you not mention this to anyone."

"If I'm calling in sick, of course I won't."

"You haven't told anyone about us, have you, hon?"

She bolted upright. "How can you ask me that?"

"That's not an answer."

"No, I haven't." Not anyone who mattered. Not any of the attending physicians—the other doctors—because that could get him fired. Although, soon enough, him being her preceptor would be a moot point. Once they were married, it wouldn't matter that they'd started screwing while she was his medical student. "I haven't said a single word to anyone except my mom and Callista and I swore them both to secrecy so you have nothing to worry about."

The room fell silent, apart from the sounds the baby was making.

Gurgling, cooing.

"Zach?"

His Adam's apple worked in his throat. His eyes seemed strangely squinty when he looked at her. "You told your mother. And who's Callista?"

THE MARRIAGE SECRET   101

"My best friend. I introduced you at the student meet and greet."

"What, precisely, did you tell them?"

"That we're in love." He looked miserable, so she put her hand on his shoulder. "Don't worry. I didn't tell my mom you were married. She'd freak out."

"Call them today. Tell them you made it all up, that you have a crush on me, and you were fantasizing. Tell them that I've never given you any indication the feeling was mutual."

"But it *is* mutual." She jerked her hands away.

"Be a good girl, and do as I say." He flicked his thumb against her chin. "Make sure you convince them."

FIFTEEN

Holly didn't call ahead for a reason. If Zach was here, at his mother's house, playing puppet master, Holly didn't want to give him a chance to whisk Jolene away before she arrived, nor did she want to put Frances on the spot in case he'd coerced her into lying for him.

Holly jabbed the doorbell and, at that very moment, the automatic irrigation system came on. One irrigation line must be missing its sprinkler head because, suddenly, hot, Arizona-in-August water reached the porch, spurting her like a geyser at Yellowstone.

She yelped and ducked behind a stucco pillar.

When Frances finally answered the bell, Holly was drenched, scalded and boiling mad.

"What in the—" Frances covered her mouth and motioned Holly inside, slamming the door on the gushing geyser. "Wait right there. I'll get you a towel."

Holly did as she was told, skulking in the entryway.

As she twisted her wet hair into a knot behind her head, she clamped her teeth together and suppressed the urge to curse.

Water dripped down the back of her neck.

She could feel a vein pulsing at her temple.

By the time Frances reappeared with an armload of towels, a pair of shorts, and a T-shirt, Holly's temper was hot enough to steam press the lot of them.

Take a breath.

Frances turned her back while Holly stripped.

She shed her drenched outfit and changed into dry clothes, focusing on the task at hand, using the moment to regain control of her temper.

Zach had, no doubt, intended to knock her back into line by sneaking Jolene out of the house this morning, but what he'd actually accomplished was the opposite.

Holly was done deferring to his majesty.

But taking her anger out on Frances would be counterproductive. If only Holly could get Frances to see that they both had Jolene's interest at heart that would be a starting point.

A starting point for what? Some kind of alliance?

Holly and Frances against Zach?

Frances would never go for that. Not even if she knew Zach was the one who'd engineered the Facebook fiasco. And Holly didn't dare tell her because Frances would never believe her, and she'd probably run straight to Zach who would deny everything. So then, Holly would've been no real help to Frances, but Zach would know Holly had been snooping on his laptop, and that would be a disaster for her and for Jolene.

So no. Holly and Frances against Zach wouldn't fly.

But Holly and Frances *for* Jolene?

Maybe they could build a better bond based on their mutual love for the baby—Holly would like that, and she preferred not to make an enemy of her mother-in-law.

Holly tugged the I ♥ Mercy General T-shirt over her head and kicked her wet things into a pile in the corner. "Is Jolene here?"

Frances whirled on Holly, her cheeks sprouting red patches. "I told you on the phone she wasn't."

"Okay. Sorry. But I thought maybe..."

"That I was lying? Why would I?"

"No, no, no. I thought Zach might've dropped her off after we'd spoken." She back-peddled as fast as she could. "I should've known you would've called me if he had. I'm sorry. I'm just so anxious to know where she is. You understand, I'm sure. You're a mother, too."

"That I am. And it can be a challenge at times—like this one. Zach's not returning either of our calls—and why would he take Jolene without telling you? Although he did leave you a note." Frances posture loosened. "You look a fright. I'll have to ask Zach to get the landscaper over here again. This is the third time this summer that sprinkler head's come off. Come with me, and I'll get you a soda or something."

"Water would be great."

Frances' formal living area was small but well appointed. Zach recently had the floors redone for her in terrazzo. The walls were freshly painted, and the furniture was sleek and new. Selected and paid for by Zach, of course. The older items —relics from the years Frances barely had enough income from teaching to support them—had either been tossed, given to charity, or relegated to the den Zach had added on.

One thing about Zach, he was hell-bent on providing for the women in his life.

Holly believed that was a reaction to his father, Russell, taking off and leaving his mother with no child support, and maybe it was, but now she was beginning to realize it was also one of Zach's surest means of controlling both his mother and her.

It takes courage to bite the hand that feeds you.

"Sorry to barge in on you like this." Holly took a sip of refreshingly cool water, intentionally sitting back against the couch cushions, uncrossing her legs, and letting go of the tension in her body, hoping that the physical relaxation would soon calm the frenzy in her mind.

"Not like I have anywhere to go these days," Frances said, taking a place on the love seat adjacent to the couch.

It occurred to Holly that with Frances isolated from her peers, she was more reliant on Zach than ever, and he was deliberately neglecting her. "If you ever want to catch a movie or go to the mall or something, you know I'd be glad to tag along."

"Who would watch Jolene?"

"I can ask a friend to babysit." Maybe Tamara would be willing. She was on her own, too much, these days, and caring for Jolene might bring her some joy. "But I hope your friends will reach out soon. If not, maybe you could make the first overture."

"Why? I've done nothing wrong. They're the ones who should apologize."

"Mmm. I see your point, only the whole incident has to be terribly upsetting for all of you. None of you is really to blame. Except Dina's husband, of course."

"And she forgave him without blinking an eye. But me, her best friend of thirty years, she kicks to the curb. And you know the thing that really makes me sick to my stomach?"

That Zach was responsible?

"Is that someone did this to me deliberately. You may believe it was random, but I'm not buying that. I think I've finally figured out who got into my Facebook account and sent those awful messages."

Holly held her breath. Was it possible Frances was beginning to see through Zach?

"Russell!"

"Your ex-husband, Russell?"

"Do we know any other creeps by that name?" Frances shook her head. "You're lucky you never met Zach's father. He's an awful man, and any flaws that Zach may have, I blame on Russell. You can't expect a boy who grew up without his father's attention and affection to be perfect."

"No, I don't suppose we can. But, Frances," Holly lowered her voice and tried to make her tone gentle. "We can't give him a free pass to do whatever he pleases, either. Zach is a man, not a little boy, and while I understand your instinct is to protect him, we have to think about Jolene, too."

"I think about my granddaughter every day. And I'm not giving Zach a pass—but what has he done that's so terrible? Yes, he took Jolene, today, and yes, he's giving us both his signature silent treatment, but these are small things, and we have to forgive him. We have to be understanding."

Oh, I understand him, all right.

"It's not as if he were like his father. Zach simply isn't capable of..."

Holly leaned forward, attentive. "Of what? What kinds of things has Russell done that Zach couldn't?"

"This Facebook incident for example."

"I don't know why you think your ex-husband would be involved after all this time."

"Three reasons. First, he could easily guess my password. It's Zach eleven eleven. November eleventh is the day our divorce was final. Second, the whole unsavory episode has Russell's fingerprints all over it—getting between me and my friends at church with a lie that makes me look like a hussy."

"I'm afraid I don't understand. Did he do something like that in the past? There was no Facebook when you two were married."

"That's true. But back in the day, Russell didn't want me going to Wednesday night Bible study because it meant his dinner wasn't waiting for him, and he had to watch the baby. Wednesday was my one night I went out for a couple of hours. Otherwise, I was on duty twenty-four seven with Russell and

Zach. So Russell found a way to ruin it for me. I had to change churches after." Frances got up and went to the window. "One night, Russell told me he was going to the Wednesday Bible study, so I couldn't go—I needed to stay home with the baby. Well, it was Russell's first time to go to church in years, so I was in favor, and he went instead of me."

Even though Holly knew Zach was the culprit behind the Facebook sham, this story had her on the edge of her seat. Could Zach somehow be taking cues from his father, a man who'd left him and his mother when Zach was only a baby? How was that possible?

"Anyway, Russell goes to Wednesday night Bible study, and when it comes around to prayer requests, he asks the group to put both me and Pastor Johnson on the prayer list because, he says, we're having an affair! *Pray for the fornicators!*" Frances threw her hands in the air. "Miserable son-of-a-bitch."

The similarity between the two incidents was impossible to deny. There had to be a connection. Maybe Zach knew the story, and that's what had given him the idea to ruin his mother's reputation with her friends and at church. "You said there were three reasons you suspect Russell. What's the third?"

Frances looked over her shoulder, as if Russell might pop up out of nowhere. "I think I saw him the other day."

"But would you even know him? He must've changed after all these years."

"I can't be sure for that very reason. But I was at the bank, and there's a revolving door. As I was coming out through that door, a man in the compartment ahead of me turned around— he was the spitting image of Russell—only old. He was staring right at me and laughing."

SIXTEEN

The automatic doors to JR's Fine Foods Gourmet Market parted before her.

It had been two weeks since Zach had spirited Jolene away in the early morning hours, and even though he'd brought her home before dinner, as promised, Holly had been sleeping with one proverbial eye open ever since. If Zach was home, she even brought Jolene into the bathroom with her. And whenever possible she kept Jolene close, carrying her in her arms or, like now, in a front pack.

As Holly entered the market, she pressed her mouth against the riot of curls atop her daughter's head, treasuring the gentle, life-affirming pulse of the soft spot against her lips, and inhaling her scent. Today it was "rainy afternoon" mixed with "essence of baby". Because of Jolene's sensitive skin, Holly avoided bath products with artificial dyes and perfumes, and so the fragrance Jolene gave off was uniquely hers. Holly could easily find her way to Jolene in a crowd, even if she were blindfolded. Her daughter's scent was as familiar and as essential to her as the rise and fall of her own breathing.

Jolene shifted her weight, stirring, but didn't awaken.

Holly grabbed a cart, her ears perking when the manager interrupted the overhead music to announce a special on beef in the butcher department. The deal was a good one, and she considered, briefly, the possibility of purchasing the standing rib roast, but quickly decided against it. She had a list, and digital coupons loaded for her trip to a different, cheaper store in another neighborhood. The prices there were worth the cost of the extra gas. She had her groceries budgeted out and knew that with her discounts she could purchase all she needed, including a rib roast, for pennies on the dollar compared to what those same items would cost here at JR's Fine Foods Gourmet Market.

With Jolene still slumbering, she headed down the condiments aisle to the quiet soundtrack of classical music, the *click click click* of the cart's wheels adding its own percussion section, and selected a JR's brand name bottle of salad dressing —something to bolster the illusion she'd purchased all their groceries here.

Jolene, at last, opened her eyes and cooed up at her mama. Holly shielded the baby's eyes from the glare of fluorescent lights and cooed back. "Hello, sleepyhead," she said, and then looked up to find a tall woman in a Lululemon tracksuit, similar to one Zach had picked out for Holly, heading their way.

The woman squeezed past them, and then paused to admire Jolene. "How old?"

"Five and a half months."

"Amazing hair! What a lot for such a tiny thing."

"I know!" Holly glanced at the woman's nearly full cart where a box of French chocolates rested on top of a six-pack wine carrier. Fine wine, she assumed, since nobody came to JR's for the cheap stuff.

"She's simply gorgeous."

"Thanks so much. I think so, too."

The woman puckered her lips as if she could eat Jolene up before continuing down the aisle.

Holly bent to kiss Jolene once more, then steered her cart to the front, taking her time, browsing the displays near the registers. When a cashier gave her the once-over, she moved to the in-store Starbucks and took a seat at a table, as if waiting for a latte. After a full thirty minutes, the barista behind the counter was eyeing her suspiciously, but Holly ignored her until, at last, the woman in the Lululemon tracksuit pushed her cart, now literally overflowing, toward the checkout lines.

Holly caught up to her, wheeling her own, cart, empty save the JR's dressing. Offered up a smile and wave.

The woman waved back.

Just do it.

This wouldn't be Holly's first attempt—she'd been turned down last week at this same store, but she had a good feeling about this one. Earlier, the woman had seemed quite taken with Jolene.

Holly cleared her throat. "Excuse me. I'm Holly, by the way."

The woman stopped, no doubt expecting an inquiry about where some esoteric item like escargot was located. "Nice to meet you, Holly. I'm Deirdre."

"I don't mean to bother you, but may I—may I use my credit card to pay for your groceries?"

"You want to buy my groceries?" Deirdre took in a quick breath of air—almost a gasp—then shook her head. "I've got a week's worth of stuff in this cart. That's really kind of you but I don't need money."

"Please don't misunderstand. I don't want to *buy* them. I just want to *pay* for them with my credit card. I need cash, and I wondered if you could possibly help me out."

Though it must've been no more than seconds it seemed enough time passed to finish that tome on Roman history Zach wanted her to read before the woman replied. "You need money?"

"Not exactly. I have credit. What I need is cash. I could always get an advance on my card but, you know, the fees are such a rip off." Holly pulled Jolene tightly against her chest.

The woman—Deirdre—frowned.

Please don't ask any more questions.

Then Deirdre's eyes flitted over her. Taking in Holly's expensive outfit, her highlighted brown hair with its stylish cut, her well-manicured nails. Even the baby carrier was designer.

"My husband doesn't approve of all the fees," she tried again.

"Your *husband* doesn't approve?" Deirdre's eyebrows rose and then, in a flash, her entire demeanor changed. Her back straightened, her eyes went wide and her lips parted. She left her cart and stepped closer to Holly, lowered her voice and said, "Some men are too particular by a mile. And you can't track cash spending like credit, can you?"

Holly nodded, feeling both shame and gratitude that this stranger had caught on, at least somewhat, to her predicament.

"I'll help you," Deirdre said. "But this load is going to cost *at least* five hundred dollars, and I don't have that kind of cash on me. There's an ATM right outside the door, though."

Holly clasped her hands to stop their shaking and wet her dry lips. "Thank you, so much. I really appreciate your help."

Deirdre touched her wrist. "It's no problem, Holly. We ladies need to look out for one another. Maybe someday you'll be in a position to do something for another woman in distress."

She flushed. "Oh, no. I'm not in distress."

Deirdre arched an eyebrow. "You don't owe me an explanation, and you haven't asked for my advice, but I'm going to give it to you anyway. Whatever is going on at home, if you have to sneak around like this that's a red flag—an entire field of them, honestly. One way or another, you need to get out of your situation."

"I'm afraid I've given you the wrong impression." Holly was about to say her husband only wanted the best for her, when Jolene looked up, her lovely, sweet blue eyes the picture of trust, and suddenly, the lie got stuck in Holly's throat.

Today's market run, after using her digital coupons and paying cash for a mountain of groceries at the Foods For Less across town, had netted Holly $260 dollars—just enough for a one-way fare to visit her great aunt in Abilene, Texas. Jolene's ticket as a "lap baby" wouldn't cost much, if anything. But Holly needed a few more scores. The money, currently hidden in a baby wipes container—Zach would never go near that—wasn't enough. Even if they lived rent-free at her aunt's, she didn't know how long it would take her to find temporary employment. Something that paid well enough to cover living expenses and a sitter. Aunt Bessie was ninety, so she couldn't manage Jolene without help.

Of course, Holly didn't plan to keep Jolene away from her father permanently. It was a trial separation she was after, a little time to give Zach a chance to adjust to the idea of a divorce. But she believed it would be safest to initiate the discussion from a distance.

Not that he'd ever hit her—but last week she'd burned the muffins and he'd muttered under his breath how he'd like to knock the daylights out of her, then raised his fist to within an inch of her face while she had Jolene in her arms. And after what he'd done to his own mother... the way he'd twice taken Jolene without telling Holly...

She bowed her head and steadied herself against the

kitchen counter—yes—Abilene was definitely the place to be when she asked for a separation.

But that meant she had to save more cash and find a way to get out of Phoenix without raising Zach's suspicions. She needed to be on her best behavior, stick to her schedule, keep the house immaculate. Jerking upright once more, she stared at the plates scattered on the table and the dishes in the sink.

She'd better get this cleared up right away.

After finishing putting away the groceries, she puttered about, clearing and rinsing and avoiding the kitchen trash, where she'd stuffed the Foods For Less receipt. Time to bag that up before Zach got home. She'd take it outside herself and hide it under the other garbage, already in the can. She dumped the tall kitchen trash liner into a larger, heavy-duty bag, accidentally ripping the liner in the process. Through the tear, she could see a paper with an official-looking logo, and she knew she hadn't thrown it away.

The hair on her arms prickled.

She wasn't the only one burying things in the trash.

When she peeled it off the liner, the paper was damp and stinking of sour milk, the print blurred. As she studied the document, heat rose to her cheeks, her pulse pounded in her ears.

This *couldn't* be what it looked like.

Zach would never stoop this low.

She read it twice to be sure she understood, and then crumpled it in her fist and kicked the kitchen trashcan across the room.

SEVENTEEN

Holly took a deep breath, "Darling, we need to talk."

Zach was currently kicked back in his recliner watching the golf channel on mute. He indicated mild curiosity with a raise of the brow. "That sounds ominous."

She had a roast in the oven, and the smell of herbs and meat drifting into the family room from the kitchen made her stomach clench. Behind her back, she clasped the crumpled paper she'd dug out of the trash.

Zach's eyes remained glued to the television.

She came around to stand directly in front of him, blocking his view. "I have something to discuss with you."

"Can't it wait? Mickelson's about to take his swing."

She lifted the remote and hit pause.

"No, it can't." The paper trembled in her hand. "What's this?"

"I won't know until I look at it, darling."

He took it, stroking his chin, considering. Then he met her gaze and smiled. "It's the paternity test I ordered on Jolene. You remember, we discussed it."

A tingling sensation started up in her lips and tongue. Her

mouth felt funny when she tried to speak, like she'd just gotten a shot of Novocain. "Bull."

"Pardon?"

"I said that's bull. We never talked about a paternity test."

"Darling, you know how confused and forgetful you've been these past months."

That was the biggest whopper of all. The awful lie he'd been peddling to anyone who'd listen, including her, since the day Jolene was born: that Holly was too feeble-minded to know up from down.

"I don't know anything of the sort."

All the conversations she'd supposedly forgotten? Every one of them had been between Zach and her. He'd lied about Craig Paulson, so maybe he was lying about other things, too. And as for the baby monitor, who could say *she* had been the one to stick it in the freezer? There were two adults living in this house, and only one of them had a track record of trying to make the other one seem loony. "We never discussed it. But even if we did and I forgot—which I can assure you I would not have—that doesn't answer my question."

"Which is?"

"Why did you order a paternity test? What is that about?" She looked down on him, hands on her hips, aware of how aggressive she must seem, but she didn't care. There was nothing she wanted more than for him to give her an explanation that would make everything okay, but she knew, deep in her heart, that was impossible.

Still, she waited, hoping, desperately wanting to be wrong.

No matter what the future held for the two of them, Zach was still Jolene's father.

Chuckling, he got to his feet. "Darling, oh my precious. You should see the look on your face. I don't know what crazy ideas are going through your pretty head, but it's merely documentation. For my records."

"What records?"

"You know. Legal papers. I've visited my attorney to revise my will. Think, darling. I *told* you I was going to set up a trust for Jolene."

She backed away from him. "Yes."

"Oh good. You do remember."

"Stop it."

He stepped closer.

"We talked about a *trust*, not a paternity test. You don't need this to set up a trust for Jolene. That's absurd."

"Actually, it's not. I admit it might be overly cautious, but you know me, I like to prepare for the worst-case scenario. Have you thought about what might happen if you and I were both in an accident? It's unlikely, but think about poor Tom and Tamara. She never expected to lose her husband in a car crash. So imagine this—we're both killed in an auto accident and my father turns up and contests the will. I would want ironclad evidence that Jolene was my blood on record. My attorney—"

"You expect me to believe your attorney advised this?"

"If you'd let me finish I was going to say my attorney said it wasn't necessary, but if it would give me peace of mind regarding challenges to the will, I should go ahead with it. And so I did. And as you can see, everything is in order. I *am* Jolene's biological father. You're getting yourself all worked up over nothing."

Her head was pounding. Every neuron in her brain was screaming at her to get Jolene as far away from Zach as possible. And the minute she had the funds, she would.

How many more grocery runs did she need? Three probably. Two if she found another understanding, big-spender like Deirdre.

"It's strictly for Jolene's protection." He wrapped Holly in his arms, and she felt her entire body recoil from his touch. "I'm terribly sorry if you thought this was anything else. I never doubted your faithfulness. And, I'm sorry, too, if I didn't mention it before. I just realized you're right. *I'm* the one with the memory problem—in this case. Yes, I did tell you about the trust, but it was only *after* I thought about Russell that I ordered the paternity test. So you see? You're not the only with baby brain."

Baby brain.

She wanted to strangle the next person who uttered that phrase. "There's nothing wrong with your brain... or mine either."

"No, darling, of course not. Hey, listen, can we put this subject to rest now? I'm happy to revisit the matter later, but it smells like dinner's about ready." He tugged on her arm.

Her head was still spinning as she turned his words over in her head. They didn't make complete sense, but she could, in fact, see Zach worrying about his father challenging the will. Especially after hearing what he'd done to Frances—in spite of the fact he hadn't been in contact with either of them since Zach was a little boy.

Zach sighed. "Listen, there's a bit more to the story."

As in Zach had just invented a new twist?

"I didn't want to worry you, but the fact is I heard from Russell. He showed up at my office a few days before Jolene was born, and he made quite a scene. I ordered that test to protect Jolene... and you. You believe that, don't you?"

Frances had said she thought she saw Russell at a bank, so maybe he really had come back to Phoenix and tracked Zach down. Maybe Zach really had been trying to protect Jolene... *or maybe* Russell had planted the idea that Holly might've been unfaithful and that Zach should get the receipts before willing any money to Jolene.

At this point, Holly had no idea if anything her husband told her was true.

She nodded, marching woodenly into the kitchen, and then

robotically pulled the roast from the oven and set it out to rest before carving. "Darling," she heard her voice as if someone else were speaking. "I got you a gift."

"Whatever it is, I'm sure I'm going to love it," he said.

"I hope so." She tiptoed up and planted a dutiful kiss on his cheek. "It's a framed photo of Jolene. I think it will look nice in your office at the hospital."

EIGHTEEN

Two unbearably long weeks and three shopping trips—that's how much longer it had taken Holly to get together the cash she needed to leave Zach. But she'd done it.

And now, she was packed and ready to go.

Her timing couldn't be better.

Zach had come home from his clinic day in a great mood.

Holly had served him his favorite lasagna and plied him afterward with lemon pound cake.

Unbelievably, the Cardinals won against Dallas, and he'd just hung up from a high-five call with his mother, who was also a big football fan. It was the first time he'd phoned Frances, that Holly knew of, since Christopher Creek, and the enthusiastic way he'd spoken to her made it seem he was ready to let go of whatever grudge he'd been holding.

There would never be a better opportunity.

Holly stood in front of him, smiling and pouting her lips. "You remember I told you my great-aunt Bessie is turning ninety next week. Anyway, I was hoping we could—"

He rolled his head back and forth in a slow-motion shake. "Sorry. I can't take leave now, sweetheart. A week is not enough notice for me to take off. You know I have to plan well in advance. I couldn't even get coverage when Jolene was born. Besides, I don't want to spend my precious time off with a bunch of old ladies sipping tea in hell-hot Texas."

"Arizona is hotter," she said.

"But it's a dry heat."

She pasted a disappointed look on her face. "Oh, honey, please? Aunt Bessie is so excited to meet Jolene, and we have to be realistic. This could be her last birthday." Another reason she wanted to go. Bessie was more of a parent to Holly than her own folks had been. "Knock wood it won't be, but couldn't you at least try? Take a look at your schedule? What about Craig Paulson? After all, he owes you."

"Sorry. I said, no, and that's final." He licked his lips. "Is there any more of that cake?"

She hurried to the kitchen and returned with an oversized slice. Waited for him to take a big bite, and then released her breath. "This is Aunt Bessie's recipe, you know. And I under-stand, darling, I do. I'm just so disappointed."

"We're not going."

"I see now, it was too much to ask. But..."

He took another bite.

"You don't suppose? What if you save your time off for us to go to Hawaii this Christmas? And I'll take Jolene to Texas for Bessie's birthday."

"By yourself?"

"How else will Aunt Bessie get to meet her? She's too frail to fly here, so I don't see any other way. It would be so much better if you could come, too. But I get it. It's too big of an ask."

His cake finished, he slowly swept his tongue across his lower lip, all the while holding her gaze, then lifted his arm high, dish in hand, flicked his wrist and sent the plate spinning like a Frisbee. It clattered onto the floor, unbroken. "Oops. Didn't mean to drop it. Pick that up, will you?"

He wanted her to cower?

Whatever it takes.

She deliberately rounded her shoulders and meekly retrieved the plate, then took a seat beside him on the couch. "Would you like another piece?"

"You're not good at this, Holly. So cut the crap."

"I want to see Aunt Bessie on her birthday. I don't see how that's *crap*."

"You have a tell. Whenever you're lying you twist your hair."

She unwound the strand that was strangling her index finger and dropped her hands into her lap. "I'm not lying. Her ninetieth birthday is next Sunday. I can show you on Facebook."

"You're lying about wanting me to come with you. You knew, before you asked, that I wouldn't be able to go."

"It seems you don't want to come with me." She was trying, but it was difficult to keep swallowing the truth and playing his game. But this was too important, she *needed* to make him believe her. Careful not to let her hand drift back to her hair, she wiped away a tear—a real one. She softened her voice, hoping to take down the temperature. "I shouldn't have said that. I'm sorry. It's just that you and I haven't been anywhere since I got pregnant with Jolene, and I was looking forward to some time with you, just the three of us."

"You, me, Jolene *and your aunt*." His words were terse but his tone had a bit less bite. Flattery often worked on Zach. Hopefully, this was one of those times.

"Well, yes. But you and I would still have time together. And you'd get a well-deserved break from work. I truly want you to come along." She reached for something, anything to make him believe it wasn't a ploy. "Jolene needs time with her daddy."

"Uh-huh." He looked at her, seeming to be genuinely considering the idea for the first time.

She knew he'd *never* travel across the country for her benefit. So that meant he was thinking about letting her go alone. "Darling?"

"Hang on a second," he said. "I'll be right back."

Her hand fluttered up to her heart. *Please, please, please.* She'd already bought a one-way ticket to Abilene.

Zach returned to the family room with a *gotcha* smile on his face—dragging her suitcase behind him.

Her heart plummeted.

He wheeled her suitcase up to the couch. "Shall I help you with this?"

He kicked the luggage, and it fell over, landing with a thud. He knelt above it. The latch made a clunking sound, and he opened the lid, began tossing her clothing, her underwear, her pajamas everywhere. "What's this? Looks like you've already packed."

"I was hoping you'd say yes."

His eyes flared, and he crawled over and grabbed her legs, then he pushed her skirt up to her thighs. "But I *didn't* say yes."

Her thigh burned where his nails dug into her skin. This wasn't good. He hadn't even been drinking. He opened her knees with his elbows and groaned. When she tried to push him away, he grabbed her wrists.

"Let me go!"

"I'm your *husband*."

"I said, *no!*"

"I want you, Holly." His face was contorted, his eyes smoldering, his breathing ragged.

Her heart thumped in panic, but if she showed him her fear it would only embolden him. "Not tonight."

"You're mine, and I have a right."

"I'm not *yours*. A marriage license is not a bill of sale." She couldn't believe the words that had just come out of her mouth, but it was too late for regrets. He was too smart, and she was a lousy actress. She didn't want a separation, she wanted a *divorce* and while she'd have preferred to tell him from a safe distance, there was no way in hell he'd let her go to Abilene or anywhere else without him. At least, tonight, he hadn't been drinking. "I'm leaving you. I didn't want to tell you like this, but there is no good time or place."

He froze.

She'd expected him to yell, or... His reaction could've been much, much worse. But he just stayed there on his knees, deadly quiet. And then, suddenly, he groaned again. "I like it when you stick up for yourself."

He was getting off on her resistance. Letting go of her wrists, he slid her underwear down to her ankles and unzipped his pants. "You're not going anywhere except where I tell you to go, darling. Have you forgotten?"

He jerked her to a stand and pressed himself between her thighs, almost purring as he whispered in her ear, "If you didn't want to stay until death do us part, you should never have told me your secret."

NINETEEN

The tension between Holly and Zach was at an all-time high, but in a way, things were better for her than before. She still walked on eggshells, but at least she didn't have to pretend to be happy about it. The morning after the awful night when she'd asked for a divorce, she'd tried to initiate a frank discussion between them. One in which they could each openly express their concerns, but Zach had asked flatly: *What makes you think I care how you feel?*

He still controlled her spending and what she wore, but he was so confident his threat to use her terrible past against her had thwarted any attempt to leave him, he no longer bothered to follow her comings and goings. It'd been days since she'd texted him photos of her location, and he hadn't complained.

Not all shackles were made of chains, and they both knew it.

As far as Zach was concerned, he'd won.

Game over.

But was it?

She hadn't given up.

So, here she sat, in a voluminous office, the walls populated with elaborately framed portraits of sundry old men, opposite Les Larson JD. An immaculately groomed man with a full head of silver hair, a keen look in his eyes, and a reputation for winning battles in the courtroom. A semi-famous divorce lawyer to whom she'd shelled out $500 from her baby wipes jar, in exchange for fifty minutes of his time.

He'd be happy to take her case with an initial $5,000 retainer, however, the odds of her wining custody were long. Generally, the court would lean heavily in favor of a mother in a custody dispute. Especially given Jolene's tender age. But *in this circumstance*, and with Zach's resources, it would be a long, hard-fought battle, which they were more likely than not to lose.

"Has he ever abused you?" Les showed her his phone to indicate they were still recording.

"He raised his fist, once, while I was holding Jolene."

He arched one eyebrow, expectantly. "And?"

"And that's it. He didn't actually punch me."

"But you felt threatened."

She nodded. "And I no longer have access to our bank accounts and credit cards."

"Do you work outside the home? Contribute to the accounts?"

"No."

"That's okay. No worries, this is a community property state. Where did you get the money to pay my fee, today?"

"I saved it. Sometimes I pay for other people's groceries with the card Zach provides for food purchases. Then they give me cash in exchange."

"That must be very difficult for you." He shook his head. "Sounds like your husband's a real shit."

She straightened in her chair. "He hasn't always been, but yes. Did I mention he gave away all my clothes to the Salvation Army?"

Les scoffed. "You're very well dressed."

She crossed her legs and shifted in the big leather armchair. "He hired a personal shopper to replace them with items he preapproved. He wants to control me."

"Sorry, but I'm afraid a husband filling your closet with new clothes doesn't count as abuse. Is that everything? Has he been unfaithful?"

"Not that I know of. He's..." she felt her cheeks flame, "... he's very interested in me sexually. And sometimes—most times—he won't take no for an answer in the bedroom."

"That one's going to be a problem, unless you have bruises or other marks. I'm not saying we can't argue it, but any *he said she said* in a custody battle is usually a wash at best."

"What do you mean *at best*?"

"I mean the court often has a jaded outlook when one parent accuses another of things that can't be verified. Frankly, the accuser can sometimes be viewed as trying to manipulate an outcome."

"You mean they aren't believed."

"Yes. That's it. If you have evidence of physical or emotional harm, that would be a different matter. Do you have any evidence of such?"

"No. He's never physically injured me. And if trying to control me doesn't count as emotional abuse, then I guess I've got nothing. Except that he's *blackmailing* me into staying in this marriage. He's threatening to keep me from our child because of my past." Holly's eyes drifted to a painting of Blind Justice hanging above the lawyer's head.

He checked his watch, then reached across the desk and patted her hand.

She pulled it away.

"As I said before, if you want to go through with this, I'll do my best. But I'm a straight shooter and there are two things you should know. First, I'm good at what I do, but I'm not cheap. Second, your past, combined with that ransom note incident, can be spun by a good attorney to make you seem unfit. I could make promises I can't keep and line my pockets with money you can't afford to spend, but you look like a nice lady. I assume you're a good mother. You seem to care an awful lot about what happens to your baby. And those awful things from the past are just that—things that happened a long time ago, so *I* don't judge you. But a judge—that's a different matter—that's their job. And your husband's a respected doctor. Think of all the people who would testify as to what a caring man he is, what a terrific father he'll make, whereas you..."

"I was a *teenager*."

"But it was a terrible, terrible thing. And he has witnesses, even a police detective, who can testify you were impaired recently, in the days after your daughter was born. My best advice to you, unless you feel unsafe around him, is to go home and try to work things out—for the baby's sake. I'm sorry, but I cannot honestly say you have a decent shot at winning custody of your daughter."

* * *

As soon as Tamara opened the door, Holly felt a rush of guilt. This was the first time she'd stopped by Tamara's place since Tom's funeral. They'd spoken on the phone, of course, and Tamara had brought flowers to the hospital when Jolene was born, but the lunch at Kandel's Delicatessen, just about a month ago, had been their first and last get-together since Tom died.

Before the accident, Holly and Zach and Tom and Tamara had been practically inseparable. So after Tom died, why hadn't they invited Tamara over for dinners or to the movies?

Holly pulled in a deep, sad breath.

This was on her. She'd been so wrapped up in her own affairs, so busy basking in the glow of her happy marriage and

Jolene's impending birth that she hadn't done enough to help Tamara get through her grief.

Superficial gestures?

Sure—a funeral wreath, a sympathy card, a gift basket and, once in a blue moon, a call or text.

But now that Holly was in trouble, she was on Tamara's doorstep, expecting her friend to advise and comfort.

"Holly, this is a nice surprise." Tamara gestured for her to follow her into the living room. "I get to see you twice in one month. To what do I owe the honor?"

"I was just thinking of you." Her cheeks caught fire at the lie. She should simply admit she needed someone to talk to, and that was what finally brought her here, to Tamara's door. Suddenly, she felt awkward, unsure of how welcome she'd really be.

In the past, she and Tamara had spent a lot of time having fun together, but were they *really* friends? The kind who could not see one another for a while and then pick up where they left off? The kind who could forgive each other for their short-comings?

As the person in this relationship who'd been the most neglectful, Holly certainly hoped so, because Tamara Driscoll was the closest thing she had to a best friend. And right now, she could really use one. "I've missed you. I'm sorry I haven't been around much."

"Please. You have a baby—I wish you'd brought her." Tamara waved off the apology. "You want a soda or coffee or something?"

"Don't you have anything stronger?" Holly laughed.

A tiny crease appeared above Tamara's nose, and she narrowed her eyes. "Of course. Is everything okay?"

And that quickly, all those tears Holly had pushed back a thousand times during her meeting with Les Larson, began to stream down her face.

Tamara threw her arms around her and hugged her until Holly could barely breathe. "It's okay, honey. Tell me what's wrong."

Holly nodded and swiped her eyes, then collapsed on the couch next to Tamara. The obvious concern on her friend's face created a veritable tsunami of shame inside her.

Tamara's husband had been gone a little more than a year.

He'd gotten behind the wheel of his brand-new Porsche, drunk, and crashed it into a telephone pole, leaving Tamara a widow—at twenty-seven. Holly's problems paled in comparison. And, now, she suddenly wondered if she was putting too much on Tamara's shoulders.

One last bone-rattling sob, and then Holly regained control, pulled a tissue from a box on the coffee table and cleaned her face up. "It's nothing. I shouldn't be burdening you with my problems."

"Seriously, Holly. You're scaring me. Take a breath and tell me what's going on. Did something happen? Is this about the baby monitor?"

Holly shook her head. "Not that, but it is about Zach."

"Okay."

"I went to a lawyer today—a divorce attorney." She twisted the hem of her blouse, the thought suddenly occurring that Tamara and Zach were friends, too. It was one thing to complain about him at a girls' lunch, another to admit she wanted a divorce.

"Divorce." Tamara's voice came out a whisper, and she grabbed Holly by the hands, forcing her to look up. "I know what I said at lunch. That you should be looking out for yourself. That you need your own money, but I was thinking along the lines of your going back to work part-time. Jolene's what... almost six months old?"

Holly barely managed to hold in another sob.

Tamara squeezed her hands. "Hey, I'm not trying to

dissuade you. It's just a shock—that's all. But I know you wouldn't make a rash decision, and I'm here for you. *Whatever* you need. Things must be pretty awful for you to want to leave him while Jolene is still a baby. You just tell me what I can do to help, and I'll do it. I've got plenty of room here if you need a place to stay."

She shook her head. "That's generous, but I don't want to put you in the middle and—"

"I'm putting myself where I belong—on the side of my friend. I'd love to have you stay here. It would be wonderful to spend time with Jolene—I hardly see either of you. And to be completely honest, the thought of having a baby around warms my heart."

That was genuinely kind of Tamara, and Holly would take her up on it if only she could, but... She pulled up her shoulders. "I'm not leaving him."

"I'm not sure I understand," Tamara said.

"The attorney says I might... I *probably* would lose custody of Jolene. Because of, you know, my past."

Tamara was a year younger than Holly, and they hadn't been friends back then, but they'd attended the same school. Like everyone from Scottsdale High, Tamara knew the story—the public version, anyway. But only Zach knew the *whole* truth. Only Zach and, now, Les Larson.

"I'm not sure what happened back then, so long ago, would matter. Maybe you should get another opinion."

"It isn't only my past. It's that, combined with more recent events—my so-called confusion about certain things. And besides, that one visit cost five-hundred dollars."

"I can lend you the money to consult someone else."

"The attorney is Les Larson. They say he's very, very good. I think he knows his business. So I trust his opinion more than others."

After a few moments, Tamara released Holly's hands and

let out a sigh. "My offer to let you stay here is always open. And, listen, I don't want to make this about me, but after Tom died, I saw a psychiatrist for a few months and it really helped. Have you talked to a therapist?"

"About Zach?"

She nodded. "Yes, of course, that would be part of it. But from what you told us at lunch, you've been going through some things. Maybe it would be a good idea to talk with a doctor. Maybe you need to see someone about *you*."

TWENTY

Holly and Zach sat close together on the psychiatrist's couch, as if they were the same as any other couple with a few minor issues to work out.

But the loss of Holly's happiness in her marriage was like a death.

While Zach talked, she silently ticked off the stages of grief she'd learned about in college—denial, anger, bargaining, depression, and acceptance. She was currently bouncing around among the stages. One minute, she'd accepted her fate, resigning herself to living out the next eighteen years, until Jolene was an adult, with a man she couldn't trust. The next minute, she was bargaining with Zach, trying to negotiate her freedom. Then back to denial, wondering if the problem was really her and not him.

So when Tamara had joined the chorus of those suggesting she see a shrink, after all the strange things that had transpired, Holly decided she needed someone outside the bubble to weigh in. Had she misconstrued the facts, misjudged her husband and her own ability to look after her child?

They were twenty minutes into an exploratory session with

Dr. Terrence Washington, a psychiatrist Holly had selected, in no small part, because of his *lack* of affiliation with Mercy General.

Zach didn't know Dr. Washington, and Dr. Washington didn't know Zach.

She hoped that would level the playing field—that Zach's credibility wouldn't automatically be elevated above her own. And this man came with a pedigree. He'd recently left his position at McLean—a psychiatric hospital affiliated with Harvard Medical School—to begin winding down his career in the Valley of the Sun. His office location, in the swank Biltmore district, appealed to Zach, as did his academic bent. Zach was clearly smitten by Dr. Washington's connection to Harvard and had been tap-dancing for him since they'd entered the room.

At this very moment, he was prattling on, and Holly was drifting.

"What's your take on that, Holly?" Dr. Washington slipped his glasses off and aimed an inclusive look her way.

"I-I'm not sure." She had no clue what he was referring to— it was so difficult to listen when the sound of her husband's voice set her teeth on edge and turned her stomach.

"Perhaps you'd be more comfortable and able to speak more freely if Dr. Bancroft stepped out," Dr. Washington said.

She laced her fingers through Zach's and felt his hand tighten, crushing hers.

"I want to make sure we address all of your concerns." The loose skin on Washington's forehead formed itself into pleats as he addressed her husband. "But I think I've got a good picture of them. At this point, I'd like to hear more from Holly. We've got beverages and snacks in the waiting area."

Zach cleared his throat.

"I understand you're worried about the toll your daughter's birth has taken on your wife. A one-on-one conversation with her might be helpful. I don't like to push, but..."

Zach nodded. "Nobody's pushing her. It was her idea to get a psychiatric evaluation done."

"An evaluation?" She wouldn't have phrased it like that, but it was true she wanted a professional opinion. If this man thought she needed treatment before she could be trusted with her own daughter, she would be devastated, but she would enroll in therapy right away.

Her number one priority was Jolene's welfare.

"That's not what I meant, and this isn't a formal evaluation. We're just talking here." Washington lowered his palms like he was braking a runaway conversation. "But, if you had to put it into your own words, Holly—" he looked pointedly at her rather than Zach "—what do you hope to gain from this session. Why are *you* here?"

"I want to know—" *Who's the crazy one in this relationship? If I leave Zach, will that be the best thing for my child?* "—whether or not you recommend therapy."

"Therapy to help you with what problems? Are you feeling sad? Do you have trouble sleeping? Again, I'd like to suggest your husband step out—"

Zach's hand locked down on her fingers. "Tell him, honey. That's why we're here."

"But haven't you covered everything already?" She was sure that somewhere in Zach's long-winded speech he'd said she was paranoid, that she'd accused him of interfering with her labor because he wanted something bad to happen to the baby. That she'd been so convinced of his malicious intent she'd deliberately shattered a Baccarat vase to get the nurse's attention. And he'd recounted the ransom note incident. Said that she'd taken too many pills and summoned a detective because she was acting under a delusion Jolene had been kidnapped. That the detective worried she might have taken an intentional overdose. She remembered him mentioning the strollers... so what was left to tell?

Zach leveled a gaze at her, his eyes full of concern.

She shuddered.

"Holly, I'll leave the room if you want me to. I'm only here to support you. But if you don't tell Dr. Washington about what happened to you in high school, I will."

"Stop right there, please." Dr. Washington rose on his haunches. "This is supposed to be a safe place for both of you. Your wife will *not* feel safe with you threatening to reveal her secrets. And I cannot allow such tactics in my office."

"She needs to talk about it. If she doesn't, how can you possibly help?"

Holly put her face in her hands. She didn't want to relive that terrible day, but she'd faced the memories not long ago in Les Larson's office. For Jolene's sake, she could dust them off again. It would be simple enough to lock them back up once she got Dr. Washington's take. "When I was in high school—"

"I'm going to stop you right there. Dr. Bancroft, you need to wait in the reception area." Washington was clever. Bringing out Zach's title, now, even though he'd been using first names earlier. It showed respect and allowed Zach to save face. "I appreciate your desire to support your wife by remaining, but I know what I'm doing. I wouldn't tell you how to deliver a baby. I'm sure you'll extend me the same courtesy."

Zach put an arm around her. "Do you want me to stay?"

If she told him to leave, Zach would be angry. Later, he might be suspicious about what she'd discussed when he was out of the room. But she couldn't bring herself to say she wanted him here, so she just sat there, crossing and uncrossing her legs.

"This is my decision. I prefer to speak one on one with Mrs. Bancroft. Thanks for understanding," Washington said firmly, and then he got up and ushered Zach from the room.

Anticipating tears, Holly pulled a tissue from her pocket, but her eyes were dry, her mind numb. The last thing she wanted was to go on record with a full accounting of her past mistakes, but if she didn't, Dr. Washington's input would be meaningless, and she desperately wanted an objective opinion. Still, she didn't dare give Zach more ammunition for a custody battle, and Washington wasn't an attorney. She wasn't sure what kind of privilege would apply under these circumstances. "Is what I say here protected information?"

"Are you planning to commit a crime or to hurt yourself or someone else?"

She let out a shaky laugh. "Of course not."

"Then yes, whatever you tell me is protected by doctor–patient privilege."

Where to begin?

The office seemed to contract around her. She felt like a mouse that had been lured into a box, and then the opening had been sealed shut, and now her oxygen was running out. "I was sixteen."

Why did she start out with that? Her age was no excuse.

Her mouth tasted like metal.

She squeezed her eyes shut before continuing, pretending it was a movie. Just a story she was going to tell. A curtain parted to reveal the big screen, and the first scene scrolled across her mind.

"I used to babysit for the family next door. John and Linda Peterson. Their baby's name was Nora—Nora was nine months old."

Holly inhaled, smelling the lavender baby lotion she used on Nora after the bath, rubbed her fingers together, feeling the ridge of two tiny teeth that had just broken through Nora's gums. Nora hated it when she'd clean those teeth with a soft washcloth, but then Holly would cover Nora's eyes, and she'd squeal with delight.

Where's Nora? Peek-a-boo! There she is!

"It was springtime. March nineteenth."

Jolene was born in March.

You're talking about Nora—Jolene is safe.

"Mr. Peterson said Mrs. Peterson needed a break, and he wanted to take her to Sedona for the day. They planned to shop and have a nice dinner before heading home. He asked if I could stay until nine or ten p.m., and I said that would be fine."

Her eyelids fluttered open.

Dr. Washington's arms were crossed over his chest. He was listening intently, not taking notes. "How do you feel?"

"I'm okay."

"Can you continue?"

She nodded. "They asked me to stay late—until nine or ten. But earlier, we had agreed on six, and I was supposed to meet someone—my boyfriend. I didn't really want to stay later, but I didn't know how to refuse. The Petersons were adults, and I was just a teenager. Anyway, after they left, I called him."

"Your boyfriend?"

"Yes. Brian Sanger. I told him I couldn't meet him after all, and then he said he wanted to come over to the Petersons. I said he had to be gone by eight o'clock so they wouldn't find out, and he said that was plenty of time."

"You weren't supposed to have visitors while you were babysitting."

"Right. I should never have agreed, but I didn't know... I mean how could I have known what was going to happen?"

"But you knew he shouldn't be there."

Pretend it's just a story. You can tell it.

"Yes. I knew what we were doing was wrong. By the time he got there, Nora was asleep. We went upstairs and..." She felt moisture on her face.

Dr. Washington shifted in his seat, waiting.

"He brought brownies with him—they had marijuana baked in. It wasn't legal back then, but we thought it was harmless. We got pretty high, and we fooled around a little, and then we both fell asleep."

"So no one knows Brian was there?"

"Everyone knows that, now."

"But I thought this was a secret."

"The secret is that we got high. That we were asleep when the fire started."

He picked up his pad. "A fire... Go on."

"I told the police that we were in the living room studying when the smoke alarm went off, and that we both ran up to get Nora. But that was a lie. We were *asleep* upstairs in the primary bedroom. So you see, now, what a terrible person I am. It doesn't matter that I never meant for anything bad to happen."

Washington got up, came around to the other side of his desk and took a chair in front of her, offered her a water bottle. "Do you need a break?"

"No." She tried to keep pretending she was watching a movie of herself, sixteen and terrified, but then she felt her heart pounding out of her chest. "The smoke is burning a hole in my lungs, and Brian is lying beside me..."

It wasn't a movie anymore.

Wake up! Wake up!

Brian's on his feet, stumbling around.

He opens the door and flames burst into the room, and he runs to the window.

"What are you doing? Don't jump!"

Brian's got one leg over the windowsill.

"Nora! Nora!" Holly screams.

She grabs the bedspread and wraps it around her; she's crawling, making a tent of air beneath the blanket; she has to get to the nursery but she can't find her way. The smoke is too thick!

And then she hears Nora.

She crawls through the smoke and flames, guided by Nora's crying.

She grabs Nora and wraps her in the blanket and runs like hell—down the stairs and out the door.

She hears sirens blaring.

They made it!

"We made it!" Holly jolts back to the moment, her face wet with tears, her pulse pumping from adrenaline. And then she sags back against the couch. "I thought we'd made it. I thought I'd *saved* her."

Dr. Washington's eyes were moist, like he knew what was coming, but he remained quiet.

For a long time, they sat in silence.

Eventually Washington said, "Let's have you breathe in and out while I count."

She put her hand on her stomach.

"Inhale. Two, three, four, five. Hold it, and now exhale two, three, four, five."

She cycled through a few more breaths, and then reached for the water. Took a few sips. Started to talk. "I really thought we were all going to make it. Brian jumped from the second story. The fall wasn't so far, but he hit his head on some stone pavers. He seemed all right the first day, and then suddenly, he wasn't. The doctors said it was an epidural hematoma—a brain bleed that killed him."

"And Nora? What happened to Nora?" Dr. Washington asked softly.

"She died from smoke inhalation. The home was new construction. The investigators never found the exact cause of the fire but they suspected faulty wiring. The homebuilders settled the case out of court. Brian's family got some of the money, too. You understand why I couldn't tell anyone about the marijuana. Or that we were asleep. His family might not have gotten a settlement if people knew it was our fault. And I was so ashamed. So horrified at myself."

"But it wasn't your fault," Washington said.

She shook her head. "Nora's death is my doing. She was my responsibility, and I was in the bedroom sleeping instead of taking care of her. If we hadn't been high, we wouldn't have fallen asleep, and if we'd been awake we would've smelled the smoke or heard the alarm sooner. Until I met Zach, I never told anyone the truth about that day. And what's worse—the Petersons actually thanked me for getting Nora out of the house, even though she didn't survive. They blamed themselves because they stayed late in Sedona, and because the wiring was faulty in their home. Some people in the community even said I was a hero for crawling around in a fiery hallway to get to the nursery."

"This is a terrible, terrible tragedy, Holly. But you didn't cause the fire. Yes, you ate the brownies and invited your boyfriend over. But when the fire broke out, you did your best to save Nora. You deserve credit for that."

"I'm not looking for credit, or for absolution. I know the pain I've caused others, and I've accepted, a long time ago, that I can't undo it."

"If not absolution, Holly, then what are you looking for? Today? From me? How can I help you?"

"Just tell me the truth. I understand I did wrong, and that I have to live with the consequences, but I don't want my past to hurt my daughter. I'm trying so hard to be a good mother. Do you think I'm capable of being one?"

"From the things I've learned about you today, yes, I do."

"What about the things Zach told you—the pills, the strollers? Don't those things worry you?"

Washington took off his glasses and met her gaze. "The strollers? That was a clerical error. We wouldn't even be discussing it if they hadn't been expensive. And, as he told it, Zach was the one who brought you those first pills. You were confused when you woke up alone in your house and found the baby missing... and with what you lived through before, it's no wonder you jumped into action and called the police. I don't think you're delusional—at least not from anything that's been outlined here today by you or by your husband, or from what I've observed in your behavior. But..." He tapped his glasses against his hand. "What does concern me is your hand."

"What do you mean?"

"How does it feel?"

She looked down where it lay curled in her lap, throbbing, aching. "It hurts."

"Zach seems too possessive to me. He gives you very little room, and I watched him crush your hand right in front of me. He didn't want to let you speak with me alone—it was very hard to convince him. So my advice to you, Holly, is this. Trust your gut. Be the smart capable woman you are, and do whatever you need to do to keep yourself and your daughter safe."

TWENTY-ONE

Holly backed away from the crib, exhausted. Jolene had finally gone down for a nap after a rough morning. Maybe the applesauce Holly introduced for the first time didn't agree with her.

Holly hoped it was something that simple. That Jolene wasn't picking up on Holly's distress and mirroring it. She'd read that babies are highly tuned to their mothers' emotions, and, since her session with Dr. Washington, Holly's mood had gotten progressively more morbid.

It was no longer possible for her to imagine things would get better at home, but at the same time, she couldn't figure a way to leave. Not one that would guarantee she wouldn't lose her daughter in the process.

She tried to tell herself she could tough it out, tolerate Zach's controlling behavior. That, eventually, the discomfort would become so familiar she wouldn't mind. Like when you put on a pair of tight jeans that chafe at the waist, but after an hour of wear you don't notice it anymore.

But with every day that went by, her marriage pinched her more and more until sometimes she felt she'd been cinched so tight she was going to explode. Unbidden, an image flashed before her eyes, a vision of her entrails bursting from her body, plastering the white walls of the nursery.

She raised her hand, drew it back and then slapped herself in the face.

She'd discovered that the sting distracted her and stopped macabre thoughts like these from circling her brain—at least for a few minutes. Last week, she'd hit herself hard enough to bruise her cheek, leading Jolene's pediatrician to ask if she felt safe at home.

Was that what she'd intended?

Was she trying to communicate her distress—create an evidence trail she could use against Zach?

Dr. Washington said she should do whatever it took to keep herself and her child safe.

Les Larson said if she wanted the court to believe Zach was abusive she needed evidence: photographs, witnesses.

Only trouble was, Zach wasn't *that* kind of an abuser.

In the small mirror above the nursery's changing table, Holly stared at her reflection. Even though it was past noon, her hair was unbrushed. Red welts in the shape of her hand stood out against her white skin, dark circles shadowed her eyes, and her lips were cracked and dry.

Her collarbone jutted out beneath her neck. She needed to eat more and stay hydrated, keep up her milk supply. The pediatrician recommended breastfeeding Jolene until she switched to regular milk at one year and Holly wanted to do that for her.

Zach, on the other hand, *hated* the fact that she was still nursing Jolene at six months.

He had plenty of reasonable arguments for why she should change to formula. Though Jolene was thriving, Holly was losing weight and tired all the time; and this wasn't a third world country where Jolene couldn't access the nutrition she needed.

But he was so adamant, so angry about it, Holly had suspected there was more to it.

Then one night, he'd gotten drunk, crawled into bed and yanked up her nightshirt. He'd growled and lurched for her, painfully squeezing first one breast and then the other. "I'm tired of sharing these, sharing *you* with the baby," he'd moaned before climbing on top of her.

The next morning he'd denied it.

Holly was *delusional*.

Nothing like that ever happened. Just like he hadn't put his hand over her mouth when she was in labor with Jolene.

Right.

And that's when she'd recognized yet another painful truth about her husband—Zach was *jealous* of his own baby.

Providing one more reason she didn't dare risk his winning custody.

No matter how he appeared to the outside world, to their friends, to his colleagues, his patients, she was living with the truth.

The real Zach was the kind of man who would kill your spirit while no one was looking.

But he wasn't going to kill Jolene's spirit.

Not while Holly still breathed.

In her bathroom, she splashed water on her face, and with sudden energy picked up her hairbrush, jerked it through her hair. Then she put Vaseline on her lips and marched to her closet. It didn't matter what she chose, it would meet Zach's approval because every stitch she owned had been curated by him. She grabbed a collared blouse and a pair of cream trousers and slipped them on. She glanced at the matching suede loafers that coordinated with the pants and decided not to bother. Barefoot, she slipped downstairs, hoping to bypass Zach's den without drawing his attention. But just as she snuck by, a sharp knock sounded at their front door.

Zach looked up and smiled, apparently pleased she'd brushed her hair and dressed for a change. "Shall I get that for you, dear?"

As if she weren't capable of answering the door.

As if it were her responsibility more than his—as if she were his employee, his housekeeper. She imagined a faceless, gender-less person, standing on the stoop and herself whispering in their ear: *My husband's evil.* "No thanks. I'll get it."

* * *

Minutes later Holly was poised on the couch in their formal living room with her dutiful husband, Zach, next to her, and Detective Don Denton sitting, legs sprawled over the edge of their Bertoia bird chair.

Déjà vu all over again.

Today, Denton brought his poker face, as did Zach, but Holly wasn't a good actress so she tried to keep her gaze down-cast lest Denton discern her nervousness.

Though she'd done nothing wrong, she felt guilty, and certain she was about to be dragged down to the station, ques-tioned and arrested for whatever crime he'd come about.

"I can put some coffee on," Zach said. "Or is this going to be brief?"

"No thanks." Denton flipped open his notebook. "Mind if I record this?"

"You're taking notes," Holly felt compelled to point out.

"Yes. I'll be doing both. How is the little one?"

"Sleeping," Holly said, and Zach picked up her hand. Inside, she recoiled, but, for the sake of appearance, and of keeping the peace with Zach, she let her hand rest in his.

A bead of sweat was working its way down the back of her blouse.

At least she was properly dressed and not out-of-it on pain pills like the first time she'd met the detective.

Maybe there had been a break-in in the neighborhood. Or had she done something and simply didn't recall? What if Zach had fabricated some damming scenario to make her look crazy? She wouldn't be shocked if he'd used her phone to text Denton about another ransom note.

"Dr. Bancroft..."

"Please, call me Zach."

"Dr. Bancroft, I have a few questions for you concerning the night of July twenty-seventh. Not this past July, but the previous year. It was a Friday. If you need to check your calendar..."

Zach held up his hand. "No need."

Holly's heart sped up.

The detective was here to question *Zach*.

And July 27th? A little more than a year ago?

Was this about Tom? Tom Driscoll.

"Dr. Bancroft, how can you remember the night of July twenty-seventh, just like that?" Denton's voice deepened, as if that answer was of great import.

"Because—" Zach cleared his throat and looked off into the distance "—unfortunately, a friend of mine died that night." His voice broke, and Holly got a momentary glimpse of the old Zach. The one who'd made her feel loved. The one who'd squired her around town and taken her on vacations with Tamara and Tom.

"He was killed in a collision," Zach added.

"Car accident?"

"Yes," Holly said. "Is that what this is about?"

"Sorry for your loss." Denton flipped a page. "So where were you, Dr. Bancroft, that evening?"

"Pardon?"

"You said you remember."

"Well, erm, I—"

Tom had been in a single car accident. He'd been drunk. And now, more than a year later, the police were looking into it?

It didn't make sense.

"I do remember, distinctly. But before I answer, please do me the courtesy of explaining why you want to know. You wouldn't be here, asking questions, if there weren't some new development."

"Fair enough. A medical student, Beth Gunther, supposedly left town that evening. No one has seen her since, until... Do you remember Beth Gunther?"

An odd sensation was welling up inside of Holly, her throat filling. Holly remembered Beth. The young woman had worked with Zach in the clinic. He was her preceptor. Beth was Holly's middle name and that gave her some kind of small connection to her. Beth had a sweet smile—after meeting Claudia, Holly meant to inquire after Beth, but with her marriage in tatters she'd forgotten. "I know Beth Gunther, too. Is she all right?"

"I'd like your husband to answer. So, where were you, Dr. Bancroft, the night of July twenty-seventh?"

"Listen, I'm more than happy to answer, but you've got me worried. I heard through the hospital grapevine that Beth left medical school in order to travel the world. She wanted to 'find herself'. That's what people said, anyway."

"Who? Which people, specifically?" Denton paused with his pencil hovering above his notebook.

"Oh gosh, I don't recall. It was just general conversation. Beth was a good student, and I was sorry to see her go."

"Would it surprise you to learn that she's dead?" Denton said, his face betraying not a hint of remorse for ambushing them with the news, his gaze unfaltering.

Holly couldn't get her breath.

Zach's hand clenched around hers. His face drained of

color. "Yes," he said softly. "It surprises me, and saddens me. What happened? Was it her husband?"

"She wasn't married."

"A boyfriend, then?"

"What makes you say that?"

"Well, you're a detective, so the death is obviously suspicious, and you know what they say."

"It's always the husband or boyfriend." Denton arched an eyebrow. "They do say that. Are you sure you don't need your calendar, Dr. Bancroft? To refresh your memory about where you were."

"What happened to Beth?" Zach's eyes flashed, and Holly could tell he was angry. Denton was asking him for an alibi. That much was plain.

"Her parents reported her missing over a year ago, but she had a problematic relationship with them so they often went long periods of time without hearing from her. Her friends, as you mentioned, thought she might've been traveling—she'd indicated a desire to do so and had said she was fed up with school. There was no evidence of foul play until recently, but I'm sorry to report that a hiker discovered her remains in a shallow grave last week. Looks like she never made it out of town at all, and now that we have a positive ID we're questioning—"

"Everyone?" Zach scoffed. "Are you seriously questioning every doctor, every student, everyone who knew her?"

"If necessary, I will. But I'd like to cross you off my list, first."

That emotion bubbling up inside Holly began to sort itself into different packages. There was shock. Sadness. Fear... and then there was hope. The police thought *Zach* had something to do with poor Beth's murder, and murder suspects didn't get to stay on as department chairs or keep their bustling private practices, or dictate whether or not their wives could leave town with their child. Of course Zach *wasn't* a murderer but that didn't matter. It only mattered that the police thought he *might* be.

He slumped back against the sofa still clutching her hand, his breathing labored and accompanied by soft, quick little wheezes.

Zach was *scared*.

"He was with me." Holly sat up straight on the couch.

Denton nodded. "Where?"

"Here, at home. It was a very difficult night for us both. Tom was a good friend, and we spent most of the night crying on each other's shoulders, perusing old photos of our vacations with Tom and Tamara—his wife—and by then it was late, we were both exhausted and went to bed."

"If you were in bed how do you know Zach didn't leave at some point?"

"Because I couldn't sleep a wink. I'm afraid I didn't doze off until the sun started peeking through the shutters."

That was a lie. Zach hadn't come home until three a.m. She'd been devastated, pacing the house waiting for him to get home so she could tell him about Tom. She didn't want to break the news to him over the phone. And she hadn't thought much of his late arrival because that's just part of life when you're married to an obstetrician. Whenever Zach came home in the wee hours, it meant he'd had a laboring patient and had slept in the on-call room. At least she'd always assumed that was what it meant. Not once, had she suspected him of infidelity—and certainly not murder.

Her mind was really racing, now, though.

Because if, in fact, Zach had been at the hospital, there'd be ample proof.

So what was all this squirming and wheezing about? "Why the particular interest in my husband, detective?"

Denton's poker face didn't slip. "One student we talked with told us about a rumor that he was involved with Beth."

"That's a lie." Zach found his voice again.

"It's a lie that you were with your wife all evening?"

Zach dropped her hand and put his elbows behind his head, suddenly the picture of calm. "I wasn't *involved* with Beth or any other woman besides Holly. I'm a very happily married man. Ask anyone."

"How about I ask your wife?" Denton shot her a glance.

"We're in love. Happy. And as you know, we have the most beautiful little girl," Holly shifted her body to face Zach. "A little girl who means *everything*. There's absolutely nothing I wouldn't do to protect her," she said meaningfully.

"Would you lie about your husband's whereabouts the night a woman disappeared? One of his medical students with whom he's rumored to have had an affair?"

"Quite the opposite." She turned back to Denton and lifted her eyes to his. "If I believed that my husband was a murderer, I'd turn him in in a heartbeat."

"So noted." Denton rearranged himself, kicking one leg out in front, stretching it. Their Bertoia bird chair didn't seem to suit him. "One more thing, Mrs. Bancroft," Denton said. "How'd you get that mark on your cheek? Did your husband hit you?"

"What?" She lowered her gaze, deliberately feigning fear. "I-I tripped and fell, just a few minutes ago."

The detective narrowed his eyes at Zach. He didn't appear to believe her at all about the handprint on her face, and *oh good*, he was writing it all down in his little book.

TWENTY-TWO

Zach approached Holly, his hands lifted as if to choke her, but then dropped them to her shoulders and shook her until her teeth rattled. "How could you be so stupid?"

She pushed him away and rubbed her jaw. "You mean how could I give you an alibi when you clearly needed one?"

He scoffed. "I mean slapping yourself in the face. You've got to stop this nonsense, or I'm going to have to cart you back to that shrink."

"Cart away. Dr. Washington says I'm sane."

"Then I'll get a second opinion. I've got to do something... Detective Denton thinks I hit you."

"He might. But more to the point, he thinks you killed Beth Gunther. Let's focus on that, why don't we?"

He gaped at her, and for a moment, it seemed she had him on the ropes.

She clasped her hands together, hating herself for using the poor woman's death to her own advantage, but when she'd told Denton she'd do anything to protect their daughter, she'd meant it.

And, besides, she believed, deep in her heart, that Zach had nothing to do with Beth's murder. He probably hadn't even slept with her. He was far too busy obsessing over Holly for any of that. But it would be better if he didn't know she thought he was innocent. "Where were you that night?"

"None of your damn business."

He was definitely hiding something. Not murder, but something. Maybe he had been having an affair after all. If she had to guess with whom, she'd say Donna.

Fine. He could screw anyone he wanted, as long as it wasn't Holly.

But what if?

No. Not possible.

Zach might be a controlling creep, but he wasn't a killer.

But what if?

Then it would be all the more imperative to stop him from getting custody. Even if she thought he was the devil incarnate, if she could negotiate a deal, she'd do it.

"Where were you?" she asked again, trying to sound like a woman who actually believed her husband might be a murderer.

"I was with you." He paced the perimeter of the room.

Holly heard Jolene whimpering through the baby monitor. She lifted it, watching her daughter on the screen as she rolled onto her side and drifted back to sleep, a beautiful smile playing on her lips.

She steeled her spine.

There was no turning back, now—not when she'd already lied to the police. "Stop playing games. You weren't home. That night, I was sick with worry. Tamara called me in shock, and all I could think of was how devastated I'd be if anything happened to *you.* I was pregnant with Jolene, and I spent the entire night crying. I texted you, but you didn't respond. I thought you were at the hospital."

He paced in ever narrowing circles around her before

coming to a halt, just inches away. "What are you talking about? I was with you."

"No. I thought you were delivering a baby, but obviously you weren't or you'd have simply said so when the detective asked your whereabouts. Maybe you were murdering your student that night. That would explain why you didn't answer your phone."

"Sweetheart." He turned his palms up. "I'm so very sorry for snapping at you. But I'm sure, if you think back, you'll realize that what you told Detective Denton is the truth. We were home grieving together."

"We were not. It's sunny outside, and today is Saturday, and I refuse to let you tell me that it's raining and it's Wednesday. I'm not crazy. I *remember* that night."

He clucked his tongue. "You're confused. Think about it, Holly. You're calling *yourself* a liar. Why would you tell the detective we were together if we weren't?"

She pulled up her chin. "Because you're a suspect, or at least you're a person of interest, in a murder investigation. And whether you did it or not—"

"You cannot possibly believe that I killed Beth."

"Oh, but I can. And whether you did it or not, just the hint that you might have will cost you your practice. No one wants a 'person of interest' delivering their baby or running their department. *No one.* Innocent or not, this could ruin you. So instead of lecturing me, you should be thanking me."

He tugged at his hair. "I never killed anyone, but you're right, the taint of suspicion would ruin us. Which is why you did the right thing telling Denton we were together."

"Not us." She smiled and drew in a long breath, the air suddenly tasting sweet. "*You.* It would ruin *you.* So here's the bargain I'm willing to make."

She paused, expecting him to protest, to keep up the pretense that he'd actually been home, but instead, he kept his mouth shut. Leveling a steady gaze at him, she continued, "I want a divorce."

"Still?"

"More than ever."

"This is the first I've heard since that night you tried to take Jolene to Abilene. I thought it was settled."

"You're mistaken. We're going to settle it now."

"I can't let you take our daughter. You're too fragile to care for Jolene on your own."

"Stop saying that—it isn't true. Here's what we're going to do. I'm going to stand by my statement to Denton. The police will move on to other suspects, like her boyfriend if she had one, and surely she did, she was so lovely."

He sighed. "Poor Beth."

"And after a respectable amount of time, just enough so it doesn't look fishy, I'm going to file for divorce. You won't contest it, and you'll sign over full custody of Jolene to me."

He frowned, considering. "We'd have to keep up appearances. You'd have to show the world you have faith in me. That means going out in public together—holding hands."

"So we have a deal?" She picked up her phone in one hand and Denton's card in the other. "Or shall I amend my statement now? Gosh, I hate to think of your mother getting wind of this."

"Yes, but I'll work hard to be a better husband. You'll change your mind—I'm sure of it. I love you, and you love me."

"To be clear: I make public appearances as a loving wife and provide an alibi for the night of July twenty-seventh. In exchange, once the police turn their attention away from you, you'll agree to a no contest divorce, and I'll get full custody of Jolene? Yes or no?"

He opened his arms and beckoned her. "That's a yes from me, my darling."

"Good." She turned her back and fled the room.

TWENTY-THREE

Holly couldn't deny the idea of a steak dinner at one of Phoenix's finest restaurants appealed, especially since fulfilling her "public appearances" clause, as well as the celebratory nature of the meal, served to cement her deal with Zach. But once she got into the weeds, the drawbacks became apparent.

At The Cuts, a place Holly had never been but Zach frequented for high-end business dinners, the problem was both the company (her husband, though, that was inevitable) and the presentation.

"Fit for a king!" the waiter declared, waving a hand above the selection of raw display meats he'd wheeled over.

Holly pulled her cardigan tight around her shoulders, and then noticed a skosh of moisture above her lip. The cold air blasting from a vent above their table and the scent of bleeding beef was making her nose drip.

"May I recommend the Tomahawk cut? It's one of our most popular—taken from a little used muscle—"

"The longissimus dorsi, if I'm not mistaken," Zach interrupted. "Highly marbled with delicious fat as compared to the hypertrophied muscles."

Did his imperiousness know no bounds? He couldn't bear to be bested by a waiter? He had to brag about his knowledge of *cow* anatomy?

"My husband's a physician." She beamed at him, then dabbed her nose with a tissue as surreptitiously as possible, though she didn't know why she bothered with subtlety when the ribcage of a dead cow, scraped not-quite clean, with bits and bobs of shiny white tissue clinging to it, rose from the display table, quashing her appetite for a juicy steak.

"Ah, bravo!" The waiter gave a quick, deferential bow. "Shall I describe the other selections?"

"I know what I want," Zach said. "But perhaps my wife will be interested."

"You choose for me, darling." She offered up a demure smile and was rewarded with Zach puffing his chest.

"I'll have the tomahawk and the lady will have the wagyu fillet. Medium rare for both. Caviar to begin. Wedge salads; blue cheese dressing. Oh, and a bottle of your two-thousand-eight Dom Pérignon, please."

"Excellent choices, sir. My compliments."

"Sounds wonderful." Zach wouldn't have forgotten that she hated caviar anymore than she could forget his love of it. Usually, she'd order her own appetizer, say the chilled cucumber soup, but tonight, in the spirit of everyone living up to their end of the bargain, she was determined to partake of the Beluga and moan with delight at each bite.

Tonight, she would put on as good a show for him as he had, until recently, done for her. Never would she have guessed that as the years passed, her husband would come to barely resemble the man she'd vowed to love, honor and cherish. That the groom who'd encouraged her to remove the word "obey" from her wedding vows, would later act as if she'd promised before God to do every single solitary thing he commanded, no questions asked.

. . .

"Fit for a king, indeed." Zach dropped his black, limit-free credit card on the little tray that contained the bill. "Thank you so much for a fantastic evening."

"Yes, it was so very lovely," Holly managed. After two and a half hours of public gushing over and flirting with a man who made her skin crawl, she was ready to leap onto the table and scream her head off until someone called the men in white coats to take her away.

Zach turned a benevolent smile on her, as if she weren't his prisoner, and she smiled back because ticking off your jailor didn't make for a pleasant stay in the big house, and she was planning on an early parole.

Until then, she would smile and giggle and flirt in public... and in private?

She could stomach a little charade; give him just enough hope to make life bearable while this played out. "Thank you, Zach, this was generous of you. I want you to know how much I appreciate the olive branch."

A sparkle in his eyes let her know she'd succeeded in one thing—he believed he had her right where he wanted her—and that was right where she wanted him.

"Darling, I meant it when I said I want us to be happy. Just like we were before..." He seemed to catch himself and left the thought unfinished.

Before the baby, was what he'd been about to say—Holly was sure of it.

Making her all the more certain she would not have peace of mind until she and Jolene could get away. Even with primary custody, she might not be able to exclude him totally from Jolene's life, but perhaps once Zach no longer had a use for Jolene as a pawn in his scheme to control Holly, he'd manage to be a decent parent for a few days here and there. Maybe once he'd accepted that it was over between them, once he no longer saw Jolene as competition for Holly's affection, he *might* even grow to love his own daughter.

"Would you like to stop in at Scottsdale Lapidary? I spotted a *to-die-for* diamond tennis bracelet I think might please. Delicate, like you."

If she accepted the bracelet could she return it to the shop? Yes, but the money would just go back to his credit card, which would do her no good, and he'd be mad as hell. Pawning it would surely bring very little compared to its value—but maybe she could get a decent price for it on eBay.

"You're spoiling me, Zach." She reached across the table and let her fingers dangle within his reach.

He leaned over and took her hand, brought it to his lips. "I plan to keep on doing so for the rest of your life."

Until death do us part? No, thank you.

"Have you forgotten our bargain, so soon?" She batted her lashes, toying with him, her words saying one thing, her body language another. Let him have his hopes. It would be all the more satisfying when she dashed them.

"Have you forgotten my promise to show you the error of *my* ways? You'll change your mind, just wait and see."

TWENTY-FOUR

Holly burrowed her bottom into the curve of Zach's body, gritting her teeth and fighting back the nausea that threatened to gag her and spoil her recent virtuoso performance.

After dinner, he'd bought her a gelato and a diamond bracelet. Later, at home, once Frances had said her goodbyes, and they'd peeked in on Jolene in the nursery, Zach had taken her by the hand and led her into the bedroom.

She'd changed into a nightgown and crawled under the covers, let him kiss her, with tongue, before shyly lifting his hand from where it had strayed between her legs.

Oh, Zach, I just can't. Not yet, I'm so confused! But wouldn't it be so lovely to spoon? I'd love a good cuddle.

As soon as she felt his body loosen, his breathing slow with sleep, she'd ease out of bed and go shower in one of the guest suites. Scrub his touch and tonight's lies from her skin. Let the clean water wash away her tears. But for now, she tucked in close and sighed. "Mmmh. This is nice."

He tightened his hold on her.

Not what she was expecting. Unlike Holly, who was a hopeless insomniac, Zach usually drifted right off. He'd told her once he'd trained himself to fall asleep on command because he often had to sleep in short snatches of time in between deliveries.

But tonight, his breathing was heavy, his body tense.

He clamped a hand around her arm. "Did you hear that?"

"No." Nothing out of the ordinary. A branch scratching against the window, maybe.

His fingernails dug painfully into her skin. "I think someone's outside."

She rolled away and sat up, concentrating. The windows were well insulated against noise, and other than that scratching branch, she heard nothing at all coming from outside the house. "You must have dog ears. I don't hear anything."

He threw off the covers, then dangled his feet from the bed, glancing back over his shoulder at her with a look that made her blood freeze. Maybe it was the way the night turned his eyes to blue-back, hard and slick, like the shiny cover of a casket. Perhaps it was the way the shadows played menacingly across his mouth, transforming his lips into a seeming snarl, but whatever it was, his expression filled her with dread.

This man in her bedroom was a stranger.

She didn't know him, or what he might do.

A crash sounded downstairs.

"Did you set the alarm?" she asked. But of course he had. Zach *always* set the alarm.

He shook his head.

"You didn't?" One hand climbed to her throat, and she reached for her phone on the bedside table.

He stood, took a step toward the door, and then froze, his eyes scanning the room. "I might have. I'm not sure."

She touched her screen, opening the app to their home security system.

Enter your password.

What? She made sure she never signed out of the app so she could access it quickly in an emergency—like this one.

Don't panic, it's probably nothing.

She tapped in the last code she could recall.

Did you forget your password?

"Zach," she whispered, straining her ears for sounds, suddenly fearing someone was really inside the house. The baby monitor's feed showed Jolene sleeping soundly in her crib.

"I'll get the baby," he said in hushed tones, then slid open the drawer beside his bed. Now, something glinted in his hand.

He kept a *gun* in their bedroom? Since when?

"Don't move."

Heart in her throat, she jumped out of bed and raced for the nursery, but Zach got there ahead of her.

"Give her to me," she said to Zach's turned back, as he crept down the hall with Jolene in his arms and a *gun* in his hand.

"Zach," she whispered, not daring to raise her voice, "do *not* take her downstairs. Give me the baby."

He didn't stop. He didn't turn.

She hurried after him, slipping on the stairs, then leaping back up, following him into the kitchen. Once her eyes adjusted to the ambient light, she saw it.

The back door was open.

Zach raised his arm.

No!

Boom!

A flash of light spotlighted Jolene's perfect face. The smell of burnt powder filled Holly's nostrils. She felt her jaw open, her vocal cords strain, and then darkness covered her mind like a blanket.

TWENTY-FIVE

Zach held Holly's forearm stretched over the kitchen sink beneath a running faucet. Red water poured from the split in her skin like fruit punch from a beverage dispenser, and her insides felt like they'd been stirred in a mixer.

Above the whooshing of the faucet and the sound of Jolene wailing, she heard pounding at the front door.

"Police! Open up!"

Holly jumped, jerked her arm from Zach's grasp and raced to Jolene, whom Zach had positioned on the floor atop a baby blanket. Jolene was still upright, her little legs spread wide, her arms braced between them like a tripod, her face distorted from crying.

Holly scooped her up, pressing Jolene's head against her chest, and frantically searched the kitchen for a place to hide. Then her heartbeat synchronized with her daughter's. Jolene's soft mouth puckered against her skin. She stopped crying, and Holly's trembling subsided. Her racing thoughts settled into a holding pattern.

"Police! Open up!"

Police.

Not a robber.

She let out a shuddering breath, and Zach left the kitchen.

Holly saw the front porch light come on, and then, a moment later a uniformed officer was standing in the kitchen, hands on his hips.

"I'm Officer Harry Vesper, Mrs. Bancroft. Your neighbors heard a gunshot and called nine-one-one."

"I also called nine-one-one," Zach said.

"Mrs. Bancroft, are you all right?"

She followed Officer Vesper's gaze to her arm, which was still dripping watery blood.

"The paramedics are on their way. Let's get you lying down."

"I prefer to sit." She blinked rapidly, and the walls stopped spinning. On steady legs—steady enough—she made her way to the kitchen table, and Zach pulled out a chair for her. He opened his arms for her to hand off Jolene to him, but she shook her head, clasped her closer, and dropped down in the chair, landing with a thud. "We don't need the paramedics, I don't think. Do we, Zach?"

"No. The bullet only grazed Holly's arm—thank goodness. I've flushed the wound, and I was just about to apply a dressing. In fact, I'm going to do that now, while we wait."

"Wait for what?" Holly still didn't quite have her bearings but she held her arm out, obediently, while Zach pulled a shiny pad from his doctor's bag.

"Don't worry, honey, this won't stick to the wound." He placed the shiny square over the abrasion, and then wrapped the bulk of her lower arm with gauze, fixing it in place with white medical tape.

"Shouldn't you have put some hydrogen peroxide or something on that?" the officer asked.

The strained look on Zach's face told Holly that the present, exigent circumstance had not impacted his ego one whit. "I've flushed it clean. An antiseptic might delay wound healing."

Officer Vesper puffed out his cheeks. "Huh. Anyway, the paramedics will be here, soon."

"Can you cancel the call? We don't need them," Zach said.

"Ma'am? What do you want me to do?" The officer was barrel-chested with smooth skin on his face that made him look too young to shave, too young to be a cop, really.

"Call them off. My husband's a doctor, so if he says there's no need, then there's no need. But..." Holly thought she heard a noise overhead and her heart jumped in her chest. Was someone upstairs? "Shouldn't you clear the scene or something?"

"It's okay, my love. I scared the guy off when I fired that shot. He ran out and hopped the back fence," Zach said.

The guy.

She hadn't seen *a guy*, only the open door to the kitchen—that led to the backyard.

"What if the guy wasn't alone?" Jolene was starting to fuss and Holly shifted her in her arms. "Maybe check the house to be on the safe side?"

"Not to worry, ma'am. My partner's clearing the premises as we speak."

A moment later, another officer, Lana Dibrell, reassuringly older and probably more experienced, explained she'd cleared the outdoor perimeter and done a walk-through of the entire house while Officer Vesper stayed with them in the kitchen.

Apparently that's what Zach had meant by *while we wait.*

In short order, they were permitted into the living room and instructed to wait again for a detective while Officers Vesper and Dibrell collected evidence outdoors and in the kitchen alongside a crime scene technician who'd recently pulled up in a van.

When the detective finally arrived, he'd turned out to be Denton.

Holly wasn't surprised.

It made sense the police would send someone who'd already had contact with the family, but it meant her bargain with Zach was going to be put to the test.

Her back went rigid, as she realized, for the first time, that Zach's story of an intruder hopping the back fence didn't add up. And yet she'd seen the back door open, and she was certain it had been closed before they went to bed.

But why hadn't it been locked?

And why hadn't Zach set the alarm?

Denton was taking written notes and also had a recorder on —like the last time he'd questioned them. "Walk me through it one more time, Dr. Bancroft."

"My wife and I had dinner at The Cuts while my mother, Frances Bancroft, stayed here with Jolene. After dinner we had ice cream—gelato rather—and stopped by Scottsdale Lapidary where we bought a diamond bracelet. Holly and I got home around ten p.m. Mother left and Holly and I checked on Jolene before retiring. Sometime after that, maybe twenty minutes later, I thought I heard someone in the yard. I went first, of course, to the nursery to make sure the baby was safe, and then came downstairs to check things out."

"With the baby and a gun." Holly was still shocked about that, but if he'd really scared an intruder off like he claimed, she knew she should be grateful.

"Remind me about the gun."

"I grabbed my Glock from a gun safe in my dresser drawer before I went to Jolene's room. Naturally, I wanted to be prepared in case an intruder was trying to take my daughter."

Denton squinted at his little book, and then grimaced. "No ransom note this time, eh?"

"Is that a joke, detective? Because this is a very serious matter. My wife's been wounded."

"I'm just pointing out the irony." Denton looked up. "So you were carrying Jolene and you had your Glock in your hand when you came downstairs."

"Correct."

The tension was building in Holly's chest, making her breath quicken.

Denton directed his gaze to her. "Are you sure you're okay? Do we need to get you to a hospital?"

"I'm fine." Her head felt light, and her fingertips tingled. She wanted to shake Detective Denton and scream *help me!* But she was concealing the truth from him for good reason.

Jolene felt substantial and heavy in her arms, and she kissed the top of her head.

This was a perfect opportunity to prove to Zach that she would stick with the plan.

Denton couldn't help her. Dr. Washington couldn't help her. Les Larson couldn't help her.

But she could help herself.

She wasn't blind to the fact Zach was a liar, or that he didn't want to let her leave. It was possible he was trying to teach her some kind of a lesson, or possibly make himself look like a hero in front of her. But as long as he needed her to alibi him, he'd eventually have to let her go.

And if he'd meant to kill her tonight, he wouldn't have missed.

Not at such close range.

"I mean, yes. Yes, I'm okay. But I'm upset and unnerved; I'm sure you can understand that," she said.

Denton nodded. "If you're sure, then let's continue."

"I'm sure."

He turned to Zach. "You say your Glock's registered?"

"Of course, but I'm sure you'll check it."

"I will. It was foolish for you to bring your baby downstairs, much less with a pistol in hand. Why didn't you give Jolene to your wife and have them wait upstairs?"

"Heat of the moment. I didn't think it through, and quite frankly, I didn't expect to find anything. I thought there might be an animal in the yard or at the door. I was quite surprised when I saw a person, a man in a hoodie, and the kitchen door wide open."

"But you grabbed your pistol before heading downstairs."

"As a precaution."

"And you shot your wife."

"I shot at an intruder. Holly reached her arm out, I believe to get Jolene, just as I was aiming at him."

"Where was he, exactly?"

"The door was open, and I saw him lurking off to the side on the back porch. Like he'd been about to enter when I came into the kitchen." Zach paused, and reached for Holly's hand. "I'm so, so sorry."

She laced her fingers through his. "I'm all right, darling. I promise."

Sniffling, he rubbed his hand across the back of his eyes.

Those were real tears, she thought.

"I feel positively horrible the bullet nicked Holly. I wish I had been the one shot and not her, but if it drove away an intruder and possibly saved her life and Jolene's... then I guess it was worth the price."

TWENTY-SIX

"Words fail me, and that's a first." Tamara scraped the chair at her kitchen table back a foot or so and peered at Holly over the rim of her Wedgwood teacup. Took a sip and set it down, stirred it with her spoon, even though she didn't take sugar in her tea. "Are you absolutely sure you're okay?"

"Physically, yes." Holly touched the gauze wrapped around her forearm. "It looks more like a cat scratch under here than a bullet wound. It whizzed by me, barely grazed the skin. I'll probably lose the bandage later today because it's not even bleeding anymore."

"Where did you get your titanium nerves? I'm sure you're right—that it was an accident, but, man oh man, if Tom had ever pointed a gun at me, I'd have been gone in a flash. You know, this might be a good time for you to take me up on my offer for you and Jolene to stay here."

There was nothing Holly would like more, but she didn't have that luxury. She had to wait it out, keep her end of the deal, if she hoped to walk away with her daughter. And staying with Zach, pretending to be happy until the police cleared him of Beth's murder, was part of that deal. But it was good to know

Tamara was on her side, because she could really use her help for her backup plan. "To be fair, Zach wasn't pointing the gun at me. He was aiming at the intruder."

"I know. It's just scary is all I'm saying. Have you heard any more from the police? Did they find the hoodie guy, yet?"

"Not yet, but Detective Denton told us, as he was leaving, that there was a burglary down the street last week, and apparently they have footage of someone jogging nearby in a hoodie, so maybe they'll catch him."

"Fingers crossed, and I'm glad you stopped by. I was worried I'd offended you last time you were here."

"Not at all." Holly shook her head. "Thanks for suggesting a therapist. Zach and I went, but not much came of it. I told him about everything that's been going on, even talked about the fire, and Dr. Washington, that's his name, reassured me I was handling things well enough, considering."

"Have you ever wondered what your life would've been if you'd never met him?"

A shiver worked its way up Holly's back leaving a feeling of cold dread in its wake. "Who?" The question had seemingly come from nowhere, but she was only pretending not to know whom Tamara meant.

"Zach, of course."

"Well, I wouldn't have Jolene, so no matter how bad things are between Zach and me, I can't let my mind go there. But I do wonder what my life would be like if it hadn't been for that fire."

"That fire was caused by bad wiring. You were an innocent kid, but you're still blaming yourself for everything. You should never have told him. It's your guilt that's given Zach this hold over you."

Holly hunched her shoulders and leaned forward. "No, it's the fact that people *died* that gives Zach his hold over me. And he may have the power, *now*, but I'm not going to cower under him, or shrink into a corner and just let him order me around. I've got Jolene to think of, and I'm going to get us out one way or another." She put her hand on the tabletop. "I don't want to get you involved in my troubles, but—"

Tamara curled her fingers around Holly's and squeezed, just for an instant, before pulling her hand away. "Whatever you need, I'm here. You're not in this alone. I promise you."

Holly pulled in a breath. She hated to involve Tamara in something illegal, but she needed her. "If you really mean that..."

"I do."

"Then how would you feel about helping me break the law? I mean *you* wouldn't actually be doing anything illegal... at least I don't think so."

"Holly, what are we talking about here? I'm not hiring a hit man for you, if that's what you mean."

"I should hope not. I want to get away from Zach—not kill him. Though, if I'm being one hundred percent honest, I have fantasized about him dying in a car crash."

Tamara tipped back in her chair, nearly falling over at Holly's words.

Holly slapped a hand across her mouth. "I'm so, so sorry. I don't know why I said something so stupid." Even though it was the horrible truth, it was incredibly insensitive given what had happened to Tom.

Tamara blinked hard and wiped her eyes with a paper napkin, then looked up at Holly. "If we're telling the truth? I've fantasized about the same thing."

"I-I don't understand."

Tamara lifted one shoulder, holding Holly's gaze. "I'm saying that more than once I've wished it were somebody else's husband who'd died in a car crash. Specifically, I wished it were Zach. Sometimes, I lie awake in bed, all night, asking myself why did it have to be *my* husband. Why my Tom?"

Holly reached across the table again.

This time, they sat there in silence, holding hands like a couple of third grade girls who've just agreed to be best friends. Then they both sighed simultaneously.

And after that, they also laughed, at exactly the same time, just like those third grade girls would've done.

"I guess we're both reprehensible," Holly said through her giggles. "Birds of a feather."

"Should stick together. So, no hit man—that's good, because even though I love you, Holly, I'd have to bow out of that one. But tell me what you have in mind? Exactly how illegal are we talking?"

"Class one misdemeanor."

Tamara rubbed her hands together. "Oh, goodie. Are we going to throw away your photo-radar ticket? C'mon girl, that's not even illegal."

"May I borrow your laptop?" Holly didn't dare search the topic on her own computer.

They scooted closer together and moved the screen between them on the kitchen table. Holly opened the internet browser and typed in, "How to get a fake ID".

A list of sites popped up, instantly.

"Oh, wait a minute. I know something about this. I saw a feature on the news about a flood of fake IDs in Arizona—and how *easy* it is to get one." Tamara took over, scrolling to a specific page. "These here—these are the good ones." Suddenly Tamara's shoulders stiffened. "Honey, what exactly are you going to do with a fake ID? You don't need to sneak into a bar, and if you're planning on kidnapping Jolene, that's hardly a class one misdemeanor."

"I'm not planning on fleeing with Jolene—this is just a backup."

"*How* is it a backup?"

"In case I have no other choice."

"You'd take Jolene?"

"It would only be temporary. I don't want to go to prison, and I don't want a life on the run with my child. I wouldn't be able to use my degree to get a job. We'd always be watching our backs, and I'd have to create a fake identity for Jolene too."

"You'd have to cut ties with your family and—" Tamara's eyes were moist again "—your friends."

As difficult as her relationship with her parents was, Holly loved them, and the idea of never seeing them again hurt more than she'd care to admit. And it would painful for them, too. No parent would be unaffected by a child and a grandchild disappearing into thin air. And what about Frances? Holly wanted her to be part of Jolene's life. Her hands were tingling and she shook them out. "This isn't even my plan B. It's my plan Z. But when I think about the other night, when Zach ran downstairs with a pistol in one hand and Jolene in the other... when I think about the way he treats his own mother, and how I never know if I'm going to wake up and find Jolene gone and a cryptic note in her stead... I realize I absolutely need the means to get away from him, in a dire emergency, until I can figure a way to come back home safely."

"Holly." Tamara looked at her earnestly. "Are you telling me you think Zach might hurt you?"

"I can't say for certain that his anger won't escalate. And he's taken Jolene away from me before."

"The last time he brought her home before dinner, just like he promised, though. Isn't that right?"

"Yes, but what if next time he doesn't? I can't say what—it's better for you if you aren't involved, but I am working on another plan. The IDs are just for my peace of mind. If you don't want to help me, I understand. I can do it myself." She was reading the instructions on the website. "I need a good, realistic driver's license photo, but anyone can take my picture."

Tamara put her hands on her cheeks. "No. Tom bought a

top-of-the line digital camera for our trip to Hawaii a few years ago. You go make yourself look like you've been waiting at the DMV for an hour. Mess up your hair a little. Wipe off your lipstick, and I'll look for the camera. If you're going to do this, I don't want you to have a subpar photo. It says right here, that's one of the easiest way to spot a fake. You can use my credit card to pay, and we'll have them send the ID here, to my address."

"You mean it? You'll be my partner in crime?"

Tamara waved her hand in the air. "I will. But I'm going on record as warning you that this is a bad idea. And not only because it's against the law. You better keep this thing well hidden, honey, because if Zach catches you with a fake ID there's going to be hell to pay."

Holly was already mussing her hair and wiping off her lipstick. "No worries. Zach thinks I'm too stupid to trick him. He'll never suspect a thing."

TWENTY-SEVEN

Claudia hung back, peering around a pillar, hidden, observing. Thousand-pound water-filled glass orbs dangled from the ceiling of the aquarium's sea-blue lobby, and as Holly pushed a sleek, expensive-looking stroller beneath them, Claudia imagined one of the "raindrops" smashing down on Holly's head.

Freak accidents happen—it wasn't as if she *wished* an orb would fall and kill the woman.

She'd been tailing Holly all morning, always careful to stay just far enough back to escape notice. When Zach had let it slip that Holly was bringing the baby to the aquarium today, Claudia had scoffed—Jolene was only six months old so what was the point? But now, after a morning of observation, she understood. Touring the aquarium was way better than being cooped up at home with a bawling baby. And Jolene had been a good girl—alternating between dozing quietly and squealing at some of the livelier exhibits. Claudia had been surprised at how interested a six-month-old could be in what was going on around her. The baby had laughed in delight at Penguin Point and Claudia had been tempted to dash over to join the fun.

Pick her up. Poke a finger in her cute little dimples.

There was something irresistible about a baby's laughter.

And that was reassuring. Sometimes Claudia worried that she might not enjoy mothering another woman's child. She pinched her arm to punish herself for the thought. She had to keep reminding herself that once she and Zach were married, Jolene would no longer belong to another woman—she'd be *hers*. A child she could mold in her own image and, besides, Zach could easily afford both a nanny and a full-time house-keeper. Why Holly employed neither was beyond her. Claudia was in medical school, but even if she weren't, hiring help would be her first order of business upon moving into the Bancroft mansion.

Now, Holly approached a bench in front of a large fish tank.

Claudia sighed.

The bright, showcase lights bouncing off Holly's perky ponytail made her highlighted brown hair look all shiny and pretty. And how irritating that she'd lost the baby weight so soon. That short-sleeved fuchsia T-shirt showed off tanned arms, and Holly's butt looked amazing in a pair of jeggings. She was disconcertingly pretty in that *girl-next-door, oh gee I've got such a friendly smile*, kind of way.

During Holly's pregnancy, Claudia had felt okay about how her own looks compared, since she was younger by at least five years and her body was smokin' according to literally everyone. But now that Holly was trim again—only with bigger boobs, it was easy to imagine Zach succumbing to her charms. And, occa-sionally, it popped into her head he might find his wife *more* desirable than he found her.

He swore he wasn't having sex with Holly, though, and Claudia trusted him... but not completely. That was one reason for her little reconnaissance mission today. At the very least it would give her a chance to assess the state of Zach and Holly's marriage for herself, and at best, she could turn up the heat and bring this thing to a boil, maybe accelerate the timeline of getting Holly out of the way for good.

Hang on. Holly was bringing out the nursing blanket. That meant she'd be sitting on that bench a while, and when Claudia came over, it would be hard to jump up and leave. Holly would have to disconnect Jolene, strap her into the stroller, pack away the blanket and so forth.

So this was it: the perfect time to accidentally bump into each other.

"Oh, hey!" Claudia marched past Holly, and then stopped and turned, as if just realizing who she was. "Mrs. Bancroft?"

Holly jerked her chin up, and the blanket slipped, revealing a happily latched Jolene, slurping away with a rivulet of milk dripping down one pink cheek. Holly quickly moved the blanket to cover everything up again. "Oh, uhm, hello."

There was enough hesitancy in her voice to make Claudia think she might not recognize her. "It's me, Claudia."

Holly flashed that ridiculously friendly smile of hers. "I know. Thank you again, so much, for the lovely flowers you brought when the baby was born. Are you here with someone?"

Claudia noticed another woman eyeing the bench and quickly sat down, placing her purse beside her to ensure there was no space for anyone else. "I'm solo. I've been dying to see the aquarium but I didn't know who would want to come with me," she said, hoping the plaintive note she added to her voice would make it more difficult to dismiss poor, friendless her.

"Ha. Well, me too, I guess. So I decided to bring Jolene. She can't exactly decline the invitation. But I think she had fun." She peeked beneath the blanket and made clucking noises. "Didn't you, sweetie?"

Ugh. She'd used a high, pouty voice. Claudia would have to be sure not to talk baby talk to Jolene in front of Zach.

It screamed *Mommy* not *mistress.*

"Are you coming or going? We're just about done," Holly said.

A hint for her to hit the road? But she knew Jolene would be eating for a while. "I'm leaving, too. But I don't mind keeping you company while you... erm... how long are you going to breastfeed Jolene—not here—I mean how many months?" Maybe Zach was waiting for that to wrap up before getting the hell out of his miserable marriage. *Please don't say a year.*

"My pediatrician recommends one year if feasible," Holly said, looking only a little taken aback.

Crap. Claudia had no intention of waiting another six months.

"Are you interested in pediatrics, then?" Holly asked, misinterpreting Claudia's interest in her baby's feeding patterns.

"Who, me? No. I'm thinking dermatology—if I can make the grade."

"Mm. I've heard it's tough to get those residencies, but I'll bet you're a great student. You didn't want a dermatology preceptor, though?"

Was Holly onto Claudia and Zach? Surely not. It was a perfectly logical question—too bad there was no logical answer for why she'd chosen a mentor from a different specialty. "Not really. I'm sure dermatology's the road I want to take, but I'm trying to figure out my second choice in case I don't get a spot. I've got another year to decide on a plan B, and like you said, derm is very competitive. Obstetrics will probably be my backup."

"Those are certainly very different paths."

Time to get off the subject. Claudia had no interest in obstetrics. It was too messy. And all those deliveries in the wee hours? Not for her. She was, however, interested in Zach—and that was the one and only reason she'd requested to work *under him*—ha ha. "Zach—I mean Dr. Bancroft—is a fantastic mentor. I'm so lucky to have him for a preceptor."

"How long have you two been working together?" Holly asked.

"Not long." They'd been at it for months. Since well before Jolene was born, but Claudia wasn't here to give information, she was here to obtain it. "Would you like me to babysit sometime? So you and Dr. Bancroft can have a date night?"

"Oh, that's so sweet of you. But we have his mother on speed dial."

"That's good. Then you can go out whenever you please."

Holly didn't seem to be paying attention. She was bringing Jolene up to her shoulder. Patting her on the back.

"Do you go out a lot?" Claudia asked. "On dates?"

A little line formed between Holly's brows.

"I think it's important after a baby's born to make sure your husband gets enough attention. Don't you?" Zach was always complaining, but the last thing she wanted was for Holly to suddenly step it up as a wife. Claudia might have regretted giving Holly that tip—if she wasn't enjoying the look on her face so much.

That's right, bitch, I'm calling you out.

If Holly had been half the wife she should've been, Zach wouldn't have needed to look for someone else.

"Sure. It's important not to neglect each other." Holly's lips were moving but Claudia could tell her heart wasn't in her words.

"I babysat for another couple over the summer last year," Claudia lied. "She spent all her time thinking about the baby, talking about the baby."

Holly's mouth twisted. "If you were taking care of the infant she must have spent *some* time on other things. And babies are much more vulnerable than husbands. Husbands are grown. They should understand."

"Maybe. But this one didn't. The couple wound up getting a divorce. Isn't that sad?"

"I don't know. I don't think I want to judge another person's marriage. Especially someone I don't know. Maybe the divorce was for the best."

Oh! Good answer.

Happiness welled up, turning the room brighter, the exhibits more interesting. They sat in silence, and while Holly got Jolene latched onto the other side, Claudia studied the descriptions of the fish in the tank beside them.

Then Holly's phone chimed with a text message. "It's from Zach. He says he's got big news."

It stung to know he was texting his wife, but it was probably about something mundane. If it were actually *big news*, Claudia would be the one he would call. "Hey, look at this guy." She pointed at a crusty, orangey-brown lump with barely discernable eyes at the bottom of the fish tank.

Holly's gaze followed Claudia's pointed finger. "Where? I don't see anything."

"That's because it's camouflaged as a rock."

Holly squinted, and then smiled. "There? That's a fish?"

"Uh-huh. I just read about it on the card. That's *synanceia verrucosa* also known as a reef stonefish. It lurks quietly, ready to ambush its prey, inject them with poison at the first opportunity. Its poor victims never see it coming." Claudia beamed. "That right there is the deadliest fish in the sea. How cool is that?"

TWENTY-EIGHT

As soon as Holly had gotten away from that cloying Claudia woman, she'd called Zach and learned that his news was indeed *big*. Lying to the police hadn't come easily for Holly, but in the end, providing Zach with an alibi had been worth it.

People get away with murder all the time, and Holly was glad, in this case, justice had been served. Maybe not the kind of justice that happened in a court of law, but poetic justice.

Beth Gunther's killer had been found.

Based on an anonymous tip that a man had recently bragged about murdering a young woman with a hunting knife around a year ago, the police arrested a vagrant. He was found to be in possession of a ring that had belonged to Beth and a suspicious knife. A clever detective disassembled the knife's wooden handle to check for traces of old blood that might have seeped inside. After the test results had come back showing that blood from inside the knife handle matched Beth's DNA, the suspect had hung himself in his jail cell—case closed.

A horrible end to a horrible ordeal for that poor woman's family.

But it was over.

Detective Denton had dropped by the hospital to let Zach know he was in the clear.

And that meant it was time for a new beginning.

Knowing for certain that Zach wasn't guilty was a load off her conscience, and he'd sounded almost giddy with relief when she'd agreed to drop Jolene at his mother's and meet him at Pinnacle Peak.

By now, it was close to sunset, and the other hikers were thinning out, so she and Zach had all the wide-open space and privacy they needed to conclude their deal. As the blood-red sun slipped toward the horizon, the aroma of cedar and palo verde filled the air. Holly and Zach stopped near a towering saguaro to admire the view, and Zach suddenly scrambled onto a giant boulder.

"Zach!" What the hell? If there were a ranger around he'd surely be ticketed for a move like that. But he was grinning and motioning to her. "C'mon. You don't want to miss this view."

Had he'd forgotten why they were here? It was time to call in her marker. They were here to discuss the divorce. At least *she* was. "Can you come down please? We need to talk."

"Up here."

She folded her arms across her chest.

"I'm not moving from this spot until the sun has set," he told her.

For heaven's sake. Even though there was a good supply of Holly's milk in Frances' freezer, she'd greatly prefer to get back to Jolene sooner rather than later. And technically the park closed in an hour. "If the rangers lock the gate we won't be able to get the car out."

"You worry too much. I doubt they'll lock us in."

"Do you want to pay a fine for trespassing? You don't think the ranger will come drag us off the trail?"

"At least we'll have seen the sunset. Get your ass up here."

She counted to ten. *Don't let him bait you into an argument.*

When he got like this the only way around him was to let him think he'd won. Climbing up that boulder might be illegal, but it was a lot less illegal than giving your husband a false alibi. "Fine."

She wiped the sweat off her palms and dusted them with dirt for a better grip, then choosing her hand and footholds carefully, hoisted herself up the boulder. The top was flat and made for good sitting, and he'd been right about the view. "It's beautiful."

"Told you so." He reached for her hand.

Her stomach knotted, but she'd been playing this game for a while. She could stand it a bit longer. She relaxed her arm, allowing him one moment of hand-holding before pulling herself free.

"Remember the good old days? Before Jolene was born? We used to hike here every weekend if the weather was right. So many times, we've seen this sun go down over these hills."

"Mm hm. I'll always treasure those memories," she lied. "Just because we're divorcing, doesn't mean we didn't have something good. I'll never regret what we had together." That part was true—without Zach there would be no Jolene.

He coughed, and then turned to meet her eyes. "We're not getting divorced, sweetheart."

She held his gaze, not letting him steal the upper hand. "We agreed I'd give you an alibi, and once the dust settled, and the police moved on, you'd grant me a divorce without contesting it."

"But I don't need an alibi. They caught the guy. So the deal's null and void."

She gritted her teeth. He was trying to back out, but she wasn't going to let him. "Zach, listen to me. We had an agreement, and I expect you to keep it."

"I agreed to a divorce because you had leverage. Now that leverage is gone. So, like I said, I don't need the alibi. Go ahead and tell the cops you lied about being with me that night. That'll make you look even worse to a judge than all the other stuff you've pulled."

The clouds in the sky soaked up the blood-red color from the sinking sun. The wind whipped up, stinging her cheeks, and blowing dust in her eyes, but she didn't dare blink. She would get him to see reason.

She had to.

"Why do you want to hold me if I don't want to stay?" she asked.

"I know you love me. You always have."

"I did, once, it's true. But not anymore."

"I won't let you go. This... *this* is why I never should've let you have a kid."

She kicked her foot against the boulder. He was the one who'd pushed her for a baby, but reminding him of that would be a mistake. "Explain what you mean. I want to understand your point of view, I really do. For Jolene's sake, I want our divorce to be as amicable as possible."

He scoffed. "Jolene?"

"What?"

"Everything is always about *Jolene*. I did want a family, I admit. What man doesn't? It's necessary for appearances if nothing else. But I should've known you were one of those women who, once they get what they need from a man, will try to leave. You've got Jolene and now you don't need me anymore. I sensed it the day she was born—that very morning, while I was driving you to the hospital, I just had the feeling that our relationship was going to go to hell."

Her head was spinning. Her heart was clenching in her chest. "I wasn't using you to get a baby. I have no idea why you'd think that. But you're correct that our relationship isn't what it once was."

"Whose fault is that?" He bared his teeth.

"I don't think assigning blame is productive. I want a divorce, and I'm going to get one."

"Then you shall have one. But you will not take Jolene. In fact, I'll make sure you don't even get visitation."

The sun dropped below the horizon. It would be dark soon. No one had passed them on the trail in a while, and he was sitting dangerously close to the edge of the boulder. "Let's go back. We'll finish talking at home," she said.

"We'll finish talking now." He slipped forward a few inches.

From instinct, she reached for him, tugging him back.

"See. You still love me." He grabbed her wrist, yanking her toward him.

"Zach!"

"Give up this foolish idea. I don't have to concede anything to you anymore. I'm holding all the cards. But if you promise to stay and, really, honestly, try to make things work, I'll change. Just tell me what you need, and I'll deliver."

"Step one: let go of me and get away from the edge of this boulder."

He threw back his head and laughed. Then he yelled, "You hear that, world, my wife doesn't want me to die. She's afraid I'll jump."

He gripped her wrist so hard she thought it might break.

"Let me go now!"

"And she's afraid I'll take her with me when I do."

She jerked her body, and her hand came loose from his grasp.

Zach looked at her, grinning, and then scooted away from the edge. "There you go. Step one."

"Thank you."

"What else do you need?"

A divorce and full custody. But she didn't know how the hell she'd get that unless she had leverage. She needed *something* to fight back with. "I want to know where you really were the night of July twenty-seventh. You weren't with me, and when the police asked your whereabouts you looked scared as hell. I know for sure, now, you weren't busy killing poor Beth, so where were you and why didn't you just tell the police?"

"And if I answer you this riddle, will you stay?"

What choice did she have? At least for the time being. "I want my credit cards back and access to the bank account."

"Done."

"I'm going to wear whatever I want, go wherever I want, without checking in and out. *And* I want separate bedrooms."

"The separate bedrooms won't last, but I won't touch you again until you ask me, no, until you *beg* me. If I agree to your terms, do you promise to not only stay, but to try to make our marriage work for real?"

"I promise to try." *I'll say whatever it takes to get you out of my life for good.* "Now, then, where were you the night that Beth Gunther was murdered?"

TWENTY-NINE

Zach had climbed off the boulder before her, and now his hands steadied her waist as she made her way down. Holly focused on her footholds and how the rock's hot, wind-hewn surface rubbed against her belly where her shirt had ridden up; the small shock to her knees when her feet hit the ground.

The gritty taste of dust in her mouth.

The sudden breeze that cooled her arms.

Anything and everything *except* her husband's touch.

You can do this.

For Jolene.

Fake it till you make it. He hadn't yet told her what he'd been up to the night Beth Gunther was killed, and she had to gather enough dirt on him to give her a fighting chance against him. Whatever intelligence she got from him today, she'd take to her attorney, Les Larson—maybe it would be enough and she wouldn't have to keep up the charade of "working things out".

And if it wasn't enough? She'd stick it out until she had all she needed to bring him to his knees.

Failure was not an option.

Quitting was not an option.

Feet firmly on the ground, she leaned into the boulder and took a deep breath, then spun around to face Zach. "So, where were you?"

"We should hurry." Suddenly, he seemed to recognize the danger of getting trapped behind the park gate—not an insurmountable obstacle but a damned inconvenient one. He stuck out his hand, and she took it to walk side by side with him.

Thankfully, the trail quickly narrowed, which put an end to the hand-holding because they needed to march single file. The trek was mostly downhill, and she was tempted to run it, but she didn't want to lose the moment. "Darling—" the word tasted bitter on her tongue "—I made you a promise that I intend to keep. But you promised me something, too."

His foot slipped and he stumbled, but caught himself. "We can go to the bank together, tomorrow, and I'll call the credit card companies as soon as we get home."

"Thank you." She waited, but he volunteered nothing more.

He started putting distance between them.

She hustled and easily caught up. "Where were you, Zach? Part of the deal, remember? You do still want to try to make our marriage work, for *real* this time? Not just pretending for the cops."

He halted, looked ahead and behind.

"There's no one here. Whatever it is, you can tell me." What was he so skittish about? An affair seemed the obvious answer. She'd always believed he wouldn't cheat on her, that he was too possessive, but recently she'd come to see that possessiveness isn't about love. A man like Zach would feel entitled to satisfy his urges wherever he pleased, and then come home to his perfect family. He probably told himself he loved his family, and he might even believe it—but it wasn't true.

Possessiveness is not love.

"We're almost to the car," he said.

She checked her watch. They'd been making good time.

They still had twenty plus minutes before close, and the parking lot was just around the bend. "Tell me, Zach."

He stepped off to the side of the trail, dug his toe into the dirt. "I was with Tom."

She held her breath, letting the words sink in. Her legs, tired from the hike and the rock climbing, began to tremble. She put her arms out to steady herself and regained her balance.

"Tom Driscoll," he whispered.

"You were with Tom before his accident? Why didn't you just say so when the police asked?" It was too hard to breathe. She needed to stop and rest a minute. "Oh no, Zach. Did you know Tom was drunk when he got behind the wheel?"

He grimaced, tugging at his hair. "Just listen, baby. It wasn't my fault."

Poor Tamara.

Holly was too stunned to process all the implications, but it sounded like Zach might have had a chance to prevent Tom's death. "Of course not. You're not responsible for Tom driving drunk." Was he? "Tell me everything. It must've been a terrible burden to keep this to yourself all this time."

"It was. Believe me, I wanted to tell you, so many times." His eyes turned a watery blue. "But, I couldn't bring myself to admit it. I was afraid you'd think less of me—I love being your hero. And then, when you offered me that alibi, I almost started to believe what you told Denton was true—that you and I were together the whole night."

A wave of compassion—for Tamara not Zach—washed over her. She could use that, she thought, and channeled the emotion, as best she could, directing it into her voice. "I'm sorry, darling. But I'm glad I can be here for you, now. I want to know everything. I want to be strong for you like you are for me."

Nodding, he swiped at his eyes. "I'd had a rough day. A difficult delivery—shoulder dystocia."

"A stuck shoulder?"

"That's right. I had to break the baby's clavicle in order to deliver him safely. And as you might well imagine, the parents didn't understand. Not at first. The father was yelling, threatening to sue. But after I explained everything to him, he understood. In the end, he thanked me for saving his baby. But it was a lot."

"I'm so sorry." She reached out, rubbed his arms with her hands.

"Anyway, I called Tom and I asked him to meet me for drinks." He glanced up sheepishly. "He suggested a gentleman's club."

"A what?"

"A strip club—that's what they call them. I never go to places like that. I don't know why I went along with the idea, except I needed to let off steam, you know? He said he'd pick me up because he wanted to take me for a spin in his new Porsche."

She gripped his arm, unable to stop herself. Never mind about the strip club... "You didn't take your own car?"

His Adam's apple worked. "No. I left it at Mercy General. Tom drove like a maniac all the way to the club. Scared me, if I'm being honest. He was into it, though—the speed. Showing off. At the club, he got wasted pretty fast. I think he was halfway there before he even picked me up. I had a few too many, myself. I'm not proud of anything that happened that night, but since we're telling all, I'll own this part, too. Tom and I both got lap dances. I'm sorry, so sorry, Holly. I-I just wanted to forget the day. I'd give anything to undo it now."

"I don't care about the lap dance, darling, go on."

Zach had a faraway, glassy look in his eyes. "Tom seemed unhappy. He mentioned something about him and Tamara having a dry spell—and I don't think he was talking about booze. Next thing you know, he's crying. Imagine that. A grown man.

That's when I knew we'd had enough. I wanted to call a cab for both of us, but he wouldn't hear of it."

"Didn't that seem strange? He's always been conscientious about having a designated driver."

"I know. But he said he'd be damned if he'd leave his new ride parked at Baby Doll's. Bad part of town and all. Neither one of us was fit to drive, but we let the booze take control. He slid behind the wheel, and I didn't stop him." Zach shuddered. "I got in, too."

Her fingertips were tingling, her thoughts swirling and diving.

"We tore out of the parking lot. He didn't even have his seat belt on. The curves just kept coming at us. We had a couple of near misses with oncoming traffic, and I reached across. Tried to snap on his seat belt, but he swerved off the road, just about drove us into a ditch, before getting back onto the pavement. I kept yelling at him to stop, to let me out of the car, but he wouldn't listen. It was like he had a death wish or something. I tried to stop him. I swear I did. And then..."

His voice was husky, his face bloodless. "There was nothing I could've done."

Breathe, Holly. "You were in the car when it crashed into the pole?"

"I don't know how I got out unscathed, but I did."

Choking on her disgust, she asked, "What happened next?"

"Nothing. Tom was dead. It was obvious there was nothing I could do for him."

"You left the scene? You didn't even call nine-one-one?" She was going to be sick, and there was nothing she could do about it.

Zach held her hair while she heaved up her lunch. Then he pulled out a handkerchief and wiped her face. "It was too late for Tom. And I was drunk, on the way back from an evening at a strip club. If word got out, someone might start to question if I had a drinking problem. Maybe even file a complaint with the medical board. I couldn't risk it. Not with you at home, pregnant."

"He was your best friend." Her cheeks were wet, her chest aching, and her mouth filled with the sour aftermath of vomitus.

"What I did, I did for our family. The truth is Tom almost killed the both of us, and I don't see how *I'm* the bad guy in this scenario. He was our friend, but you need to dry your eyes, and do what I've done. Learn to live with it. And Holly, my love, I do want this to work between us, I truly do, but if you breathe *one word* of this to Tamara, our deal's off. I'll cut off all your money and send Jolene away with a nanny for weeks on end. I'll make sure you barely see her, and I will make your life a living hell. Is that understood?"

"Understood," she said, squaring her shoulders, eyeing a sharp rock near her foot and stoically fending off the urge to scoop it up and smash his face with it.

He reached for her hand, and she took off running down the trail.

THIRTY

Holly had invited Tamara for a visit. It was definitely her turn to play hostess, not to mention logistically simpler, because Jolene could nap upstairs while Holly kept tabs on her via the baby monitor. Now that Holly had her credit cards back, she'd gone all out, shopping at JR's Fine Foods for real. She'd served her friend shrimp cocktail, followed by thinly sliced prime rib sandwiches and gourmet cookies. It was the least she could do after all Tamara had done for her—including obtaining a fake ID for Holly, which Holly had just now slipped into the baby wipes container along with her secret stash of cash.

Now, she joined Tamara in the "bonus room", a space where, when Tom was alive, they'd sipped cocktails and played pool on their many couples' nights. She found Tamara standing still, staring, as if transfixed by the photographs that adorned the "wall of fun". In their glory days, Tom and Tamara and Zach and Holly had engaged in all sorts of activities: summer hikes, couples ski trips and disco-dancing to name but a few.

A wistful smile played at the corners of Tamara's mouth as she reached out and straightened a picture that Holly had snapped on one of their adventures: a candid shot of Tamara and Tom strolling ahead, Tom's arm draped across Tamara's shoulder, her elbow bent, reaching up; her hand captured in his, their fingers entwined. A flash of moonlight glinted off Tom's gold wedding band.

The poignancy of the simple shot caused Holly's heart to squeeze.

How long could she keep Zach's secret from Tamara?

Why was she lying to the only person who was truly in her corner—the only person who understood what she was going through?

Despite having known each other longer, Holly and Tamara had never been as close as Tom and Zach, but, in these past months, Holly had grown to love Tamara and appreciate her friendship more than ever.

If you breathe one word of this to Tamara, our deal's off. I'll cut off all your money and send Jolene away with a nanny for weeks on end. I'll make sure you barely see her, and I will make your life a living hell.

Tamara had lost the love of her life, and Holly had information about his death that she didn't. No matter how miserable Zach could make her life, she owed it to Tamara. She didn't want to use her fake IDs, she didn't want to lie to the police, she didn't want to run away in the dead of night with her innocent child, but she was prepared to do *all* of those things if necessary

So why wasn't she prepared to tell Tamara the truth?

Tears brimmed in her eyes, but she blinked them away. "Tamara," she whispered. "There's something I need to tell you."

At first, Holly thought Tamara hadn't heard or understood what she'd said. She sat so still, on that leather love seat, not even blinking. But slowly, as Holly spoke, the color in Tamara's cheeks faded, her chin quivered, and her shoulders pushed back so hard it was as if she were coming to attention for an entering dignitary.

"Tam…" Holly stretched out her hand. "I hope you can forgive me for not telling you right away, but I only found out a few days ago. You do see what a difficult position I'm in. If Zach finds out I said anything…" She didn't finish the sentence because she couldn't bear to. If he knew, he'd make her pay, and he'd start by sending Jolene away.

The silence was heavy, like an anvil dragging them both to the bottom of a deep dark sea.

Holly sat down next to Tamara, her fingers creeping closer, and just when their hands brushed, Tamara jerked her arm away so fast and hard she knocked over her glass of wine that had been resting on an end table.

Holly jumped up to sop the mess with napkins, while Tamara remained sitting at attention, cabernet dripping down the bodice of her bright-yellow frock like blood from a gunshot wound.

Holly ran to the bar, wet a rag, and brought it to Tamara. "You're angry," she said, her voice threadbare.

Tamara tipped her head back and laughed. "Angry? Whatever for? Oh, you mean I'm mad because Zach was with Tom the night of the accident and fled the scene? Do you think it upsets me to think about it? Or perhaps I'm a wee bit peeved that you've been sitting on this information while I—a woman who has lost the love of her freakin' life—have been worrying about *you*? Trying to comfort *you* and help you negotiate your troubled marriage?"

She rose to her feet and paced the room, finally landing inches in front of Holly—then her hand darted out.

A soft cry escaped Holly's lips, but the slap stung her heart far more than her cheek.

Holly touched her burning face with her fingertips, never dropping her gaze from Tamara's glare. "I deserve that."

"You *bitch*! Who cares if you deserve it or not? Why must *everything* always be about you? What about me? What about my pain? It's been more than a year since I've lost Tom, and I can count on one hand the number of times you've asked me how I'm doing." She yanked her hair, mascara dripped off the tip of her perfect nose, her face was contorted in anguish. Then came a series of sobs and distorted, muttered words. Still, Holly could make out the oft-repeated phrase: *you selfish bitch.*

Tamara turned her back, and then bent at the waist, wailing, until after what seemed like an eternity, her cries grew softer, and finally sputtered to a stop like a car running out of gas. Then she lowered herself to the floor and propped her back against the bottom of the love seat, her legs stretched out in front of her. Carefully, she crossed her feet at the ankles, and in the process seemed to come back to herself. She looked up, wiped her hand beneath her dripping nose, and then held up her wet hand. "Okay, I'm finished."

"With me?" Holly asked, bereft. She and Tamara had known each other in high school. Their husbands had been best friends. They'd vacationed as couples. They'd served on charitable committees together. They'd shared innumerable lunches and shopping trips. They'd been through the death of Tamara's husband and the birth of Holly's daughter, and yet, in all that time, Holly had never really gotten to know Tamara. She knew her middle name—Anne, and she knew her favorite Mexican food place—Macayo's—but she didn't know the important stuff.

Like how she felt when Tom died.

Like whether she had someone she could call when she got lonely at night, or if she drank herself to sleep instead.

After all this time, Holly should know these things.

She eyed a box of tissues on the coffee table.

Tamara motioned that it was okay to come closer.

Holly lowered herself to the floor beside Tamara, and held

out the box, her arm cautiously extended like she was approaching a wild animal.

"Thank you." Tamara blew her nose loudly and unapologetically. "I need time to process this. I can't believe you've kept it from me, but I'm sorry for slapping you... and for calling you a bitch."

"That's okay," Holly said. "I am a bitch."

Tamara shook her head. "Not really. A bitch delights in other people's pain. You don't do that. You're just too wrapped up in your own problems to notice anyone else's."

"So you're saying I'm a narcissist."

"Not even that. I wish you were so I could hate you. But I don't. For a minute I thought I did, but frankly, that takes too much energy, and I'm exhausted. What I am saying is you're selfish, sometimes, and you haven't been as good a friend to me as I've been to you."

"Can we change that?"

Tamara shrugged. "I guess that's up to you. But if you're asking if we can get past this, the answer is I don't know. But one thing I do know is we need to go to the police. Holly, do you realize Zach could've been *driving* in the crash that killed Tom?"

That *had* crossed her mind. Who was to say Zach hadn't insisted on getting behind the wheel, if he thought Tom was too drunk?

Tamara seemed to have come back to reason, but just moments ago she'd been out of control, and furious. And Holly could *not* allow her to go to the police about Zach. Her relationship with him was far too tenuous, too *dangerous*. He'd surely talk his way out of it, and then take it out on Jolene and her. Whatever plan she came up with had to be designed to succeed. Otherwise it wasn't worth the risk.

Somehow, they needed to get through this conversation and Holly, though she wanted desperately to be a better friend to

Tamara, was going to have to keep on being selfish—for Jolene's sake as well as for her own. Holly steadied her breathing, choosing her words carefully. "I understand. You think the reason Zach left the scene without calling for help was because *he* was driving. But we don't know that for sure. And I don't see how we ever can."

Tamara rolled her eyes. "He was the driver. Zach fleeing the scene doesn't make sense otherwise. And *if* all he did was flee the scene without rendering help, I'm not sure if that's illegal or if it is a minor charge. So why go on lying about it even after he became a suspect in Beth's murder? Don't you see? His being in the accident with Tom was a legitimate alibi. But instead, he continued to lie. And now you're saying he offered you a divorce in exchange for that fake alibi when he had a real one the entire time?"

Holly suspected Tamara was right. Zach might have been—no, he'd *probably* been driving that car. And if so, that was manslaughter, but it would be damn hard to prove. "I want him to be held accountable, I do. But proving it will be difficult—maybe even impossible without a confession, and Zach is not going to confess."

"I can't let him get away with this. I owe it to Tom."

Right now, Holly had *nothing* to hold over her husband. He'd given her room to breathe, but if Tamara went to the cops, if they showed Zach their hand when they didn't have the high card—when they didn't have *any* cards, they would lose. "I can't risk it, Tamara. I can't lose Jolene."

"And I can't let Zach walk away."

Holly shook her head. "We can't go to the police."

"If he gets jail time, that's your ticket out. And if I'm the one behind it, it will soften some of his rage toward you."

"What makes you think he'd get jail time? He can afford the best attorneys. Rich people sometimes get away with murder even when there are eyewitnesses. And here, there's no evidence at all. Zach probably wouldn't even be charged, much less convicted."

"It's the job of the police to find the evidence. And Zach told you he and Tom were drinking together. He admitted it."

"He admitted to being in the car, not to driving. And I've already told the police we were together all night. Zach will deny everything. He'll say I'm delusional or lying to get custody of Jolene. My leverage is gone."

Tamara's jaw hardened. "Your leverage is gone? My husband is dead and still, all you can think about are your own problems."

"I haven't told you everything. You have no idea what it's like to live with that man, but I promise you, he's ruthless. We both want him to pay, but I'm the one with the most to lose."

Tamara turned hard eyes on her. "Because I've lost everything all already."

"I'm asking you for time. If I can get more dirt on him, then I can file for divorce and win custody, and *then* maybe... Tamara, I *lied* to the police. *That* is a crime. Don't you see?"

Tamara climbed to her feet and planted her hands on her hips. "We have to take him down, Holly."

"Please—" Holly got on her knees "—I'm begging you."

Tamara extended a hand to Holly and pulled her to her feet. "Stop groveling. I'm not saying we *have* to go to the police. I happen to agree, after listening to your points: We'll never prove that he was driving that car, and it will cause major problems for you if the cops find out you gave him a false alibi. But there's more than one way to make a man pay for his crimes, and one way or another, you and I, *together*, are going to take Zach Bancroft down."

THIRTY-ONE

This morning would be *the* test of Jolene's fancy stroller. If it held up to the rigors of the dusty path that edged Phoenix's manmade canals, Holly would gladly cough up a five-star review.

Ahead, already at the bridge, Holly spotted Frances, one hand on the guardrail, dressed in purple Lululemon, stretching out her quads. "Ahoy!"

Frances turned and waved, "Ahoy!"

Holly wheeled Jolene over. "Are you sure you're up for our walk today? What does the ankle say?"

"Definitely—but let's take it slow."

"Sounds like a plan." Holly was a bit relieved. Frances had a tendency to take on too much, and though she was an adult and could make her own decisions, Holly hated to think what another fall might do to her. "Let me lather this lady with sunscreen, and then we're off."

With Grandma blowing kisses, Jolene gurgled her approval and tried to grab the lotion. Holly covered her from head to toe —they didn't call this the Valley of the Sun for nothing—then she pulled the stroller's built-in sunshade into position. Given

the high price she'd paid for this thing—in more ways than one
—she'd be damned if she'd spring for a separate, cheap stroller to
take Jolene to the farmers' market.

Allowing Frances to set a comfortable pace, they headed
out. The sky was cloudless and blue. What the route lacked in
scenery—it was a flat gravel path, winding through commercial
streets—it made up in camaraderie. Like most Saturdays, the
path was busy with casual joggers, cyclists, and serious runners
training for competitive events, most of them ready with a
wave and a friendly smile. It was around a mile and a half from
the bridge to the farmers' market, plenty of time for conversation, and just ahead, Holly knew the palm trees held a
surprise.

As soon as she heard the *cheep cheeps*, Holly slowed her
pace. "Frances, stop. Do you see, there, in that tree?"

Frances removed her big square sunglasses. "My goodness!
What colorful birds."

"Rosy-faced lovebirds—escapees from the African pet trade.
They seem to thrive in Arizona, and they love that palm. I used
to see them in this spot almost every day, back when I ran the
canals." Yet another pastime she'd given up after meeting Zach.
He'd complained it took too much of her time. And since Jolene,
she definitely didn't have time for competitive running.

"You sound like a regular ornithologist."

"I looked them up after seeing them along the canal."

"Do lovebirds talk?"

"Not like a pet parrot, but they know how to converse with
each other."

They kept moving, enjoying the day, Frances prattling on
about her knitting and her favorite television programs. So
different than only a few months ago when she was full of
stories about her friends in the Red Hat Club and her church
group. Holly had hoped the situation with Dina's husband and
the fake Facebook messages would be forgotten quickly, but it

seemed the ladies had long memories. It was one of the things Holly wanted to discuss with Frances this morning.

But, for now, that could wait.

Even before they spotted the market's white pop-up canopies, the aroma of sizzling meats drifted to them on the breeze. With its fresh flowers and homemade crafts, the Saturday market never disappointed. But Holly's favorite part was the food. For an exorbitant price you could support your local vendors and fill your belly with your choice of kabobs, crêpes, burritos, and so on.

Holly ordered a large power drink and a spinach omelet while Frances stood in line for shrimp tacos. Then they grabbed a shaded table off to the side to enjoy their brunch. There were people around, but everyone was talking, and the general buzz of voices in the air masked the conversations of others. If one really tried, they might overhear bits and pieces, but in general, this was a safe place to share secrets—and Holly was hoping that's exactly what Frances would do.

"How are the shrimp tacos?" Holly asked.

"Best I've ever had." Frances grinned. "I guess that long walk makes them all the more delicious."

"The market is a nice reward for the exercise, I think."

"Thanks for inviting me. It's been a little lonely if you don't mind me saying. I was thinking I might try going back to church soon, but I'm not sure how it will go."

"What's the worst that can happen?"

"I can be shunned." Frances dropped her taco, an apprehensive look on her face.

"I suppose. But what if Jolene and I go with you? I'm pretty tough, and who would shun a baby?"

That drew a smile from Frances. "Not me. She's basically irresistible. Better than a puppy."

"Then let's give that a go, tomorrow."

"Tomorrow?"

"I think it's time. Whatever Dina's issues with her husband are, they're not your fault. And you didn't send those messages, that should be clear to them by now. It's possible they're just embarrassed about the way they jumped to conclusions, and that's why you haven't heard from them."

"I'm not expecting any apologies."

And she probably wouldn't get one, but Dina and Alfre and Frances had been friends a long, long time. Holly had to believe there was a chance they could revive that. It wasn't just a loss to Frances, it was a loss to all of them.

"I'm convinced Russell was behind it. I consider myself a forgiving person, but if I ever bump into him again, I'll probably smack him to kingdom come, and I won't be sorry, either."

So, clearly, Frances still didn't suspect the truth, that her own son was the culprit, and it was probably best she didn't find out—or at least not until Holly found a way to protect her from his wrath. "We'll probably never know who did it—I really think it was random. But I understand your anger."

Frances began to gather her trash—apparently she'd just lost her appetite for the best shrimp tacos she'd ever had.

Holly reached out and touched her fingers to the table, a few inches from Frances' hand. "Before we go, there's something I wanted to talk about, if you don't mind."

"You don't need to ask permission to speak."

"It's about Zach."

Frances folded her arms across her chest and tucked in her chin. "What about him?"

"Can we keep this between us?"

"No idea. Depends on whether I think he needs to know."

Holly cast a glance at her daughter, sleeping peacefully in her stroller. "It's a delicate matter, but I think you may know something about it. He said something odd to me about Jolene, and I have absolutely no idea where he got the notion."

Frances leaned forward.

Just as Holly suspected it would, the mention of Jolene got Frances' full attention. "He said that shortly before Jolene was born he wondered if—" she stopped and turned her palms up in disbelief "—once I got what I wanted from him—a baby—I'd leave him. Now the honest truth is, starting a family when we did was Zach's idea. I was perfectly happy with my career, and our relationship was, frankly, wonderful at the time. So I'm baffled. Really mystified why he would think such a thing, and I wondered if there might be some family dynamic, something in his history, that could explain it."

Frances pushed back her chair, rose on her haunches, then plopped back down in her seat. "You think it's my fault. Because I left his father when he was six months old."

She crumpled her napkin, then started to shred it, dropping it piece by piece onto her plate. "I'm not saying it's your fault at all." Holly could certainly relate—more than Frances knew. "I'm sure if you left with a baby that young, you must have had a very good reason."

Frances sighed. "It's true. No woman would leave in a situation like that unless she was desperate. Certainly not because she'd gotten what she wanted out of a man. But to hear Russell tell it, that was the gist. Russell and Zachary haven't seen each other since he was a baby, though. I don't see how Zach could've gotten that bizarre idea from his father unless..."

Unless Zach's father *had* come to his office and caused a fuss. "That man you saw at the bank—the one in the revolving door—I suspect it really was Russell. Zach later told me his father came to see him a few days before Jolene was born. Afterwards, Zach ordered a DNA test on Jolene, and I think Russell must've convinced him it was necessary."

"That jackass!"

Which one? Holly swallowed hard, working up her courage. "You told me once that you thought Russell wanted to hurt Zach, but that the doctor said you were delusional, put you on medication. Is it possible it wasn't a delusion? That what you were sensing about Russell was the truth?"

She shook her head. "I don't honestly know."

"But you didn't want to risk it. That's why you left Russell when Zach was so young, isn't it?"

Frances sat silent, staring at her hands.

She didn't deny it, and that was enough for Holly. "I just have one more question for you. You and Zach were together when you fell and broke your ankle. Were you arguing? Did Zach shove you? Maybe he stuck his foot out and tripped you? Did Zach cause the fall?"

"I've had enough of this, Holly. I like you, I really do. But I won't stand for this kind of talk, especially not in front of Jolene. If you drop the subject right now, I won't mention this to Zach."

Once again, her mother-in-law hadn't denied the charge.

Frances slapped her fist on the tabletop and stood up so suddenly her chair fell over. Then she pulled her hand across her face, the way Zach sometimes did, transforming her expression completely. "Now, then. What a nice morning for a walk. I hope we see those lovebirds again on our way back."

THIRTY-TWO

A good wife lunches with her adoring husband in full view of his colleagues. And Holly was playing the part. She was getting so good at this she could almost believe she had Zach fooled.

Maybe she did.

Or maybe he was simply playing his part as well.

Frances had been thrilled to babysit her one and only grandchild, allowing Holly to meet Zach at the hospital, where they headed straight for the doctors' lounge.

Zach swiped them in with his badge and, upon entry, Holly nearly bumped into a pillar.

Fixed onto the pillar were two notices.

The first, a temporary-appearing paper sign, read:

Doctors, we APPRECIATE everything you do!!

Next to it, a larger sign, laminated for staying power, admonished:

Doctors, *DO NOT TAKE MORE THAN ONE BAG OF CHIPS as this may result in loss of your lounge privileges. If you see someone take more than one bag of chips please report the offender to Donna in medical staff services IMME-DIATELY!*

Frank Calletano, a white-haired, retired orthopedist who still hung around on an emeritus basis—he'd once been hospital chief of staff—struggled to his feet and proffered a half-bow. "Hey, Zach. Don't take that little beauty to the cafeteria! Sit down with us in here. We'll happily make an exception for her."

"You know me, Frank. I'm a rules guy." Zach saluted him.

"Oh c'mon. You don't want Holly to miss the creamed corn."

Frank was a dinosaur, and his flirtation bordered on the inappropriate at times, but he was pushing eighty and Holly had a soft spot for him. His wife, Judy, had died of cancer a year ago. Holly had seen them together plenty of times, and when they'd held hands there was nothing phony about it. "It's not the creamed corn, Frank; it's your company I'll miss."

The doctors' lounge was strictly for physicians—no families allowed, though Holly knew the rules were sometimes broken. Zach had groused a time or two when a young doctor, usually a woman, settled a child in the lounge with a book and snacks because of an early dismissal at school or some such.

Holly suspected this stroll through, on the pretense of Zach grabbing a free granola bar, was doing double duty. Not only did it announce to everyone that Zach had his perfect wife at his beck and call, he was setting an example: no family dining in the lounge, no exceptions.

Next, they made their way to the hospital cafeteria where Zach signed for his free lunch and dutifully paid for Holly's grilled cheese and fries with extra pickles. A perk of hospital dining was that Zach didn't criticize her food choices at his place of work where someone might overhear and realize what an asshole he really was. At home, or even at a restaurant, he'd have cautioned her about watching her figure.

"Enjoying your lunch?" He smiled magnanimously, as if to say: *see how nice I'm being, not mentioning the calorie count?*

"Mm hmm. Delicious," she answered with her mouth full, knowing that would make him crazy.

He grabbed the edge of table and red climbed from his neck to his cheeks. Bit of an overreaction, even for...

Holly followed his gaze.

Mercy General boasted a restaurant-style cafeteria including chandeliers and a wall of windows. Through those windows, she saw cop cars pulling up in front, one after another. While the uniformed officers bounded out and raced toward the hospital entrance, she counted six vehicles.

In the space of time it took her to count them, Zach's complexion changed from bright red to ghostly pale.

That was a lot of squad cars, but this was a trauma center. Maybe there'd been an accident with multiple fatalities, or victims from a drug deal gone wrong. She dropped her sandwich.

Zach's phone vibrated on the table. He put it to his ear and nodded. His brow worked up and down, causing a deep crease to set up shop above his nose. "Okay. Yes. I'm on my way."

"What's happening?"

His forehead smoothed. His contorted features softened into the look he wore when trying to reassure. "Everything's okay. But I need to go."

"Fine, but does it have to do with all those police?"

He reached across the table and took both her hands in his. "You're going to hear it on the news, but you should keep this to yourself until it's been made public."

Some kind of major catastrophe?

He leaned in.

Her heart raced, its beats tripping over one another.

"They found a body in the morgue," he whispered.

She let out her breath, blinking in confusion. "But that's where the bodies are..."

"No. It's one of the medical students."

Suddenly, she couldn't breathe. "Why do *you* have to go? Was it..."

"One of mine. Yes. You might remember her—she brought flowers to the house when Jolene was born."

Claudia!

* * *

"I need to make a quick call to my mother-in-law to let her know I'll be late." Holly checked the clock on the wall of the police interrogation room. "How long do you expect this to take?"

"That depends." Detective Denton bounced a pen between his fingers.

"On what?"

"You, of course."

They needed to turn up the air conditioner. It was certainly above eighty in this sweat box, but then that was probably by design. "I'm happy to answer all of your questions, but I barely knew the poor young woman, so I don't see how I can help."

"Perhaps you should tell your mother-in-law you don't know when you'll be home. Ask her to be flexible. I'm sure she'll understand, under the circumstances."

Holly wished she understood. What did she have to do with Claudia's murder? Zach, naturally, would be questioned since he was her preceptor. She clicked on her cell. She had no intention of dragging this out because she had nothing to offer that would be of any help. "Frances, something's come up. Do you think you can watch Jolene for another hour?"

Denton sent her a disapproving look.

"Or less," she said, defiantly, determined not to be intimidated. She absolutely wanted him to find Claudia's killer, but she hadn't done it, and she didn't like his attitude. In fact, she'd requested to speak to him somewhere other than the station. She was doing him a courtesy coming down here in the first place, and there was simply no need to corner her in an over-heated, cramped interrogation room.

"Take your time. Is everything okay?" Frances asked.

"Just running errands. Thank you!" She clicked off.

"Let's start by listing your whereabouts, to the best of your recollection, for the past seventy-two hours."

How long had the poor woman been dead?

"I don't understand."

"Which part?"

"The why part."

"Claudia Keeler was last seen three days ago."

"Yes, but I barely know her, so I don't understand." Only perhaps she did. Ah yes, obtuse of her not to see it in the first place. They had Zach in a separate room. If he tried to use her as a false alibi, this would prevent it. The police were making sure she and Zach didn't have a chance to confer on a story—and that was unfortunate because as heartbreaking as this was, it might've presented an opportunity to renew her prior deal with Zach—an alibi in exchange for a divorce.

She touched her neck. When she tried to swallow, just now, the lining of her throat burned like someone had just poured a gallon of acid down it.

The first time she'd been questioned about a murdered student, she'd been convinced Zach had nothing to do with her death.

And you were proven right.

They'd found the murder weapon, the knife, on that vagrant—and his hanging himself in jail was practically as good as a signed confession.

But Claudia makes two.

If Zach was a murderer, and of course he wasn't, but if he *was,* could she live with herself if she helped him escape justice in order to save herself and Jolene? The question was moot, because they simply had no way to confer. She picked up the pen Denton had placed in front of her and began listing her activities. It would have been easier if she hadn't made Zach tear up her schedule, but she did her best to be completely accurate.

There was no reason to lie... this time.

Denton took it from her and looked it over. "So no interaction with Ms. Keeler?"

"Not in the past three days, no."

"You say you didn't know her well, but you do know her. When and where did you first meet?"

"I recall meeting her very briefly in Zach's office at the hospital around a year ago—the interaction lasted no more than a minute or two before I asked to speak to my husband alone. But the first time we really talked was when she brought me flowers after Jolene was born."

"Why would a woman you'd only met once bring you flowers?"

Good question. "I thought it was strange myself. But not too strange. She explained that Zach was her preceptor, so I thought she was either very nice or possibly trying to win brownie points with him."

"He was also Beth Gunther's preceptor. The relationship was the same. Don't you find that disturbing?"

"I thought Beth's case was closed."

"It is." Denton tapped his pen on his teeth. "Talk to me about what the role of a preceptor is. What does it entail?"

"I think that's a better question for Zach, but as far as I know, the preceptor acts as a mentor to the medical students. They allow the student to follow them around in clinic or on hospital rounds, sometimes they're even present at a delivery, and, from the stories Zach tells, there's a great deal of dispensing of pearls."

"Pearls?"

"Wisdom they've gleaned over the years. Their secret sauce for being a good doctor."

"Sounds like you actually know quite a bit about that."

"There's a similar process for speech therapists."

"I didn't realize you were one."

"I was before I got pregnant. I'm certified as a speech-language pathologist assistant, and I hope to get my master's when Jolene's a little older."

"If your husband allows it."

If Denton was trying to rile her up, he was succeeding. "Excuse me?"

"Never mind. So, back to Claudia—Ms. Keeler. Did you invite her in?"

"The house? Of course. We had a nice visit, but not too long."

"How long would you say?"

"Thirty minutes at most."

"And since then? What interactions have you had?"

She shifted in her seat and pressed her palms into her slacks to soak up the sweat. She had no reason to feel guilty. "I saw her at the aquarium—the one near the casino. That was around a week ago. I can check the date by looking at my credit card."

"Please. And then call me with that information. But why would you go to the aquarium with someone you, as you said, barely knew?"

"I didn't. We just ran into each other."

"Quite the coincidence."

Her stomach somersaulted. She hadn't thought much of it at the time, but now it did seem far too convenient.

"You're sure it wasn't planned, because lying to the police is a crime."

She opened and closed her fists. "Not by me, it wasn't."

"Do you think Claudia might have planned it?"

"I have no idea. I was sitting on a bench with Jolene, and she walked past at first, but then she stopped to chat. Next you're going to ask what we talked about. Well, I'll save you the trouble. We talked about how long one ought to breastfeed a baby. And we talked about fish."

"Not about your husband?"

"Not much. She said he was a good mentor—a fantastic mentor—and that was all. No, wait, she also spoke of a couple she babysat for, and how sad it was that they were divorcing. I haven't seen her since. I'm incredibly sorry to hear she's—she's gone." She closed her eyes, letting the horrible truth sink in. That a young woman, with all the promise in the world, had been murdered. "May I ask what happened to Claudia?"

"That's what we're trying to determine. Was your husband having an affair with Ms. Keeler? Is that why you arranged to meet her at the aquarium?"

She could feel her cheeks flame. Did Denton think *she* killed Claudia? Did he think of her as *the jealous wife*? "You don't mince words, do you? I already told you it was a chance encounter."

"Did you confront her about the affair?"

"There was no affair. Not as far as I know."

"But you suspected one."

"I-I really haven't thought about it much. Although she did get a bit starry-eyed when she talked about Zach..."

"Let me ask again. Did you suspect an affair? *Do* you suspect an affair?"

In the beginning, she hadn't paid a lot of attention because she truly didn't care. Anything that diverted his attention, his compulsive attention, away from her would've been welcome. But nothing had. He came home every night unless he was on duty—not that she checked his schedule and could say that for a fact. But he was always bothering her for sex. If he were having an affair, she'd have expected his appetite for her to diminish.

A woman is dead.

Should she tell Denton about the picture frame nanny cam in Zach's office?

The recordings had been so boring she'd stopped watching a while ago, but what if there was something new there? She decided to say nothing. She wanted to review the footage herself, before turning anything over to the police. "I don't have any reason to think my husband has been unfaithful. If anything, I think Claudia may have had a schoolgirl crush on Zach. That's common for students to imagine their teachers as perfect and become infatuated. Or so I've heard. But I don't think Zach has been unfaithful. He's a devoted husband. If you think they were involved, I suggest you ask him."

"I certainly will."

The silence dragged on. He stared at her, and she stared at the clock. "May I go?"

"You're free to go, for now. But, Mrs. Bancroft, you're under caution not to leave town."

THIRTY-THREE

Swinging her legs over the side of the pool lounge chair, Holly dusted the crumbs of her chicken salad sandwich from her fingertips and licked the lingering taste of mayonnaise from her lips. The Desert Hotel, nestled in the foothills of the McDowell Mountains north of Scottsdale, boasted an outdoor pool with a spectacular view of Pinnacle Peak.

Pinnacle Peak—the very spot where Holly had struck her second deal with the devil.

Little did Zach know the spa day he was paying for, both for her and Tamara, would, hopefully, lead to his undoing.

Terracotta-colored umbrellas dotted the outdoor patio, protecting them from the sun. Even in September, on a cloudless day like today, the Arizona sun could be brutal. But the temperature was perfect for lounging and dipping in the pool.

Holly lifted the bottle of chardonnay from its ice bucket and tilted it invitingly above Tamara's plastic wine goblet.

"No thanks. I'm still feeling the first two."

"Should we order more food?" Holly asked.

Tamara propped herself on her elbows, the natural wave in her blonde hair on full display from swimming and sunning. "Are you sure? You've spent so much on me already."

"I love spending Zach's money on you. The way I see it, he owes you so much more than money can buy."

"True enough." Tamara took off her Dior sunglasses, and met Holly's gaze. "I know there's a lot going on but my massage did the trick for me—it was great. You, however, don't seem relaxed in the least. Your masseuse wasn't good?"

Holly removed her own sunglasses. "I'm worried I might be living with a killer—so yeah, I'm tense."

Tamara's glasses clattered onto the small plastic tabletop between them. "If you honestly think Zach had something to do with Claudia Keeler's murder, my advice is let's forget about getting the upper hand and you pack your bags today."

"If I leave with Jolene, he'll have the cops on my tail in a heartbeat. After Detective Denton interviewed me, I called that divorce attorney, Les Larson. He warned me that if I try to flee, that would virtually guarantee Zach gets full custody. He says if Zach murdered someone, I should let the police handle it. If I have evidence, or if he threatens me, I should go straight to the police. But I know they can't help me. Tamara, the man shot me and they did nothing."

"You said you thought that was an accident."

"I did, but now I can't be sure... anyway, I thought you and I were going to take him down together, and I've got a plan."

Tamara snapped her fingers then pointed at the chardonnay. "Hit me. I think I'm going to need a third glass for this."

"Look, if you don't want to help, I understand. Zach is a dangerous man, and you don't owe me a thing. After what happened with Tom, the obligation is all on my side."

"I didn't say I wouldn't help. I want to get him every bit as much as you do, maybe more. And somebody has to keep an eye on you, make sure you don't do something you'll regret. If I'm hesitating, it's only because I care about you. Whatever we do, we have to be smart about it. Neither one of us really knows what Zach is capable of." Tamara took a gulp of wine. "But if it's any comfort I don't think he killed his student —Claudia."

"What makes you say that? Because I *do* think he killed her. They were sleeping together. *I know it.*"

"You know it how?"

"I just do, that's all. I feel it in my gut."

"If he didn't kill Beth, then he probably didn't kill Claudia either."

"But do we know, one hundred percent, that he didn't kill Beth? Isn't it possible that knife could've been tossed out and the vagrant picked it up? Maybe the vagrant didn't kill himself because he was guilty. Maybe he killed himself because he was afraid of going to prison."

"They also found Beth's ring in the man's possession. And you're forgetting, Zach has a real alibi for the night Beth went missing." Tamara's eyebrows went up. "He was in the car with my husband, probably driving drunk. He might be, and probably is guilty of *that*, but even Zach can't be in two places at once."

No, he couldn't be. "You're right, he couldn't have killed Beth. But, I still believe he's dangerous, and he's not going to just let me walk away with Jolene. He's made that clear."

"So what's the plan? I'm all ears."

"My attorney says Zach has too much dirt on me—my taking pills and then calling the police about a 'ransom note', ordering all those strollers—it makes me look like a basket case. And when you add in the fact that an innocent child died while I was babysitting, I just don't stand a chance."

"But what about the fact Zach is a person of interest in a murder investigation?"

"*As am I.* But Larson says unless one of us is charged, it can't be a factor in a judge's decision. What I need is something

I can use as leverage. Something that will give me a fighting chance."

"Okay, so it sounds like what we need to do is catch him in the act. But what act? Infidelity?"

Holly shook her head. "Again, Les says that's not enough. An affair doesn't make you an unfit parent. I need something that would affect his ability to be a good father. Something like drugs."

"But Zach hates drugs."

"And I didn't order twenty strollers or take a bunch of pain pills and forget. Get it?"

"Not really."

"If Zach can make me seem unfit by making it *appear* that I swallowed a bunch of pain pills, then I can return the favor."

"A setup?"

"A sting." She scooped up her sunglasses before they could fall off her lounge chair. "I deserve an Academy Award for my recent portrayal as the good wife, trying to make things work—in every way but one. I haven't let him into my bed yet, and it's driving him crazy."

Tamara grabbed the bottle and refilled both their goblets.

"He has a conference coming up, soon, in Tucson. I was thinking I could show up at his hotel and ply him with liquor."

"And what, slip him a mickey?"

"Exactly. Then we could—"

"*We?*"

"I'm going to need help. Someone to intercept room service... and moral support. I'm definitely going to need moral support."

Tamara had a wide smile on her face. "Uh-huh. So once he's out, we plant drugs on him and call the cops—except where would we get the drugs? That sounds risky. Like it could backfire and we could get caught with them."

"We only need sleeping pills to knock him out, then we just

put a bunch of baby powder on mirrors and stuff. Take photos of him sprawled on the bed with what looks like cocaine scattered everywhere and empty liquor bottles. That, plus what we already know about him drinking at a strip club? I think it just might be enough for a new deal—mine and Jolene's freedom in exchange for his reputation."

"Have you thought about what he might do to you if he figures out what you're... what *we're*... planning?"

Holly put her hand on her heart, nodding. "That's the reason we won't let him find out."

THIRTY-FOUR

Holly was already regretting her decision to request a hotel room on the same floor as Zach's. If anyone found out, it might look suspicious, but she'd taken the precaution of booking the hotel online using a fake name and a credit card attached to a bank account she'd opened with her fake ID. And the red-headed wig and big floppy hat she was sporting would make it hard to identify her on security footage—not that it would come to that.

Cross fingers.

Tamara pulled off her own floppy hat, revealing a black wig. "These disguises seem a bit unnecessary."

Holly wasn't taking any chances. They'd left their mobile phones back at Tamara's place to support their story that they were in Scottsdale—in case anyone tracked them. And, after arriving in Tucson, they'd parked Holly's Tesla in a nearby lot, then taxied to the hotel. "They're necessary. What if Zach refuses to deal? What if he goes to the police and says I set him up? I don't want any trace of my being at the hotel at all. Then it'll just be his word against mine—against *ours* because we're not here. We're at your place, swimming, all day."

"He'll deal. I hope." Tamara sighed. "Though, I almost wish he wouldn't. I mean, for your sake, *of course*, I want everything to go just as planned. He caves in and lets you go. Your secret traded for his secret—a done deal."

"But?"

"If he *didn't* go along, and we put those pictures online, he'd lose his medical license. And that would feel like some sort of justice served to me—for what he did to Tom."

"We can't."

"I'm saying *if* he doesn't play ball."

"It's not possible."

"So then, this is an empty threat on your part? Let me tell you something, my friend, you can't beat a ruthless person if you're not willing to be ruthless yourself. If Zach senses, for one minute, that you won't go all the way, that you won't put up those pictures, he'll call your bluff."

Holly nodded, her stomach in knots, knowing Tamara was right. But what Tamara wasn't taking into account was the danger of a judge deciding both she *and* Zach were unfit after a toxic custody battle. Les had warned Holly that with her parents vagabonding it abroad, and Zach's mother in her seventies, it was possible Jolene could wind up in foster care. "Once we have those pictures, I won't let him smell the fear on me. This *has* to work. Jolene's future, our life together, everything that matters to me is at stake."

"Understood." Tamara reached out. "Are you ready?"

"As I'll ever be." Holly took her hand. "Thank you for being there for me."

They hugged.

"Signal?" Holly asked.

"Three knocks, followed by two knocks followed by three knocks on the wall. Then I come over with the set-up and this cool little instant camera, we take pictures, clean up and get the hell out."

* * *

Zach opened the door to his hotel suite and pulled her inside, grinning. "Hey, baby. I didn't know we were playing dress up."

"We're playing whatever you want, mister, as long as you have cash up front for Sugar," Holly said.

"Sugar suits you, 'cause you're sweet." He pulled her against him, and ran his tongue across her cheek. She could smell whiskey on his breath. But that shouldn't be a problem, as long as he was drinking, she could dose him with the drugs in her purse.

"Did you order the champagne?"

"I sure did, baby... I mean Sugar. Shall I pop the cork?"

"Is it too late to change my mind?"

"That's a woman's prerogative. What's your pleasure?"

"What have you been drinking?"

"Bourbon, neat."

"I'll have the same." The plan was to switch glasses, and she could use something stronger than champagne anyway.

He poured her two fingers. "How's this?"

"Keep going. And one for you, too."

Zach held up his hand. "One more, but I don't want to overdo. It's been a long time, Sugar, and I want to be able to please the lady."

She walked around the room, stalling, pulled the curtains back and laughed. "Nice view." It was of the back lot, filled with dumpsters. Strange, because Zach usually liked to stay in a primo room. A flash of doubt made her breath catch.

Was it possible he suspected something?

"The high floors were sold out because of the conference. I'm in meetings all day, so I didn't make a fuss. Of course if I'd known you were going to come down, if you'd let me know sooner, I would've done better. If you want, I'll call the front desk right now and throw some weight around."

She took a big breath, relieved. "It's fine. I'm not even spending the night."

"Are you sure?" He pulled a wad of cash from his pocket and beckoned with his finger. "I could make it worth your while."

The wig was making her scalp sweaty, and she wanted to shed it. But the role-playing was putting emotional distance between her and this wicked scheme. Holly would never, ever drug her husband. It would be easier as Sugar, the hooker.

Just keep pretending.

She was getting good at this, too good.

She strutted over to an armchair, positioned near a small table, and sat, kicked off her shoes. Zach followed and took the seat opposite. He pulled her barefoot onto his lap, began massaging, then worked his way up her ankle. "How was the drive?"

"I walked—from the street corner." She kept in character.

"Right." He grinned. "So you're not tired?"

"Not me." Winking, she raised her glass, lifted it near her lips but didn't sip. Not yet, she didn't want to get lipstick on this one. "But I do have to tinkle. You don't mind if I freshen up, do you?"

"Please." He motioned toward the bathroom.

She slipped her leg from his lap, gathered her purse, her overnight bag, and her untouched drink, and then, swinging her hips to give him a nice show, she headed for the bathroom. Locked the door behind her.

Be Sugar.

You can do this.

She unzipped her dress and let it slide to the floor, changed into a black lace teddy with a built-in bra; her breasts needed the support, and she knew the push-up effect would get Zach lathered up and distracted. The more distracted the better.

Next, she snapped open her purse and stared at the glass of bourbon, sitting on the counter.

Everything is at stake.

She dug out the drugs, sighing. How many sleeping capsules would she need to put in his drink to knock him out quickly? The longer it took, the greater the chance she'd have to have sex with him. Four was the number of pills he'd supposedly given her but he was bigger, so the powder from *five* capsules would do for him. After stirring the drink with her finger, she looked in the mirror, pushed up her cleavage and adjusted the wig. Then applied thick liner to the corners of her eyes and an extra coat of mascara to her lashes. Eye drops. Next, she pulled a tube of midnight red lipstick from her bag, and painted it on thick.

Sugar twirled in front of the mirror, satisfied.

"How long you gonna be in there, baby?"

"Coming." She made her voice low, purring as she entered the room.

His belt and shoes were off and he sat, legs wide apart, on the edge of the bed. His bourbon, still untouched, was on the nightstand.

This was the tricky part.

She set the dosed drink next to his, noting its position, and straddled him without making contact. "Would you like a lap dance, sir?"

He groaned.

"That's what I thought, but no touching. Those are the rules." Holly had never given a lap dance, but Sugar seemed to be good at it. Soon Zach was writhing and reaching, with Sugar teasingly slapping his hands away.

"That's enough fun, Holly," he said. "It's time for Sugar to leave. I want to touch my wife."

Then he pulled her down onto his lap and yanked off her wig.

"That's too rough, Zach," she whispered. "Play nice and we can do all the things."

"All the things?" he asked and pressed his lips to her cleavage.

Please, please, please hurry.

A loud knock sounded at the door. "Room service."

"Go away!" Zach yelled over his shoulder, and Holly took the chance to climb off and back out of his reach.

"Just leave it at the door, please." She raised her voice loud enough to be heard.

Zach pushed off the bed, his face red, his breathing labored. "You ordered room service?"

"On my way up. I assumed that was okay. I haven't eaten all day. Would you mind bringing it in?"

"Now?"

"I ordered a hamburger—there's one for you, too. I don't want it to get cold."

He squeezed his eyes closed, then drew his hand across his face, changing his expression from irritated to magnanimous. "Whatever you want, darling. I'm nothing if not a patient man."

Even as he moved toward the door, Holly's heart started to race. Her hands trembled and she wished, oh how she wished, time would slow down, give her time to consider, re-evaluate whether this was the right thing to do. But there was no time, so the instant Zach slipped into the hallway, she picked up the drug-free glass and pressed her lips on the rim.

Just in time.

He wheeled a table into the sitting area, and she brought over the drinks. Plunked a bourbon on his side, lifted the warming cover and grabbed a burger. "Oh, man, I'm starving," she said, her mouth already full.

He picked up his glass. "Is this me?"

"Mine's the one with the lipstick." She laughed and showed him the mark on her glass. "Does it matter?"

"Not at all."

"How about we toast to us?" She lifted her arm.

Their glasses clinked.

"To us," he said, and tossed back his bourbon in two big gulps.

THIRTY-FIVE

Tamara hung back in the hallway. "Are you sure he's unconscious?"

"Get in here." Holly grabbed her hand and tugged her inside Zach's hotel room, then hung the Do Not Disturb sign and set the dead bolt. "He's out cold. He drank it too fast and started getting groggy right away. I was barely able to walk him from the table to the bed before he collapsed. Imagine if I'd had to lift him off the floor."

Tamara shrugged. "We could've left him there. I don't know why you care about making him more comfortable."

"I don't," she said. But she actually did. What she was doing was reprehensible enough. She didn't need to deliberately make Zach suffer more in the process. "Have you got everything?"

Tamara dumped the contents of a tote on the bed: a mirror, razor blades, baby powder, instant camera, whiskey bottle. "Guess I didn't need to pour out this good whiskey after all. Looks like he provided the empty bottle on his own. How much did he have to drink?"

Holly eyed the virtually empty bottle at the bedside. No

way to know how much he'd drunk today versus earlier in the week. "Not sure—he'd been at it before I got here though."

"We should hurry." Tamara handed her the mirror and a small bag of baby powder. "Set this up on the bed, near him, and stick the bottle in his hand. I'll mess up the room, and then we can start taking pictures. This camera's fun."

"Fun? Tamara, this is serious."

"You're right. I'm sorry. But try not to act so guilty—Zach would do this to you in a heartbeat."

"He *did* do it to me. I'm almost certain he drugged me the morning of the ransom note incident with who knows what. I don't know if he meant for me to the call the cops, but I think he was trying to scare me with that note, make me doubt myself."

"And think of what he did to Tom. He deserves this."

"Uh-huh." Holly wished there was another way, but she'd wracked her brain and weighed all the consequences, and eventually she'd come to accept that this was the only way she could keep her daughter safe. But that didn't mean she felt good about it. That she didn't have her regrets and self-recriminations. If she didn't, she'd be a monster.

"Should we undress him?" Tamara asked.

"Why? Him passed out surrounded by drugs and booze is what we're after."

"It would be more humiliating. Give you more leverage because of his pride."

"This is enough." She crept behind Tamara, looking over her shoulder as she began snapping photos. As Tamara got closer and closer, Holly's stomach began staging a revolt. Doubling over with cramps, she forced herself to breathe through it.

Tamara eased the mirror with lines of baby powder on it near Zach's face, and Holly squinted, straining her eyes. Her heart thudded heavily in her chest, and then, her vision darkened.

The mirror wasn't fogging up, not at all.

She backed against the wall, slid to the ground. "Tamara?"

The camera kept whirring and spitting.

"Is he breathing? I don't think he's…" She was going to be sick. She catapulted to her feet, raced to the toilet and heaved up her burger and booze. Moments later, she staggered to the vanity and vomited bile in the sink.

Get a grip.

She had the water on, directing it with her hands, trying to flush the bile down the drain, when she saw Tamara's pale-faced reflection in the mirror.

"Holly, we need to get out of here." Tamara stepped near and put a hand on her shoulder. "He's not breathing."

"A-Are you sure?"

"Positive. No pulse, either. I checked. Honey, he's dead."

Dead.

The word rang in her ears, and then the room went silent as a tomb.

Tamara spun Holly around, shook her. Tamara's lips were moving but all Holly heard was the sound of her pulse thumping in her ears.

Tamara lifted her open palm and swung it.

Holly heard the slap, felt the sting on her cheek… and started to breathe again. "I killed him. I killed Zach."

"It was an *accident*. We'll talk about it later, though. Right now, we've got to clean this place up and get the hell out of here."

"Shouldn't we…" Holly didn't finish the sentence. *No.* They shouldn't.

"Call nine-one-one? Hell no. I'm not risking getting caught for *nothing*. Zach is *dead* and there's no bringing him back. It's ironic when you think about it, though, because isn't that the same thing he told you when he left the scene of Tom's accident?"

Tom was dead. It was obvious there was nothing I could do for him.

She'd hated Zach for that.

Now she hated herself, too.

But she understood what had to be done.

For Jolene.

"I'll wipe down the bathroom. You move the room service table into the hall, roll it back in front of our door."

They'd deliberately ordered room service for two, to their room next door, so no one would know Zach had company.

"We do everything exactly like we planned." Tamara sounded calm, and the color had returned to her face.

"We didn't plan to kill him."

"No, we didn't. This was an accident, and that's *exactly* how it will appear. Like that or suicide. Only we've got to get all the baby powder and mirrors out of here. They'll want to do an autopsy, and you'll go along. But we've got to get rid of the fake stuff. What they will find is booze and sleeping medication in his system. A lethal combination. How much did you give him?"

"More than I should have. I just kept remembering him saying *four pills never killed anyone,* and he's so much bigger than me. I wanted it to be quick." She felt the tears begin to roll down her cheeks. "I couldn't stand the thought of... him touching me. So I added an extra capsule's worth. But I never thought..."

"Of course you didn't. This isn't your fault, Holly, or mine either. If Zach hadn't drunk a boatload of booze before you got here, he'd still be alive. All of this is on him. He did it to himself, and after what he did to Tom, what he tried to do to you, I can't honestly say I'm sorry."

* * *

Was Holly sorry?

Back inside the other room, the one she'd rented with her fake ID, she leaned against the door, pressing her face against the peephole. Her legs felt too weak to support her body. It would be so easy to slide to the floor sobbing. Images of her life with Zach, the good parts, kept flashing through her head: their first kiss, cuddling under the covers, him letting her heat up her icy feet on his warm legs, Zach with his hands on her belly waiting to feel the baby kick. She'd stood at an altar and promised to love him forever, and there was a part of her that always would. But what do you do when you realize the man you married, the man you trusted with all your heart, is evil?

Whatever is necessary to protect yourself and your child.

"This place is probably crawling with doctors from the medical conference. We should keep our heads down and get through the lobby and out the doors as quickly as possible. I don't want to bump into one of Zach's colleagues," Holly said. Her words seemed cold and calculating because, after all, they were. She'd just killed her husband, and now she and Tamara were plotting their escape.

"Even if you do run into one of his colleagues, just be cool. Unless it's someone you know really well, they probably won't recognize you since you're not on Zach's arm—especially not with that red wig and heavy make-up. People are so wrapped up in themselves they don't pay that much attention. If you see someone you think you know, pretend you don't."

"The coast is clear. I say let's go now." Holly entered the hallway, wheeling her overnight bag with her. She glanced behind her—not a soul in sight. She wanted to break into a run, but if there were security cameras in the hallway, that would draw attention to herself and Tamara.

Walking slowly, they kept their heads down until they reached the elevators.

The doors opened and the couple inside glared at them,

apparently outraged someone would have the nerve to try to take up space in *their* elevator. But sharing a ride was the last thing Holly wanted to do.

"Going up?" Tamara cleverly saved the day.

"No!" The woman reached across the man's body and pushed a button. A moment later, the doors closed.

Rinse. Repeat.

By the time they'd turned down three occupied elevators, Holly's head was boiling hot under her wig. "Let's just take the next one. If we wait for an empty, it could very well take..."

Ding.

The doors opened to reveal a blessedly vacant compartment. They crossed the threshold, and, just as the doors were closing, a hand darted intrepidly between the doors. Holly heard a familiar voice say, "Hold please."

Tamara mashed the *door close* button too late, and Craig Paulson leaped into the elevator, dressed in a rumpled brown suit, with a twisted, backward-facing lanyard dangling from his neck and a mustard stain on his white dress shirt.

He smiled. "Afternoon ladies, you here for the conference?"

Holly's mouth went dry as a bone. She didn't dare speak for fear he'd recognize her voice. Please, please let Tamara be right about not being recognized out of context—she'd only met Craig a couple of times, but their last conversation had been memorable—at least to her. She tugged her floppy hat over the side of her face nearest Craig and threw a *help-me* look Tamara's way.

"We're pharmaceutical representatives," Tamara said.

Smart, because Holly's plunging neckline, booty-hugging skirt and stilettos marked her as one of two things—an expensive, high-class hooker or a big pharma rep.

"What's your specialty, Doc?" Tamara asked.

"The ladies." Craig chortled at his own wit before adding, "OB-GYN."

Holly glanced at the panel and noticed the buttons to

several floors were lit up. When she was a child she'd loved pressing the buttons in elevators, so she didn't blame the kids who'd done it, but the longer the ride, the greater the chance Craig Paulson would get a good look at her face. And that would spell disaster.

No one could know she'd been at the hotel.

"Which company are you with?" Craig's gaze travelled the length of Tamara's body.

"The best one, of course. Our product's just out. A new injection to treat erectile dysfunction."

"What's the advantage over the old ones? And with all the oral meds available, I don't see the point."

Holly's breath caught in her throat. Tamara was in over her head. Craig Paulson was no dummy. He was going to see through this act any minute.

"The point is reliability. A single injection lasts six months. We call it the UpShot."

His eyes narrowed, and he cocked his head to the side. Shifted, turning his gaze on Holly. She caught her reflection in the mirrored walls of the elevator. Red hair, long, false lashes, bright-red lipstick... Holly had no idea what to do, but suddenly, Sugar did.

Sugar clasped both hands around Tamara's waist, spun her into a position to block Craig's view of her face, and laid one on her best friend. As the elevator jolted between floors, she and Tamara worked that kiss for their audience of one, not stopping to come up for air until the elevator gods announced *lobby-level* in an eerie overhead voice, and a flush-faced Paulson scurried off, holding his hands strategically cupped in front of his trousers.

THIRTY-SIX

On the way home from Tucson to Phoenix, Holly had a full-blown panic attack—the kind where your palms sweat, your heart races and you think you're going to die, but then you somehow manage to pull off the road before passing out.

After which, Tamara took the wheel, and Holly slept for the better part of the trip, waking up just as they were pulling off the 101 onto North Scottsdale Road.

Pressing the back of her hand to her forehead, Holly said, "I think I have a fever. Thanks for driving."

"And for helping you kill your husband?" Tamara scoffed. "Aren't you going to thank me for that?"

Holly clenched her jaw. "That's on me. I'm the guilty party, and if the police find out, I promise I'll take full responsibility."

"It doesn't work like that. I supplied those sleeping capsules. I created a diversion with room service to lure him out of the room so you could switch the drinks, and then, when we realized he was dead, I helped cleaned up the mess and planned our escape." Tamara slowed for the turn into a residential area. "We're both responsible. We're in this thing together, and we need to figure out what to do next. While you were sleeping, I was thinking."

"And?"

"And I don't know what to do."

"Me either. I'd suggest brainstorming, but I don't think my head can withstand it. Let's just sit here and think quietly for a minute."

"Or we could approach it from another angle. What *not* to do—and the first thing on that list is panic." Tamara's sarcasm was clear from her tone.

"Okay, it sounds like you're reprimanding me for something I couldn't control. My heart was beating out of my chest, I couldn't see my hand in front of my face, and I felt as though a meteor was about to slam into the earth. Yeah, I melted down, but at least I pulled over." Holly could hear the faintest hint of defiance braiding into the quiver in her voice.

"We almost crashed. We could've been killed because of your self-indulgence."

"So guilt is self-indulgent?"

"At a time like this, yes it is." Tamara stopped for the light. "You have a child who's depending on you to be there for her. And *I'm* depending on you not to get us *both* locked up. So you don't get to go around having panic attacks and leave me to do the driving."

"Leave you to do the driving? Is that a metaphor or what?"

"Yes. A metaphor. I don't want to be in charge."

"You're absolutely right. I'll figure everything out. I'll get you home, and then you're off the hook."

"That's not what I'm saying. I don't want either of us to be in charge. We've got to figure this out *together*, because the stakes are high for us both. I don't want to spend the rest of my life, or even a portion of it, behind bars."

"I did this for Jolene, so we could be together, and so she could be safe. If I go to prison, then it was all for nothing. I can't tell the cops the truth, because even if they believe that I didn't intentionally kill Zach, I'd still be charged with reckless homicide or manslaughter or—I have no idea. Do you think I should discuss it with Les Larson?"

"He's a divorce attorney."

"I could find a criminal one."

"That won't make you look guilty at all."

But she *was* guilty, and they were almost to Tamara's place, and they hadn't come up with a game plan, other than the original *stick-to-the-plan*, which had already gone so badly awry. "How long do you think it will take before they discover the body?"

"We hung the Do Not Disturb sign, so if we're lucky, they won't go in that room until he's supposed to check out—which is when?"

"Tomorrow. In the meantime, I should be texting him, calling him, to make it look like I'm trying to reach him. When the cops ask where we were today, we'll say we were at your house, lounging by the pool, drinking wine."

"And no matter what, no matter how hard it is to lie, we don't cave under pressure. We don't turn on each other."

"I would never," Holly said. "But I think we're going to need a different story about where we were today."

Tamara raised her eyebrows. "Why?"

"Because that's Detective Don Denton standing in your driveway."

* * *

Denton rapped on the car before Holly had even come to a complete stop. She killed the engine, and then buzzed the window down about an inch—no more than that. She didn't want him sticking his head in for a look around. Not with bags and two wigs tossed in the back seat. "What can I do for you, Detective?"

"Good afternoon, ladies." Denton's fingers barely fit in the gap in the window but he managed to wedge them inside. A tactic Holly didn't appreciate, and one that made her want to *accidentally* hit the "up" button.

"Is everything okay?" Tamara leaned toward the driver's side. "Burglary in the neighborhood? Or are you selling tickets to the policeman's ball."

"If you'd put down the window, Mrs. Bancroft, we could speak more easily."

"I'm getting out." Holly and Tamara exchanged a quick glance. No need to discuss strategy on one point; they both knew he shouldn't get a look in the back seat. "You'll move your fingers if you're fond of them."

He jerked his hand away, and Holly quickly buzzed up the tinted window, then the two women bolted from the car, with Holly literally knocking Denton back with the door. She leaned against it and reached behind her, casually touch locking it. "What are you doing here?"

"Aren't you going to introduce me to your friend?"

"Tamara Driscoll, Detective Don Denton—and vice versa. What's going on?" He didn't look like someone who'd come to tell a woman her husband had been found dead in a hotel room, but the possibility made her knees watery. It was too soon. She wasn't ready. Until the police came knocking on her door with the news, she could still pretend this wasn't happening.

"I need to talk to you. And your mother-in-law said you'd be here, swimming. But you're not wet. Or in the backyard. Where have you been?"

"Gosh, do I need a lawyer because we decided to go to the mall instead of the backyard?"

"Which mall?"

"Kierland Commons." The upscale shopping area surely

had security cameras, but it was a massive collection of outdoor shops. It would be nearly impossible to prove they *hadn't* been there.

"Are your bags in the car?"

"Pardon?" Tamara's eyes widened.

"Your shopping bags."

"We didn't buy anything." Holly shrugged. "I just can't seem to find anything that flatters my figure since the baby."

"Oh, I thought everything looked good on you, sweetie." Tamara smiled at her and then turned to Denton. "She's too hard on herself. She looks fabulous, doesn't she?"

He flushed and shifted his feet. Somehow, working together, they'd gotten him off balance. They made a good team. "You said you need to talk; is this going to be a formal interview? Should I meet you at the station? I don't want to take anymore of Tamara's time."

"I should've said I want to talk to *both* of you. We can do it at the station, or inside, ladies' choice."

THIRTY-SEVEN

From her perch on a high-back green suede armchair in Tamara's living room, Holly crossed one leg over the other, twisted it around her ankle and dug her nails into her palms. Meanwhile, Tamara leaned back against the sofa, arms relaxed at her side, her forehead unwrinkled—though the credit for the latter probably went to Botox.

Denton circled the room, taking in the photos and mementos before dragging another armchair near Holly's and plopping down in it with his legs stretched, nearly touching hers.

"Feel free to rearrange my furniture." Tamara smirked.

"Sorry, just wanted to make sure we could all hear each other, and I've got some things to show you in a minute, so we need to be close."

"Uh-huh. I'd offer you coffee or tea, but I'm afraid if I leave the room you'll have redecorated by the time I get back."

He met Tamara's gaze. "Mrs. Driscoll, I worry we've gotten off on the wrong foot. I do apologize about moving the chair. I'll put it back if you like."

"No." Tamara softened her expression. "I shouldn't have snapped at you. It's just that I'm feeling a bit protective of my friends. I'm well aware you've questioned both Holly and Zach about that poor medical student, Claudia Keeler, and at one point you even considered Zach a suspect in a different case."

"He's just doing his job, Tam." The mention of Claudia Keeler and Beth Gunther took the vinegar out of Holly. Those women deserved justice, and while she didn't want Denton digging up dirt on *her*, she wouldn't mind seeing him solve their murders one bit. In fact she'd be downright thrilled if he did. "I'm happy to answer your questions, as always, Detective, but I must say I'm curious why you want to include Tamara."

"Routine. I think she can shed some light on certain matters."

"Happy to do what I can." Tamara pushed a lock of her hair out of her eyes and tucked it behind an ear. "Ask me anything."

Denton nodded. "I see from all these photos how close you and your husband, Tom, were to the Bancrofts."

"*Were?* You're aware my husband was killed in a car crash, then?"

"It came up in a different interview. I'm sorry for your loss."

"Thank you. And yes, the four of us were quite close. Tom and Zach were best friends."

"And you and Holly? Would you consider her to be your best friend, as well?"

Holly was interested to hear Tamara's response to that. She'd take her cue from her regarding their relationship and how much to reveal to Denton.

"Yes. Before Tom died we were friends, but not like Tom and Zach. Since Tom died, though, we've become almost like sisters."

"So that's how you met? Through your husbands."

Whether it was his plan or not, Denton's line of questioning was lowering Holly's defenses. It seemed innocuous. What did it matter how they became friends? "No. Tamara and I met at the gym we both belong to. We started chatting and hanging out, and then we discovered we had a lot in common—it turned out we both went to the same high school. I didn't realize it at first because she was a year behind me."

"I knew who she was, though," Tamara put in.

Holly wished she hadn't said that, but if Denton had done his homework, he would already know her story.

"You mean you knew Holly because of the fire?" Denton asked.

Tamara nodded. "Yes. The entire school knew what had happened, and who she was. Anyway, we started spending time together after our Pilates class and one day, over coffee, Holly mentioned her husband's best friend was single and quite a catch. She suggested a double date and the rest is history, as they say."

Out came the notebook. Denton scrawled for a minute or two before looking up again. "So you two were casual friends, and then you met and married the best friend of Holly's husband, and got closer, even more so since Tom's death. Have I got it right?"

"I'd say so. But I don't understand what this has to do with, well, anything," Holly said.

"I'm just trying to elucidate the relationships here. Trying to determine exactly how close the two of you are. Would you say, Mrs. Driscoll, that you'd be willing to lie for your best friend?"

Tamara leaned forward and looked Denton directly in the eye. "I love Holly like a sister, and if my sister needed me to lie for her, say, for instance, to tell her boss she was sick when she wasn't, I'd do it without hesitation. But if my sister had something to do with a murder, or the cover up of one, I would have to rat her out. Is that what you want to know?"

"Exactly."

Suddenly, Holly got her vinegar back. What kind of game was Denton playing? "Are you saying I'm an official suspect in the murder of Claudia Keeler?"

"I'm saying I'd like you to answer some more questions on the subject. Were you aware of an affair between your husband and Ms. Keeler."

"I told you the last time you questioned me there was no affair. Not to my knowledge."

"Were you aware of the *rumors* he was involved with the young woman?"

Holly hesitated, tried to catch her breath. It was one thing to say the thought never occurred to her, but what if he asked Tamara the same question? After all, Holly had told Tamara she was *sure* there'd been an affair. And what if Denton talked to some of the other ladies in their circle? Was it plausible to deny she'd heard gossip? "Never. If there are rumors, I haven't heard them. Certainly not from my friends."

"What about you, Mrs. Driscoll? Did you know of or hear rumors about an affair between Dr. Bancroft and Ms. Keeler?"

"Yes." Tamara was so good at eye contact. It made everything she said seem genuine. "But I haven't been able to bring myself to repeat them to Holly." She shook her head, slightly. "I'm sorry, sweetie. I should've told you. I feel awful about your finding out like this, but rumors are just rumors. I have no idea if they're true or not."

"We believe them to be true. Ms. Keeler was found wearing an aquamarine ring, and we've been able to trace its purchase. Dr. Bancroft bought the ring on March third. If I'm not mistaken that's the day your daughter was born, isn't it, Mrs. Bancroft?" Denton spoke casually, as if he hadn't just told a woman her husband was not only cheating, but he'd bought his mistress an expensive gift on the day his wife gave birth.

Holly wanted to vomit, but she'd emptied her stomach back at the hotel, and she needed to *think* before reacting.

If this were the first inkling she'd had about an affair, she should seem devastated. On the other hand, Denton himself had made the accusation during an earlier interview, so if she acted *too* surprised that wouldn't ring true, either. In the end she decided just to be real. Her emotions were running high, and even if she tried to pretend all was right with the world she wouldn't be able to pull it off. Zach, if Denton was to be believed, had purchased an expensive ring for his lover on the day their daughter was born. He must've done it, she supposed, when he'd left the hospital for a few hours to allow her to "get some rest". And then, that same lover had come to Holly's home and sat with her while she cared for her newborn daughter, deliberately flaunting the ring in her face. Holly had killed her own husband, and it was only a matter of hours before his body was discovered. If she was tried and convicted of his murder, it would be her innocent, angelic Jolene who would pay the highest price. Her eyes stung with tears. Her mouth quivered. "I-I don't know what to say. I'm stunned, really and I don't feel good. I'd like to stop, now."

"I have a few more questions, first."

"Can't you see she's in shock? Her lips are white. She should lie down."

"I'm sorry, but a young woman is dead—two young women, in fact—and there's a murderer out there who could kill again, so no, it cannot wait until everyone's feeling chipper again." He bumped his chair closer to Holly and the coffee table. "Are you planning to flee, Mrs. Bancroft?"

She felt her head snap back, like he'd clipped her jaw with his words. "Of course not."

"But you asked your friend, Mrs. Driscoll, to obtain a fake ID for you. Several copies, in fact according to the records we've obtained from the company." Denton pulled out a manila envelope and placed it on the table between them. "And Mrs. Driscoll did so. She paid for the IDs and had them mailed to her home address."

Holly's hand flew to her throat.

He removed a photocopy from the envelope. "That's your picture on this driver's license, isn't it? But that's not your name or address."

It was definitely one of her fake IDs. The ones she'd hidden so carefully from Zach.

"When did you purchase these for your friend, Mrs. Driscoll?" He held up his hand. "Oh, wait I have it right here. You ordered these *before* Ms. Keeler was murdered. So that tells me your friend was planning a getaway. The only question is why?"

Holly's head was light, and she could hardly breathe, much less speak.

"Don't be ridiculous," Tamara said. "Those are nothing more than novelty items. Gag gifts for our white elephant parties with the girls. And by the way, there's nothing illegal about ordering them or possessing them."

"That's true," Denton said, then turned back to Holly. "But if you use them to commit a crime, that *is* illegal."

She gave her chest a soft punch, forcing out a breath, which allowed her to inhale again, taking in precious oxygen that fed her heart and cleared the fog from her brain. Denton was cagey, but she wasn't going to let him get the better of her. She refused to faint in front of him. And she didn't kill Claudia Keeler, which was the only murder he seemed to be accusing her of at the moment. She drew herself up tall in her chair and, following Tamara's example, looked him in the eye. "I haven't used them for a crime, and I obviously haven't tried to flee. I'm sitting right here in front of you without a lawyer answering all your bogus questions. The IDs are a joke. That's it."

But how the hell had he found out about them?

Had he searched Tamara's computer? He couldn't do that without a warrant, and if he had, *that* would be illegal. "Where did you get that photocopy?"

"We found the fake ID in Ms. Keeler's apartment. Would you care to explain?"

In Claudia's apartment? Impossible.

"I can't," she snapped, as her mind began spinning theories. Did Zach find it and put it there? Was he trying to frame her for murder? Or had Claudia been back to the house? Did *she* find the ID and steal it for some reason—maybe to show it to Zach in an attempt to persuade him to leave Holly?

"How did your fake ID, the one that Mrs. Driscoll obtained for you surreptitiously, get into a murdered student's apartment?" he asked again.

"We're done here." Tamara held out her wrists. "Arrest us or leave."

Denton kept his eyes on Holly. "Are you refusing to answer my questions, Mrs. Bancroft?"

"Go ahead. Arrest us." Holly was on her feet, wrists out in front, in solidarity with Tamara.

"Not today," Denton said.

"That's what I thought." Her body shook from the adrenaline raging through it. "You couldn't possibly have found that ID in Claudia Keeler's apartment. You're *lying.* You're fishing in the dark because you don't know what happened to that poor woman. I wish you well going forward with your investigation, and I hope you catch her killer, I really do. But the next time you ask me questions, I want my lawyer to be present."

And she very well might need one. Because if they checked the records of the hotel in Tucson after finding Zach's body, they'd learn that the room next him had been rented by someone using the same name as the one on the fake ID found in Claudia Keeler's apartment. The only hope she had, now, was to keep to the plan she and Tamara had agreed upon. Act as if they had no knowledge of Zach's death. Holly wished they had left a suicide note near his body, confessing to the murder of Claudia Keeler—that's what a cold-hearted murderer would've done.

Too bad her heart wasn't yet frozen solid.

THIRTY-EIGHT

Last night, Holly had barely slept, and all she wanted to do now was curl up and cry while she waited for the cops to come knocking on her door—but Tamara had other ideas. So here she was in the parking lot of the Goldfinch Golf Club Grill, leaning against her gray Tesla, while, at the opposite end of the lot, Tamara leaned against her white Mercedes Sports Coupe. Both women had phones pressed to their ears. Up ahead, Lindsey and Audra descended from their golf cart at the edge of the greens, their gesticulations suggesting an argument. Lindsey virtually always accused Audra of cheating (and vice versa) but that never stopped them from lunching together or golfing again the following week.

"I don't think this is a great idea," Holly complained to Tamara via phone. This was the only chance she'd have to speak to Tamara before the gang sat down to brunch at the Goldfinch. "I shouldn't be here. Audra and Lindsey are going to know something's up. I'm no Jennifer Lawrence."

"You don't have to be. I'll meet you at the table." Tamara started for the outdoor restaurant, located at the edge of the golf course.

Holly touched her door to lock it, then dutifully marched toward the patio dining area, a desert oasis surrounded by the lush golf greens, its borders defined by flowerbeds filled with yellow marigolds and bright-orange penstemon. "You said we have to 'act normal'—that's why we agreed to meet them for brunch. But Audra and Lindsey are going to ask questions. And I'm *not* a good liar."

"Oh, I don't know. You did a pretty good job lying to me about Tom, as I recall."

Holly resisted the temptation to snap back. "I deserved that, but I thought we agreed we weren't going to let the stress make us turn on each other. And as you know, I might have lied in the beginning—"

"*Might* have lied?" Tamara's voice crackled over the airwaves.

"Okay, I definitely lied, but my point is I couldn't keep on lying to you. Just a few days after I found out, I broke down and told you what Zach did to Tom, and I'm worried I'm going to somehow break down and let something slip about Zach to the girls."

"This is totally different. You won't slip up. There's too much at stake for both of us. I know you're scared, but I have a plan."

"We're less than one minute from go time—if you have a plan I'd like to hear it now."

"Confide in us girls, just like you normally would. Your husband isn't answering your calls, so how weird will it seem, later on, if you haven't cried on our shoulders? And if they don't find the body soon—the conference ends today, right? You're going to have to report him missing. I'm sure that won't be necessary, but let's lay the groundwork, now, just in case."

Yet she didn't need acting skills? "Got it." She hung up and slipped her phone in her purse.

"Holly!" Audra motioned her to a table set for four beneath

a long cedar pergola, and then offered her the chair with the best view of the greens. "Sit here. We see you so rarely these days you can be the guest of honor."

Lindsey plopped down on her left, leaving Audra and Tamara, who'd just arrived, sitting opposite. Holly had to lean to one side to make eye contact with Tamara above a centerpiece of red gerbera daisies. Tamara suddenly stood and marched the pretty, yet obstructive, flower vase over to an empty table, then returned to her seat. "That's better. How's everybody been?"

Holly shifted, pointedly looking to Audra. "I'm dying to hear all about the new beau. You met him online?"

Holly could feel Tamara's eyes burning a hole in the side of her head, but she refused to acknowledge her. She was determined to get Audra, who had quite the gift of gab, talking, and Audra did not disappoint.

Apparently she could speak *forever* on the subject of online dating, pausing just long enough to order when their server stopped by.

"Meet 'em and street 'em. Not that you two—" Audra paused and glanced from Lindsey to Holly "—need the tips, but it's past time Tamara dipped her toe in the dating pool again."

"Do tell?" Tamara smiled and sipped the water the server had brought over when he took their order.

"Meet 'em quick, then make a decision. That's key. Trust me. You do *not* want to carry on a protracted online relationship beforehand. I learned that the hard way. One dude and I emailed for months, and then when we finally got together, there was no spark. Not for me, anyway, and when I turned down a second date, it was as bad as breaking up with a long-time boyfriend. Never again. That's when I came up with my rule: If he won't meet after two emails, I'm out. I treat finding a man like a full-time job, because that's what it is." Audra leaned back in her chair, as if exhausted by a hard day's work.

"I'll keep that in mind the next time I *don't* sign up for a dating app." Tamara laughed.

"So have you met someone special or not?" Holly didn't want to let the topic go, afraid of where the subject would turn next.

Lindsey rolled her eyes and waved at the server. "If Audra's going to start in on her stories about the widowed ophthalmologist I'm going to need a Cosmopolitan."

"Let's all have one," Tamara suggested. "The four of us haven't gotten together since Kandel's, and I feel like celebrating."

"Are you in, Holly, or are you still nursing?" Audra asked.

"I can pump and dump." One drink wouldn't hurt, and it might take the edge off.

The busboy headed over with a giant tray containing their food order.

Eventually, Lindsey would lose patience with Audra's babbling, and then it would be Holly's turn to dish.

She couldn't dodge this bullet forever.

Nothing screams *I killed my husband* like not complaining about him to your girlfriends.

And sure enough, halfway through her shrimp salad, Lindsey threw up her hands. "Audra, you talk too damn much. Did you ever think other people might have things to say?"

"Well, that's rude. Holly asked me a question."

"Twenty minutes ago. You've been yapping so long the rest of us are almost done with our lunch, and you haven't even touched yours."

"Maybe I do talk a lot but—"

"Maybe?"

"So what? At least I don't cheat at golf."

"Are you kidding me? You moved your ball three inches. I *saw* you."

"I have to do something to compensate for the strokes you forget to count."

"Stop!" Tamara waved her white cloth napkin in the air. "Or I'm never meeting you two after golf again. *Ever*. And Audra, for the record, you ought to shut up once in a while and give other people a chance. Have you thought about setting a timer?"

"Nice." Audra pushed out her lips in a pout, but then she tipped her head back and laughed. "The widowed ophthalmologist says talking is my superpower. *He* adores listening to me. But I would like to know what's going on with Holly. I never heard what happened after we bought that baby monitor off Craigslist and tried to pass it off as the original. I'm assuming it fooled Zach since Holly's not six feet under."

Lindsey widened her eyes, sending Audra an admonishing look. "Don't be stupid."

"I was only joking."

A bite of shrimp caught in Holly's throat, and she coughed into her napkin. The subtext was plain—her husband was a possible suspect in a murder investigation, and everyone at this table was more than aware. They simply hadn't gotten around to broaching the subject yet. "Oh, yeah, no, I got away clean. Zach was totally fooled by the substitute baby monitor. And I still owe Audra some cash."

"That's not why I brought it up," Audra said. "I can wait however long it takes for you to pay me back."

"Has Zach loosened the reins on the bank account, then?" Lindsey popped an olive in her mouth.

Holly's shoulders relaxed. These women might be nosy, but they were rooting for her, and they'd be easily led because they were motivated to believe her. "I'm back in business, ladies. Credit cards, debit cards, checkbook, you name it. Typical Zach; he went from one extreme to the other. Suddenly, he'll do anything to please me."

"Well done, you," Lindsey said.

Tamara narrowed her eyes at Holly signaling that this was the moment. "So everything's great at home? He's not stressed about that student he was mentoring, the one whose body they found in the hospital morgue?"

Holly took a swig of her pomegranate Cosmo, letting its syrupy sweetness slide down her throat to coat the lies. "Naturally, he's upset, but he didn't know her all that well. The relationship was strictly professional."

Audra and Lindsey leaned forward, and Holly suddenly understood this was what they'd been waiting for. She hadn't been the only one playing a part today.

"I heard the police questioned him," Audra said.

"Who told you that?" Holly asked.

"Craig Paulson. I went for drinks with the guy, and all he talked about was poor Claudia Keeler and how suspicious it seems that *two* of Zach's students have now been murdered."

Holly stuck her chin up. What would an indignant wife say? "Craig Paulson is a horrible man who's jealous of Zachary being department chair. What did you say?"

Audra straightened her back. "I told him he was full of crap. I reminded him a vagrant killed that first student, and then I said Zach was a friend, and I know for a fact he wouldn't harm a fly. He spends his time saving lives, not taking them, and that he, Craig, I mean, was no friend to Zach if he went around implying whatever the hell he was trying to imply."

"Thank you." Holly dabbed nonexistent tears from her eyes, feeling bad about the charade on the one hand, and glad it was so easy to deceive on the other. People see what they want to see. Later, if Detective Denton questioned Audra and Lindsey, they would probably recall genuine tears in her eyes.

"Go on. Tell her," Lindsey prompted.

"What?" Holly asked. "What else?"

"Nothing..." Audra lowered her gaze. "Except... well, Craig

said he wasn't Zach's friend. He said he knew him, of course, from work, but he tried to avoid him whenever possible because... and I'm just repeating what he said, mind you..."

"Spit it out," Tamara said.

"He said 'Zachary Bancroft is a skirt chaser and a pathological liar'. And that's when I dumped my beer on him. The jerk deserved it."

Holly gasped and covered her mouth. Partly for show, but partly because of the shock of hearing the truth about Zach from Craig Paulson, albeit third-hand. It always amazed her to learn there were other people—objective, reasonable people—who could see through Zach's façade and weren't afraid to say so.

Audra reached for her hand and patted it. "No one who knows Zach believes he had anything to do with those murders. It's so unfair the hospital put him on leave."

Well, well. Apparently, courtesy of Craig Paulson, Audra knew more about Zach than Holly did. He hadn't mentioned one word about a leave of absence. So how long ago was that, and where had Zach been going when he left the house every day? "Th-thank you," Holly stuttered. "This is just so hard."

"What can we do to help?" Lindsey asked. "How's Zach holding up?"

"I'm sure he'll get through it, but, can I be totally honest?"

"Yes!" the women said in unison.

"Vegas rules?" she whispered.

"What happens at the Goldfinch stays at the Goldfinch," Tamara was whispering too. "We won't breathe a word to anyone. Whatever's going on, you can trust us."

"Okay, but this stays in the vault." She pulled out her phone and passed around the thread of messages she'd been sending to Zach since returning from Tucson. All of them unanswered, of course. "He left for a conference in Tucson earlier in the week and, in the beginning, everything was great. We talked on the phone almost an hour that night, and he texted me pics of the hotel buffet. I don't know why, but he loves to send me pictures of food."

This time there were actual tears brimming in her eyes. As awful as the past months had been, she'd loved Zach, once. And without him, she wouldn't have Jolene.

She took a breath, refusing to give grief any room in her heart—she couldn't afford to. "I'm rambling. Sorry. I'm just so worried because after those buffet pics he stopped responding to my texts and calls. Ladies, I'm afraid it's official. My husband is ghosting me."

"That's not like Zach." Tamara shook her head.

"Are we talking about the same Zach who calls ten times when we go to the mall? The one who won't leave you in peace?" Lindsey asked.

"I don't understand what I did wrong." She sniffled. "We've been so happy lately. I don't know if it's me or if he just needs space because of all the pressure from the police. He was *very* upset about being put on leave." She'd gotten so good at deception she was now incorporating facts she'd only just learned.

"You don't think he's… met someone else, do you?" Audra grimaced. "Things happen when men are out of town."

"Have you called the hotel? Checked to be sure he's really registered there?" Lindsey asked.

"No, but I can see the location of his phone on my app, and he's definitely at the hotel. He's due home today, so I think the best thing to do is wait it out and confront him when he comes back. I don't want to seem like I'm desperate for reassurance— even though I am. He's the one who should be chasing after me."

"Damn straight," Lindsey said. "Show him a backbone and ghost him right back."

Holly let out a shuddering sigh. "I've tried but I just can't hold out. I miss him too much. You don't think anything's happened to him, do you? I've been wondering if I should have someone from the hotel check on him. Or maybe I should call the police."

Tamara drummed her fingers.

Audra and Lindsey exchanged a look.

"That seems like a bad idea," Audra said. "After that ransom note incident Zach already thinks you overreact. And frankly, I think you might be doing just that. He's at a medical conference. He's busy. He's a *man*. My advice is to give him his space. There's nothing to worry about. He'll be home tonight safe and sound. You mark my words."

THIRTY-NINE

Another sleepless night for Holly, and still nothing on the news about Zach.

No word from the police about finding a body, even though he should've checked out of his hotel yesterday morning.

Frances had called, concerned, and Holly felt duty-bound to rush over to her house, so now, Jolene lay on her back in a playpen, set up in Frances' den, batting at tiny stuffed lambs floating in a circle above her head. But even the sound of delighted baby squeals and the soft strains of Brahms' "Lullaby" weren't enough to dispel the tension in the room.

Seated on a dark-brown corduroy couch, Holly deliberately rounded her shoulders and relaxed her jaw.

Frances sat opposite, back rigid, at the precipice of a matching chair. "This isn't like Zach at all. He ignored me for a while, after Christopher Creek, but these days he's back to his usual habit of calling me, without fail, every morning. And it's been two days, now, since I've heard from him."

Holly saw no legitimate way to dismiss Frances' concern but she gave it her best shot. "You know those conferences.

They keep him on the run. He doesn't even have time to eat a proper meal, so we can't expect him to call us every day."

"I thought that conference ended yesterday."

"It did, but I'm just pointing out…" What? "That explains why he didn't call before."

"Stop *handling* me," Frances bit out the words. "I'm not a child, and I don't need your coddling."

"I'm sorry." More than Frances could possibly know. "You're right. I'm worried, too. And I don't know why he didn't come home yesterday, or why he's not answering our calls and texts. The only thing I can think of is that something came up, and he's simply been too busy, or…" She paused and took a breath. "He might be angry with me."

"Did you argue? I thought things were going so well between you."

"They were—they are. But you know how sensitive he is; sometimes little things set him off, and he doesn't speak to me for a few days. It's doesn't happen a lot, but it wouldn't be the first time." She pulled her bottom lip between her teeth, considering. This was good practice for the police. Things were getting to the point they might want her to explain why she hadn't reported him missing.

Although, in her mind, it might be time to do exactly that. She needed to sit down with Tamara and figure out next steps. Zach's body should've been found by now, since he'd missed his checkout. And Holly ought to have been notified right away. It wasn't as if they'd have trouble identifying the body or locating next of kin.

"All I can think is the last time we spoke on the phone, I mentioned that I wanted to go back to school next year. Start working on my master's degree in speech, and he definitely didn't like that idea."

Frances lifted one eyebrow. "Really? With Jolene still in diapers."

"Just a few classes. And I can do a lot of it online."

Her lips turned down in an exaggerated frown. "I see why he'd object to your going back to school since, obviously, if you're wanting a master's you're intending to go back to work. You should've told me this before. I'm *positive* he's mad at you. And, yes, I do know how he gets. But why is he ignoring *my* calls?" Her brows lifted even higher, opening up her eyes and wrinkling her forehead. "You didn't drag me into it, did you?"

Holly grimaced. She hated how easily the lies came these days. It was a habit she was determined to break once Zach's death was declared an accidental overdose or suicide, and she didn't have to worry about going to prison. "The truth is, I might have suggested you'd probably be willing to help out by watching Jolene, that we wouldn't need daycare, and then he jumped to the conclusion you and I had already discussed it."

"Oh boy. He still hasn't gotten over me siding with you after *the incident*—when I brought Jolene home before he thought you were ready. He might claim it was fine with him, but I know better. He keeps bringing it up out of nowhere, needling me about it and saying things like *whose side are you on anyway*? Even though I've made it perfectly clear I'm on his side... unless it conflicts with what's best for Jolene..." She threw up her hands. "That's it. He's ghosting us. Have I got the term right?"

"Mm hmm."

"And I suppose he might be bunking at the hospital in one of those on-call rooms."

Knowing he'd been put on leave, Holly didn't dare pretend to go along with that one. "I suppose he might; even though he's not on duty, he does have access. But my money's on the Four Seasons—I bet he's hitting the links at a nearby course even as we speak."

"Let's call the golf courses!" Frances' face brightened, and Holly could see she'd convinced her.

She had to talk to Tamara about reporting Zach missing. Keeping her mother-in-law bouncing between fear and hope was cruel. It was hard enough to look herself in the mirror as it was.

"I've got a better idea. If you don't mind watching Jolene, I'll go down to his favorite courses in person. I'll check Troon, and if I don't find him, I'll try the Goldfinch and Silverleaf—and then I'll hit every luxury hotel in town. Eventually I'm bound to find him, and when I do, I'll set the record straight. Explain you never agreed to help me with my plans to get my master's degree."

"You don't have to tell him that. I love watching Jolene, and he'll eventually get over it. But just find him, please. I need to know for sure that he's safe. It doesn't matter how old he is, Holly. Zach will *always* be my baby."

"See you soon." Holly hung up the Bluetooth and hit the accelerator. She was meeting Tamara at her house later, and she wanted to follow through on her promise to visit some golf courses and hotels first. Otherwise it would seem fishy she hadn't bothered to check.

A glance in the rearview mirror made her squirm. That blue Corvette had been behind her since she'd pulled out of Frances' drive, and now it seemed to be matching her speed. Naturally, she was on edge. Anyone would be under the circumstances. It was easy to get paranoid, imagine she was being followed, and if this guy was tailing her, he wasn't a professional. He was so close, if she put her foot on the brake, the nose of his fancy sports car would be sniffing her perfume from the back seat.

She mashed the accelerator.

The Corvette's engine revved and roared, and then the driver changed lanes, passing her on a curve. This stretch of

Tatum wound through desert on either side, and the speed limit was 50 mph. But she was doing 70 mph so he must be doing...

Dammit!

He swerved in front of her and slowed to a crawl.

She switched lanes, eyeing the inhospitable desert terrain on either side of the road.

He sped up and pulled in front of her again.

There was no mistaking what was happening.

Road rage.

But what had she done? She hadn't cut him off. Regardless, the best thing to do was to get away from him. If she changed lanes and sped up, that would only continue the game, but if she slowed down, dropped back, he'd likely declare victory and move on. She let up on the accelerator, which had to be aggravating to the cars behind her, but she was in the slow lane, now, and they could always pass.

Moments later, she breathed out a relieved sigh. The Corvette had zoomed off into the distance, but when she came around the curve she saw it again—at a near stop in her lane, just ahead.

She slammed on the brake, swerving right. Her Tesla jolted, and her teeth clattered as it rolled to a stop, half on the soft shoulder and half in the desert. A foot more and she would've had a giant saguaro on her hood. At least her misadventure hadn't triggered the airbags to deploy.

Gripping the wheel, she put her chin down, willing herself to stop shaking.

She shifted into reverse and heard the whir of tires spinning in the dirt.

She got out, walked around to check the tire situation, and then cursed her stupidity.

The blue Corvette pulled up on the shoulder, and before she could get back inside her car, the driver jumped out, blocking her.

He was tall, over six feet, and older. Seventies maybe. "Holly Bancroft?"

The man's voice had a disquieting familiarity to it. Normally, she wouldn't fear a man his age, but he was in decent shape, he'd just forced her off the road, and he might have a gun on him—in Arizona it was legal for anyone over twenty-one to carry a concealed firearm, and a lot of people did. Plus, there was something weird she couldn't put her finger on. Did she know him from somewhere?

"I'm Russell Bancroft."

Zach's father! She should've known it from that strong chin, those ice-blue eyes. "You ran me off the road."

"Technically, maybe, but I thought those Teslas had autopilot that would prevent accidents. I thought the car would steer itself to the side of the road and stop itself easy-peasy."

Her hands had formed into fists at her side. She relaxed them and, trying to de-escalate, said, "You're giving my car way too much credit."

"It worked, though, didn't it?"

She slowly, so as not to spook him, raised one hand to shade her eyes from the glaring sun. "What do you want?"

"Where's my boy?"

"Beg pardon?" Since when was Zach his *boy*? The man had been out of his life forever—except for that one encounter just before Jolene was born. Had there been more since? Is that where Zach had been off to when he was supposedly working? And here Holly had been speculating Zach had been meeting his lover.

"Where's my son?"

She had no idea what to say—it was hard to think on her feet when her mind was still reeling from a near accident.

"He was supposed to meet me for lunch yesterday."

Apparently there *had* been more contact. "So he stands you

up and you decide to run his wife off the road. What if the baby had been in the car?"

"I knew she wasn't. I followed you from Frances' house. I thought he might show up there, but he didn't. I've been calling him for days. I'm starting to get very worried."

The adrenaline rush was wearing off and her muscles suddenly went weak. She sagged against the side of the car, and felt the heat of it through the fabric of her blouse. "I don't know what to say. You're not part of his life. You're not part of our lives."

"I'm entitled to know where my son is." He stepped close, a mean look in his eyes.

A look that reminded her a little too much of Zach. "I don't know where he is. I'm trying to figure that out right now. So if you'll let me get back in my car, I can get on with it."

"Have you called the police?"

"Not yet."

Another step toward her. She could smell tobacco on his breath. "I expect you to keep me in the loop. And just so you know, I'm back for real. Zach and I have come to an understanding, and I am going to be part of my granddaughter's life from here on out."

Like hell you will.

There was absolutely no way Holly was going to let him bully her like his son had, or come near Jolene. "So after all this time you suddenly want to be part of Zach's life? You're suddenly interested in family?"

"At my age, you start to look back and wonder what you've missed. Jolene's my blood."

"And you would know, wouldn't you? Because you're the one who planted a seed of doubt in Zach's mind before she was born. You're the one who told him to get a DNA test to be sure she was his—to be sure she was *your* blood."

"A man's entitled to know."

"You keep using that word. Well, you're not *entitled* to a damn thing." She drew up to her full height of five feet four inches and poked her finger at his chest. "I'm not afraid of you, Russell, but you should be afraid of me. *Very* afraid."

"Oh yeah?"

She shoved him, and he stumbled out of her way. "Stay out of our lives. You come near *anyone* in my family, and that includes Frances, and I *will* make you regret it." Then she climbed in her Tesla and slammed the door, punched the SOS button and summoned roadside assistance.

FORTY

A sudden storm, a monsoon, was threatening and, outside, the thunder rumbled. The wind picked up, lashing against Holly's kitchen windows, and even though it was early evening, the sky was dark, the room shadowed.

Still no word about Zach.

She flipped on the lights.

Paced circles around the breakfast nook.

Every instinct Holly had screamed at her to pick up the phone, call Detective Denton, and report Zach missing, but she wasn't going to do that—she was going to stick to the plan. She couldn't lose her nerve now.

There is no other way.

Jolene's soft whimpers, streaming across the baby monitor, melted her heart and, at the same time, steeled her nerve.

She would do whatever was necessary to protect her daughter.

It was past time for her feeding, but Jolene still slumbered, even if somewhat fitfully, and Holly didn't intend to wake her. Jolene's first tooth had finally cut through her swollen gums, and she seemed peaceful, less restless than she had been all week.

Was it possible Jolene might sleep another hour?

Holly opened the cupboard and pulled down a box of chamomile tea—Tamara's favorite—relishing the extra quiet time, determined to banish her worries if only for a moment.

Keep calm. Focus.

Tamara would be there any minute.

The rain was coming down now, pelting the glass pane of the kitchen door, and Holly touched her heart, aware of its erratic thumping.

A sudden strike of lightning illuminated a palm pressed against the pane.

Holly jumped as a bolt of thunder rumbled through her, and then she jerked open the kitchen door.

Bringing the scent of wet earth with her, Tamara rushed inside, her damp hair hanging limply over her ears, her eyes bracketed with tight worry lines.

Holly clapped a hand over her heart. "I just about came out of my skin. Why didn't you come around to the front?"

"I didn't mean to startle you. But I figured you might be in the kitchen, and I didn't want to ring the bell in case Jolene was sleeping." Tamara unbuttoned her faux leather bomber's jacket, beaded with moisture, and draped it over the back of a chair, then took a seat at the breakfast table. "I *almost* beat the downpour."

Holly's heart ping-ponged around in her chest for a few seconds, but then settled into a less disturbing rhythm. If Tamara could meet the moment with calm, so could Holly. "I was going to make tea. Would you like some? I've got chamomile."

"Sure. Have you heard from the police?"

She crumpled into the chair opposite Tamara. "No. That's weird—bad weird, right? How is it possible they haven't found his body yet? Zach's conference ended yesterday. He was due back last night."

"I'm sure it's something simple. Like he booked an extra day and didn't tell you, so he wasn't due to checkout, and that's why he hasn't been found."

"His mother's asking about him—she's worried. I should be worried, too. How will it look if I don't notify the police or at least call the hotel?"

Tamara stuck her elbows on the table and clasped her hands. "Don't do it. Not yet."

"But don't you think, once they do find the body, the police will think it's suspicious I haven't reported him missing. The spouse is always a prime suspect."

"In a murder, sure. But Zach wasn't murdered. He overdosed—accidentally. That's how it will look. He's only a day late coming home. You've been texting him, and that story you told the girls at the Goldfinch was a good one. Stick with it. Be consistent."

"We should go over that story again." She stretched out her hand to Tamara. "And our mutual alibi, too. What if the police know he's dead? Maybe they found the body, and they suspect me of killing him, and now they're toying with me. Waiting for me to make a mistake and expose myself."

"It's not like on TV, honey. The cops aren't that clever. There's no rain-coated detective stumbling around with a cigar hanging out of his mouth while sniffing out the smallest of clues: *'Why did we find hamburger in his stomach if there was no room service tray or fast-food wrapper? This means it was no accident! He had to have had company. Deadly company. The killer drugged him and then hid the room service tray to make it appear our victim dined alone. Eureka! Find the tray and you'll have your murderer!'*"

She forced a smile. "I suppose that would be too clever by far."

At least on TV justice always prevailed. But this was real life, where innocent people got thrown in jail all the time and rich psychopaths with good lawyers walked free.

"I have to admit, though, I never thought hanging a Do Not Disturb sign on a doorknob would be all it took to keep a body from being discovered. If this goes on much longer it's going to start to smell," Tamara said.

Holly choked back the bile rising in her throat. The "it" Tamara had just referred to was her husband's corpse. Zach was the father of her baby. A sudden cry from Jolene and, at once, Holly's milk let down, soaking through the front of her T-shirt. She rose on her haunches, holding her breath, but a second cry did not follow the first. Only a soft gurgle. Jolene was self-soothing.

Thank goodness.

"Let's go over your story again," Tamara said.

Holly relaxed back into the chair and met Tamara's eyes. "You're pretty wet. Why not dry off while I make tea? And then we'll talk—we'll rehearse all night if we have to."

* * *

By the time Tamara returned from the powder room she no longer looked like a rat that had recently emerged from a river. She looked beautiful. Her naturally curly hair was doing its thing—framing her face with golden waves. Her green eyes glowed.

From adrenaline?

It wasn't in Holly's DNA to deceive, but this one last time, for the sake of her daughter, she could overcome her own nature. "Let's go through our story. I'm ready."

Tamara took the tea Holly had prepared for her, warming her hands on the cup. "Is this chamomile? Thanks."

"Of course." Holly stirred a spoonful of Stevia into her own cup.

"Zach was out of town for a conference. You two had been getting along well, but the stress of the investigation into Claudia's death was getting to him." Tamara clanked her spoon thoughtfully on the tabletop.

"He was terribly upset about being put on leave from the hospital. Without warning, and for no reason, he stopped answering my calls and texts." Holly paused. "And I could say I didn't want to mention him being out of town to the police because they cautioned both of us not to leave town. I was afraid it would cause him problems with the authorities."

"Good! I like that," Tamara said.

"So, the day that he started ghosting me, I cried on your shoulder. You and I spent the morning and afternoon together, shopping at Kierland, and then Detective Denton interviewed us at your house. And again—I didn't want to mention Zach being out of town to him, because Zach and I had been warned by Denton himself not to leave Phoenix. Zach should've been home yesterday, and I've been waiting to hash things out in person. I'm worried, of course, but it isn't the first time he's given me the silent treatment. In fact, it's his MO."

In synchrony, they took a shuddering breath, and at that very moment, Jolene let out another cry.

"Go." Tamara arched her brow and nodded toward Holly's milk-dampened T-shirt. "Feed the darling. Like you said, we've got all night."

Holly shook her head, though her arms were aching to comfort her daughter. "I want her to go back to sleep on her own. She's been learning to self-soothe."

Tamara brought her teacup to her lips, but set it down again. "Do you have any cookies?"

"Not unless you're up for teething biscuits."

At that, they both smiled.

Holly picked up her cup just as a powerful gust of wind flung open the kitchen door. Hot tea splashed, burning her arm.

Tamara's eyes went wide.

Holly followed her gaze and screamed—it wasn't the storm that had flung open the door.

There, at the kitchen threshold, lightning strikes crackling behind him like Frankenstein's monster, Zach towered, then lurched into the room—pointing a pistol straight at them.

FORTY-ONE

Holly felt triumphant as she faced Detective Denton for one last interview. As horrible and as terrifying as her ordeal had been, she'd survived.

She was alive.

And Jolene was *safe*.

Now, this detective, who'd looked at her with so much distrust, who'd said outright she needed a psychiatrist the first time he'd met her, understood that Holly wasn't crazy at all. She'd had every right to be fearful for her own welfare and her child's.

He must know this for certain, because, at this very moment, Zach and Tamara's dead bodies lay on her kitchen floor.

If that didn't prove her sanity, nothing did.

"First of all, I'm sorry for what you've been through," Denton said it gently, nudging a box of tissues toward her. He'd escorted her, not to an interrogation room, but to some sort of family area at the Scottsdale police station. The space was freshly painted and furnished with comfortable chairs, a coffee table and vending machine. She could see a camera lodged in the corner of the ceiling, and there was a microphone on the table. He'd asked her consent to be recorded and made clear she was under no obligation to answer questions. She was free to go at any time.

"Thank you." She pulled a tissue and kept it in her hand hoping the tears might come. When the first officer had arrived on scene she'd broken down, sobbed, hugged a perfect stranger until her arms ached—not from grief, but from relief. "I appreciate that. But I'm ready to answer your questions. I just want to get back to my daughter."

"Jolene's with your mother-in-law, correct?"

She nodded. Frances had been devastated to learn that Zach was dead, but even in her grief she'd come to the rescue, agreeing to keep Jolene while the police interviewed Holly.

Holly wrapped shaking arms around her waist, trying not to think about the pain she'd caused Frances. "That's right. Zach's mother doesn't know many details, yet. May I request you hold off on speaking to her until I can be present?"

He shuffled his feet beneath the desk. Cleared his throat. "I'm afraid we've got someone on the way out there now. But trust me, it's better that way. You don't want her to get her information from the news."

"Sure. I guess. But let's please take care of whatever you need quickly so I can go to her and Jolene."

"Just tell me in your own words what happened. I'll jump in when I have a question."

She breathed in, waiting for the words to rush out, but they didn't. This wasn't going to be as easy as she'd hoped. But she would get through it.

"You want a cup of tea?"

Hard pass. "I'd love a bottle of water." *And make sure it has a seal.*

Denton went to the vending machine and pulled a credit

card out of his own wallet. Brought her the water. She checked the seal. She couldn't help it. Then took a swig.

Just tell your story. You can do it.

"I had just sat down to tea with my best friend... with Tamara." He already knew Tamara was her best friend. She should stick to the important things. "Anyway, as you know, she and her husband, at one time, were very close with Zach and me. We often traveled together." She sipped her water and looked away. "I guess I should've been more on guard with such a beautiful woman spending so much time around my husband but, back then, I thought Zach and I had a great marriage. I had no reason to doubt him. Not ever—at least not until you told me Beth Gunther had been murdered. I admit that worried me, but then you arrested someone else so..."

"You never suspected him of cheating with Beth or with Claudia. Is that what you're saying?"

"I had some doubts after I found out they were missing. But only because *you* put those doubts in my mind. What I'm saying is it didn't occur to me that he'd been cheating until very recently, and never with *Tamara*." Her eyes burned, her throat tightened from the sting of betrayal. "But I learned, *today*, they were having an affair."

"And that's what precipitated the altercation in your kitchen."

"Yes. But it was so much more than a love triangle." She had to pause, gather her strength to keep going.

Denton's eyes seemed filled with compassion—so different from the way he'd looked at her, just two days ago.

"We were sitting down to a cup of tea, Tamara and me, when Zach came bursting in from outside. He'd been at a medical conference in Tucson, and he was a day late returning. Frankly, I'd been terribly worried about him, and it was a shock to see him storm in like that—he had a pistol in his hands." Obviously she wasn't going to admit to drugging him, or to mistakenly thinking she'd killed him, or that seeing him standing there, *not dead*, had given her the fright of her life. "He kept waving the gun. Yelling at me not to touch my tea."

"He didn't want you to drink the tea because..."

"He said Tamara told him that she planned to poison me with a combination of sleeping medicine and eye drops. I couldn't believe it, of course. I thought he was lying." She shuddered. "But I wasn't stupid enough to take a chance and drink that tea. Anyway, he kept ranting about Tamara, insisting she was a psychopath. He claimed *Tamara* was the one who killed Claudia and Beth, and that now she wanted to kill me."

"Why would she do that?"

"He told me, still waving his gun, that he'd had affairs with *all three* of them—with Tamara and Beth and Claudia. He said they meant nothing. That I was the one he loved, but that Tamara was out of her mind with jealousy."

"Go on."

"I was stunned. I didn't know what to do. At one point, Zach pointed the pistol at his temple, so I ran to him, begged him to give me the gun. But then, he turned it on Tamara. I knocked his arm down, and when I turned back around, I saw that *Tamara* had a pistol, too, and she was aiming it at *me*. That's when I knew Zach was telling the truth about her. Tamara was a murderer."

Holly put her head down. Her heart was beating so fast she could no longer speak. Her knees banged against the desk.

It took several minutes for her to compose herself enough to continue. "I-I was in shock. I had confided so much in her. I *trusted* her. And I froze. But not Zach. He lunged in front of me, shielding my body. I heard gunshots. Smelled smoke, and he fell on top of me, bleeding. Then his arm lifted, and I heard more shots." The tears began to flow. She couldn't stop them if she tried. "Zach shot Tamara before she could kill me, even though he was wounded. He had affairs, yes. But in the end, he gave his life for me."

Denton placed his elbows on the table, dragging his hands through his hair. "How many shots did you hear?"

Be careful. "I can't be one hundred percent sure, my ears were ringing, and I was terrified. Maybe three. Maybe four. It all happened so fast."

He nodded. "Fair enough. I'm glad you survived this, ma'am. The outcome could've been much worse. And if Tamara did draw a weapon and fire on you, then my assumption is that Zach was telling the truth. That Tamara killed the students, and then she must've planted the knife and ring on the vagrant. She certainly had access to the fake ID we found in Claudia's apartment. That sounds like she was trying to misdirect our attention onto you."

"Do you think she was really going to poison me?"

"There's one way to know for sure, we'll check the tea for toxins—you said Zach told you she was going to use eye drops to poison you?"

"Yes. And sleeping pills." She checked her watch. It was nearly midnight. Jolene usually woke up to nurse around one o'clock.

Denton reached across the table and put his hand near hers, without touching. "I'll get a statement typed up for you to sign tomorrow. The rapid swab we did on your hands was negative for gunshot residue, but the swabs from Tamara's and Zach's hands both came back positive—so that lines up with your account of events. If we do find toxins in the tea, I think we can wrap up the investigation into their deaths quickly. We'll need to look into the student murders more, but hopefully we can find evidence that connects Tamara to them now that we've homed in on her as a suspect. I haven't mentioned it before, but we have some additional DNA evidence in Beth's case, so we should be able to get a match to your friend and, as we speak, officers are at Tamara's home checking her wardrobe for a belt to match the patterned imprint around Claudia's neck—it appears she was strangled with a belt with distinctive markings. If what you're telling me is true, and frankly, I don't doubt that it is, the evidence will be forthcoming, and we'll be able to close all the cases." He pulled up his chin and met her gaze. "Mrs. Bancroft…"

"I think you can call me Holly, now."

"*Holly*, if you don't mind my adding a personal note, I think your instincts are good ones. I hope you'll always trust them. Don't ever let anyone—especially not someone like me, whose job it is to go hard at *everyone* until a case is solved—make you doubt yourself. I have no right to be, since you're not my daughter or my sister, but the truth is I'm proud of the way you handled yourself."

EPILOGUE

ONE MONTH LATER

Holly had an appointment to meet a realtor later that afternoon but first she needed to eliminate any evidence that might give away the truth about Zach and Tamara's deaths. She'd waited until all the cases, including Claudia and Beth's, were officially closed, but now it was time to get rid of everything. If the police ever found out what Holly had seen and heard on the nanny cam she'd planted in Zach's hospital office, her motive for murder would be clear.

Motive might not be evidence, but it could be damning just the same.

She sat at the back of the public library alone, safely hidden in a study room, staring at the gray carpet that had been tacked onto the walls for soundproofing. Frances was at home, watching Jolene, and Holly was supposed to be house hunting. With her only son dead and buried, Frances needed her family —Jolene and Holly were all she had left. They needed her, too, and not only because Holly planned to return to school for her master's degree. Frances was the one person Holly knew, for certain, would always be on Jolene's side, and she loved her for that.

Holly and Frances' relationship still had its kinks, its awkward moments, but Holly was confident, in time, those would melt away. The plan was for Frances to sell her house and move in with Holly and Jolene once Holly found a nice, comfortable place where the three of them could live without the stench of blood and the heartache of memories.

They'd been staying at Frances' house in the interim, since Zach's "passing"—that's how his mother referred to his violent death—and Holly also tried to use that term. Frances loved her son, like a mother should, and though she'd been forced to face some of his shortcomings during the course of the death investigation, Holly didn't feel the need to hammer her over and over with the facts: that he was a lying, cheating, sack of dirt who'd gotten exactly what he'd deserved.

After his death, Frances had finally acknowledged to Holly that Zach had deliberately pushed her, causing her to fall and break her ankle, and she'd come to accept the fact that it had to have been Zach who engineered the Facebook scandal that cost her so much. In her heart of hearts, Holly believed Frances, too, understood that, had Zach lived, he would've hurt her again, and Holly, and worst of all Jolene. She chose to believe that if Frances knew *all* the things that Holly knew, she'd forgive her for what she'd done. But she had no intention of burdening Zach's mother with the full truth of his sins... or Holly's.

Frances deserved to live out her twilight years believing that her son had gone astray but, in the end, had redeemed himself by "saving" Holly. Frances should be the doting grandmother, much beloved by her granddaughter and her daughter-in-law—and that's how Holly intended it to be.

Holly could've made different choices.

Left matters in the hands of the police.

But even with the evidence she'd discovered, she'd feared a good lawyer might get Zach or Tamara *or both* of them off. What if said lawyer managed to keep the footage from Zach's office from being admitted into trial evidence? What if the authenticity of Tamara's diary entry was challenged in a courtroom?

What was that saying? It's better to be rich and guilty than poor and innocent?

Maybe a better move for Holly's personal safety would've been to turn over the office footage and Tamara's diary entry to the authorities and get out of the house, but Holly preferred to risk her life rather than Jolene's future.

What if Zach found a way to escape the consequences of his behavior and won custody?

Jolene would *never* be safe with him.

And that was a chance Holly simply wasn't willing to take.

She wished she could say she hadn't wanted things to turn out the way they had. That she hadn't wanted Zach and Tamara dead. But that would be a lie. And she'd vowed she'd never lie to herself again. Because that was how she'd gotten into this mess in the first place.

He's a good man.

He loves me.

He loves Jolene.

He'll change.

He would never hurt us.

Dangerous, dangerous lies—all of them.

She dug out her cell phone—the one she'd purchased under her fake name using funds from the bank account she'd opened with her fake ID, and navigated to her nanny cam's application. She'd deliberately chosen *not* to store her camera's feed in the cloud.

The weight of the phone felt heavy in her hand. Once she'd erased the footage, she'd smash the thing with a hammer, and then toss it in a landfill. Afterwards, she'd forget about what really happened. She'd move forward in life with the version of events she'd told the police, which they'd accepted as fact.

She wasn't just erasing footage.

She was erasing reality.

Which is why she wanted to see it for herself, one last time, before storing what had really happened in that hard-to-reach part of her brain where she hid all her poisonous memories.

The truth had been revealed to Holly thanks to a photograph of Jolene.

The one inside the picture frame nanny cam she'd given Zach for his office at the hospital.

When she'd first watched the nanny cam footage, it had been less than noteworthy. Zach doing his chart notes. Zach reading his medical journals with his feet on his desk. Zach bombasting away to Donna or an intern or a janitor, or anyone he could convince to listen to his esoteric, jargon-filled diatribes. The footage had been unbearably dull, and so she'd given up watching—until the day they found Claudia Keeler's body in the hospital morgue.

Holly felt a sense of duty to the woman. It seemed clear that Claudia had fallen under Zach's spell. Holly had sensed it that day at the aquarium. She should have warned Claudia, then, about Zach—about how cruel he could be, still, she hadn't said a word, because Claudia's open admiration of Zach had irritated her.

But after her interview with Detective Denton, the day they found Claudia's body, Holly had gone through all the footage from Zach's office, speeding it up, skimming, and that's when she'd found *it*.

Now, here in one of the library's soundproof study rooms, Holly forwarded the footage to the relevant spot and forced herself, once again, to watch the very scene that had taken her by the shoulders and shaken her awake, called her to action and forced her to set a plan in motion to save her child:

Claudia enters Zach's office.

The intimacy between her and Zach is clear from her body language, her playful words.

Claudia slips off her underwear and twirls it on her fingertips.

Zach sniffs it.

Zach wheels his chair from behind the desk, his trousers pooled around his ankles. With no words, no preliminary, Claudia climbs him. He lifts her skirt and Claudia's bare bottom bounces, her back arches.

Holly fast-forwarded again, skipping most of the sex, resuming at the nine-minute mark, just before the door opened and quietly eased shut again, unnoticed by the couple in the midst of their rutting.

In a flash, a woman's arms snap a black strap, a belt, around Claudia's neck. Claudia's hands fly to her throat.

She struggles.

Writhes.

Gasps.

Then slumps forward on top of Zach.

Holly noted the time: nine minutes forty-five seconds.

It had taken almost a full minute for Claudia to die.

And Zach had done nothing to stop it. In fact, it looked as though he'd climaxed just as Claudia had succumbed.

It wasn't until he'd stopped groaning and untangled himself from her dead body, that he'd turned livid. Red-faced and sweating he'd zipped his trousers, tugged at his hair and raised his fisted hands at the person who'd strangled Claudia with a belt: Tamara.

"What the hell?" Spittle spews from Zach's lips.

Tamara arches a brow. "After Beth, I thought you'd get the hint. I won't be made a fool."

He backs against the wall and slides to the floor. Drops his face in his hands.

Tamara laughs. "You didn't know?"

"They arrested that homeless guy—and then he killed himself in his jail cell so I thought..."

"I guess cops aren't the only stupid ones."

He looks up, mops sweat from his face with the tail of his shirt. "What's wrong with you?"

"Not a thing. I'm just eliminating the competition."

He bangs his head, quietly, against the wall. "You don't have competition. The other women didn't mean anything."

"If I had a nickel," Tamara says. "And I'm ensuring you'll live up to your end of our bargain."

Tamara and Zach, it seemed had a bargain of their own.

"I've already told you we have to lay low," Zach says.

"Oh right. We can't be together again until things settle down. And it would look too suspicious if your wife suddenly went missing while you were a person of interest in Beth's case. Only you're not a person of interest anymore. And yet here you are fooling around with another student and Holly is still alive. You were supposed to get rid of her as soon as the baby was born."

"What do you want from me? Haven't I done enough? I killed Tom for you. You got two million dollars from his life insurance! Why not just let me go and take the win?"

"Because we had a deal."

"I thought it was all just pillow talk. We kill each other's spouses and then you and I get married? We live high on the hog off Holly and Tom's life insurance proceeds? I was just going along for the sex. And it was a cool power fantasy—but it was never meant to be real. You might have needed money but I sure as hell didn't. I don't need anything. I have everything I want."

"But as you pointed out, you did kill Tom."

"Like I said, I thought it was a lover's game. Role play. Just talk. That is until you threatened me! In the end, I did your dirty work with Tom because you blackmailed me. Do you really think I'm going to marry you when you're threatening to pin the blame on me for your husband's murder?"

"You need to finish what you started and get rid of Holly."

"I don't need her life insurance, and you and I are finished. After this, you must know it."

"Were you ever planning to kill Holly?"

"No."

She folded down beside him, picked up his hand. "Darling, you will do this for me. I still have all those conversations recorded. The ones where you promise to kill Tom and Holly so we can cash in on their life insurance, get married and live happily ever after—just like in the movies. Tom is dead, and now it's Holly's turn."

"This is all on you. I never would've killed Tom or anyone else."

"It's one thing to lie to me. It's another to lie to yourself, sweetheart. It was always your choice. You could've gone to the cops, told them I was trying to blackmail you into murdering two people. You would've likely gotten immunity. But you didn't do that. You drugged Tom and sent his car crashing into that pole, just like you promised me. And now, you need to finish what you started. Your attempts on Holly, so far, are pathetic. Four sleeping pills and a Rohypnol? A bullet that barely grazes her arm?"

"That was only to get you off my back. I thought after a couple of failed attempts you'd give up on the idea of getting rid of Holly and move on to something—to someone—else. I know you don't love me, so what's the point? I think you're just dead set on getting revenge against Holly for what happened between the two of you a long time ago."

"That, I am." Tamara climbs to her feet and walks to the door, points at Claudia's corpse. "If you don't take care of Holly, I will. I think I've demonstrated I'm quite capable. And as for us, I do want you. Neither one of us is blinded by love, the sex is great, and we're both good at getting what we want. We're perfect for each other, and we can have a perfect life together.

You just need to let go of this obsession you have with your wife."

There is a long moment of quiet. Zach crosses and uncrosses his arms. Then he nods. "I'll take care of it."

"You'll kill Holly?"

"I just said I would."

"Good. Now, if I were you, I'd flush that condom and remove this corpse before it starts stinking up the place."

"You're not going to help? What's the plan for getting her out of here?"

"I don't have one." Tamara smiles and taps the top of her head. "You'll have to put on your thinking cap. But this is a hospital, I'm sure there are some excellent places to stash a dead body."

* * *

It was ten thirty a.m. The realtor would be here, at Holly's house, any minute to look over the place. She'd said it would be a hard sell given the fact that a double homicide had taken place in this kitchen. Holly would need to drastically reduce the price if she wanted to sell it.

And Holly did want to sell it.

There were too many memories here.

Memories of Zach and his iron-fisted rules, his lies, his complete lack of interest in his own daughter. And what did she care how much their "dream home" sold for? Between his investments and the life insurance policy, Zach had left her with close to fifteen million dollars—more than enough to provide well for Jolene and to set up blind trusts for the families he and Tamara had destroyed: Tom's, Beth's, Claudia's… and Brian's and baby Nora's.

Fine by Holly if the house sold for a penny a square foot.

She hated *almost* every room in it.

But the one room she *didn't* hate was the kitchen—the scene of the very crime that was tanking her home's value—because that was where she'd taken back her life.

She walked through the kitchen, now, surveying it, one last time.

Some of what Holly had told Detective Denton about what had happened that day had been true.

Only it hadn't exactly started with Tamara and Holly having tea:

Holly had put Jolene down to nap upstairs and settled herself in the kitchen. At the time, she'd believed Zach dead by her own hand, and it weighed heavily on her heart. Taking yet another life, even for the safety of her daughter, was going to be difficult. She might not have had the will to finish things if she hadn't found Tamara's diary. But she *had* found it—when she'd decided to chance a search of Tamara's house the same day they had traveled to Tucson. While Tamara had been in the bathroom getting ready, Holly had quickly slipped the journal into her overnight bag.

Later, she'd torn two devastating pages from Tamara's diary and read those pages, yet again, while sitting in her kitchen that stormy evening, waiting for her "friend" to arrive. What Tamara had written in her diary had given Holly the courage to finish what she'd started.

Page 177

> *You have what I want. You wake up in the morning and slide your feet into cashmere slippers. The robe you toss on, so carelessly, was handmade especially for you from a bolt of silk he chose while you were honeymooning in Verona—a bad omen*

considering what happened to Romeo and Juliet—but I digress.

Tears threatened as Holly took in the resentment-filled lines —all the more ironic because she had never wanted the material things Tamara coveted. She read on, slowly, letting every bitter word sink into her bones, until she came to the bottom of the first page:

I want what you have, and I'm coming for it.

Holly's hand trembled so, she could hardly hold the next page in her hand. But, with tears of *rage* slipping down her cheeks, she forced herself to continue. For there, on that next page, Tamara revealed the terrible, unimaginable truth about the fire that took Brian and baby Nora's lives.

Page 178

Don't act so innocent. So shocked. If you'd ever really looked at me you'd have been ready. But you didn't see me coming, then, and you don't see me coming now. You're totally unprepared, and you have no one to blame but yourself.

You're blind, Holly.

After all this time, you still don't understand what you've done to me.

Brian was mine. And you took him from me.

He was my first, and I loved him.

I was pregnant with his child.

The gossip began as soon as I started showing, and when I swallowed a bunch of pills, hoping Brian would come back to me, the entire school buzzed with the news.

I lost my boyfriend.

*And when I tried to win him back with a suicide attempt,
I lost my baby.*

But you never even noticed!

*You were oblivious—so wrapped up in your own world—
head in the clouds, the pretty, popular cheerleader everyone
adored.*

*Even after I set the house fire that killed Brian and baby
Nora, you didn't know.*

Holly couldn't stop the gasp that escaped her lips, even
though she'd read the words before, knew them by heart—they
still shocked her to the core.

Tamara set that fire.

Tamara caused Brian's death, a man she claimed to love,
and worst of all—worse than *anything*—Tamara had caused the
death of an innocent child, baby Nora.

Tamara had no remorse.

Well, then, neither would Holly.

The diary continued:

*When I enrolled in your Pilates class, Holly, you didn't recog-
nize me—didn't even know me after I told you my name.*

Me! The woman who set your world ablaze!

*I had to explain to you that we went to the same high
school! And then you introduced me to your husband's best
friend, Tom.*

How stupid can you be?

*And now you're pregnant with Zach's baby. You think I'm
going to let you get away with that? You may have escaped the
fire, but you will not escape me.*

Not this time.

*I'm going to take Zach from you, and I'm going to take the
baby, too.*

Then I'll have everything, loads of money, a handsome

husband who's great in the sack, your precious little baby—it will all be mine, and you'll have nothing but a pile of dirt for a view.

Oh, wait, there's no window in a coffin so I guess you won't even have that.

Ironic, really, because all you had to do to stop this was open your eyes and see me.

Holly folded the pages and hid them in the bottom of a boot in her closet.

Oh, I do see you now, Tamara.

And I am ready.

She returned to the kitchen and pulled down a box of chamomile tea.

Let the games begin.

Tamara arrived, and she and Holly sat down in the break-fast nook, ostensibly to work out what to do about Zach's body—or the lack thereof.

But *Holly*, not Tamara, was the one with the deadly plan.

At Holly's urging, Tamara went to clean herself up in the bathroom, and then, with Tamara out of sight, Holly pulled out the sleeping capsules she'd taken from Frances' medicine cabinet earlier that day (she'd thrown out her own prescription long ago) and emptied them, along with a bottle of eye drops, into Tamara's tea. It was the same cocktail she'd used on Zach at the hotel, and it had worked—or at least she'd thought so at the time.

Holly had never planned to blackmail Zach with photos of a coked-out afternoon in a hotel room. She'd planned to kill him, and she'd believed she'd succeeded.

Now it was Tamara's turn.

If the cocktail worked on Zach, it should easily take Tamara out. Holly had a suicide note ready to print and place in Tamara's purse—confessing to an affair with Zach and to killing Beth and Claudia out of jealousy, and to poisoning Zach at the hotel after a bad break-up. Finally, the note begged Holly for forgiveness for betraying their friendship.

Ha! That was a nice touch, wasn't it?

Tamara, like Zach, would die by poisoning, all arranged by Holly, and cleverly disguised as the result of guilt and jealousy.

Only Tamara just kept on stirring her tea!

Clanking her damn spoon.

Each time she picked up the cup, Holly held her breath, waiting for her to take a sip.

When she asked for cookies, Holly's heart sank.

And then Zach burst in, a Glock in his hand.

"We've missed you, darling," Tamara said, the picture of calm.

Zach raised his arm, pointing the gun at Holly. "I doubt that very much."

"Should we tell her our little secret?" Tamara asked.

Zach's jaw clenched. He swung the pistol toward Tamara, then back at Holly, as if he couldn't make up his mind which of them to shoot first.

He was indecisive—and that gave Holly a chance. Eyeing the block of knives on the counter, she slowly, slowly climbed to her feet, then took a baby step toward Zach, playing innocent. "W-what secret?" It was easy to make her voice tremble with fear. Zach was *alive*. And she had no idea how. He really should be dead. She'd emptied an entire bottle of eye drops into his whiskey! "Zach, please. Put down the gun."

"*She* tried to kill us both." He jerked his head to indicate Tamara. "Those sleeping capsules she gave you to put in my drink were supposed to have *sugar* in them. While you were in the bathroom lacing a glass with what you thought was a sedative, *I* was supposed to put *arsenic* in my drink, knowing you would switch it for your own while my back was turned. The glass *you handed me* would then have sugar in it, while the glass *you kept for yourself* would have arsenic. Only Tamara didn't give you sugar pills for me, did she? That must've been arsenic, too!"

"I-I. Tamara, what's going on? Zach, please!" Holly's head was swimming from all the double-crossing glass switching, but she got the drift. Tamara had meant for both Holly and Zach to die in that hotel room.

"You almost got away with it, Tamara." Zach straight-armed his Glock. Took a step toward Tamara. "Except that I didn't put *anything* in Holly's drink, because she's mine. I love her, and I'm not giving her up simply because you tell me to. The only reason I'm not dead is because I had the good sense not to trust *you*. You *both* must think I'm an idiot. Don't you know by now how smart I am?"

"But how?" If Zach was right and the powder Tamara had given her to slip him was arsenic, how could he possibly have survived that *and* the eye drops?

"I took a dose of ipecac before I let you into the room, Holly, just in case Tamara planned to betray me, and it *worked*. I was almost dead. You two were obviously convinced or else you wouldn't have left me like that. But the ipecac did what it was supposed to do. I woke up in a pool of my own vomit, and I kept on throwing up until I'd eliminated the bulk of the poison from my system. I survived because I'm too damn smart for both of you."

Holly took another step toward Zach, reached out her hand. "You say you love me? Give me the gun."

Outside, lightning streaked through the sky. The kitchen door, still open, banged against the wall.

Zach lowered his arm.

"Don't move!" Tamara commanded.

Holly whirled; now *Tamara* had a pistol trained on her. She must've pulled it from her purse.

There had to be some way to defuse the situation. If only

Holly could keep Tamara talking. "I don't understand why you hate me."

That was a lie, of course, but it was the least of Holly's crimes.

"Brian." Tamara's eyes changed to green fire. "Brian was mine! And you took him from me."

"But I didn't know anything about that. It was high school. People were hooking up and unhooking all the time. You and I weren't friends. I-I'm truly sorry." Holly didn't recognize her own voice, or this body she was suddenly occupying. Her bones were titanium, her muscles steel. Her daughter was upstairs sleeping, and Holly was a woman ready to fight for her child—to the death.

From her peripheral vision, Holly saw Zach's hand shaking. He raised his arm higher and took a step toward her.

Now there were *two* guns aimed at Holly.

"Do it, Zach!" Tamara ordered. "We can still be together. And I've got everything I need to send you to prison for the rest of your life if you don't."

The thought of this man, raising her daughter—possibly with this woman—sent blood rushing to her brain and revved her reflexes. Her gaze darted from Tamara to Zach. Tamara might be the diminutive one but she was formidable. Zach might be physically strong but he was emotionally weak. And he *always* underestimated Holly. She lunged toward Zach, taking him off guard, and, with surprising ease, jerked his body in front of her. The gun in his hand went off before clattering to the floor, just as a second shot sounded.

The smell of burnt powder filled the air.

Blood spattered onto Holly's face and eyes. Through a haze of red, she watched Zach slide to the floor. Holly dropped to her knees, grabbed Zach's gun, aimed.

Tamara's hand jerked.

A flash of light.

Holly's breathing was rock steady as she squeezed the trigger, her shoulder jerking from the pistol's force.

Tamara fell to the ground, moaning. Zach too, was wounded, and both he and Tamara were writhing on the ground, *breathing*.

Any minute, the neighbors would be calling 911. Hell, they probably already had. The time for action was now.

Holly crept close and straddled Tamara where she lay on the floor.

"This is for Brian. And for Beth and Claudia. But most of all it's for baby Nora." Holly squeezed off her shot.

A pool of blood seeped from the center of Tamara's forehead.

Holly pivoted, pointing her gun at Zach, but it was too late —he was already gone.

Mechanically, she lowered her weapon. She'd tried to poison him once, so there was no absolution in the fact that she didn't put a bullet in him, now.

She would have done it if he hadn't been dead already.

Instead, she used a dish towel to wipe her prints from his gun, then with her own hand still wrapped in the towel, she carefully pressed the pistol into his palm, closed his fingers around it and then released, allowing his hand to fall to the floor and the gun to slide naturally from his grasp.

Then she scrubbed her hands with vinegar and dishwashing detergent to remove the gunshot residue. She'd hear about using vinegar and a degreaser on a crime show, and she prayed her heavy-duty dishwashing liquid could substitute for the degreaser—it was the best she could do.

She called 911.

"Hurry, please! My husband and his mistress just had a shoot-out in my kitchen."

* * *

Holly shook out her shoulders and blew out a hard breath. The past was over, and she was finally ready to let it go. Just one hour ago, she'd erased the footage from the nanny cam, but she still had the pages she'd torn from Tamara's diary to deal with. She retrieved them, now, from the boot in her closet where she'd hidden them. She hadn't wanted to use the library's shredder. She'd seen too many movies where a clever sleuth pieced the strips together to discover the horrible truth. Instead, she strode back to the kitchen sink and held the pages under running water, watched the ink stream like blue tears down the pages, and then demolished the mess in the garbage disposal.

Mixing in with the rumbling of the disposal, she heard a car's engine.

That would be the relator.

Right on time.

Holly dried her hands, and then marched, straight-backed and with purpose, to the front.

She opened the door and stepped onto the porch, watching as the realtor's blue BMW crawled up the long gravel drive. While Holly had been reminiscing and destroying evidence, it seemed a light rain had come and gone. There was a *clean* scent in the air, and the blades of grass, dampened by the recent rainfall, twinkled like green diamonds. Holly drew in a big breath, expanding her chest, filling her lungs with newly washed air.

What a beautiful morning!

A LETTER FROM CAREY

Dear Reader,

Thank you! I appreciate your taking time out of your busy life to read *The Marriage Secret*. I loved creating these characters, and I hope you enjoyed getting to know them and taking their journey as much as I enjoyed sharing them with you.

If you'd like to be the first to know about my next book, please sign up via the following link. Your email address will never be shared and you can unsubscribe at any time.

www.bookouture.com/carey-baldwin

If you loved this story, I would be very grateful if you could leave a short review. Reviews are one of the best ways to help other readers discover my books. They don't need to be long or clever. You can make a big difference simply by leaving a line or two. And guess what? I actually read every review!

Building a relationship with readers is one of the best things about being a writer. I love hearing from you, so please stay in touch by connecting with me on Facebook, Twitter, and my website, and following me on BookBub. I've posted the information below for your convenience.

Thank you very much for reading and don't forget to stay in touch!

Love, Carey

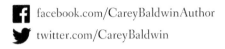

facebook.com/Carey.Baldwin.10
CareyBaldwin.net
Bookbub.com/authors/carey-baldwin

facebook.com/CareyBaldwinAuthor
twitter.com/CareyBaldwin

ACKNOWLEDGMENTS

Thank you so much to my wonderful agent, Liza Dawson, who remains unendingly wise. I want to thank my brilliant editor, Laura Deacon, who stepped up and took me on while the amazing Lucy Dauman was on leave. Both of these women are incredibly insightful and supportive, and they make writing a better book a pleasure. Thank you, thank you, thank you, to the fabulous Noelle, Sarah, Kim, and Jess. Thank you to Donna, Alexandra, Alex, Lauren and to all the individuals in marketing, art, and administration at Bookouture who championed this book.

Thank you to my dear friend, Dr. Kimberly Diana-Brooks, for her expert advice on the labor and delivery scene. Any mistakes, of course, are my own. I also want to thank my beta reader, Suzanne Baldree, for her enthusiasm and her invaluable input. As always, I want to thank my incredibly talented friends Leigh, Tessa, and Lena. You've been with me from the start, and you're always there for me whether I need to cry, celebrate, or fix a plot hole. I don't know what I'd do without you. To my family—Bill, Shannon, Erik, and Sarah. I love you truly, dears. And dear little Olivia, please hurry up and get here. I cannot wait to meet you!

Printed in Great Britain
by Amazon